The Emerald Knight

A Dark Divide

Ade McBain

To Louise

Thank you for the journey. I am grateful for every step we take together.

Copyright © 2023 Ade McBain

All rights reserved.
ISBN: 9798853111875

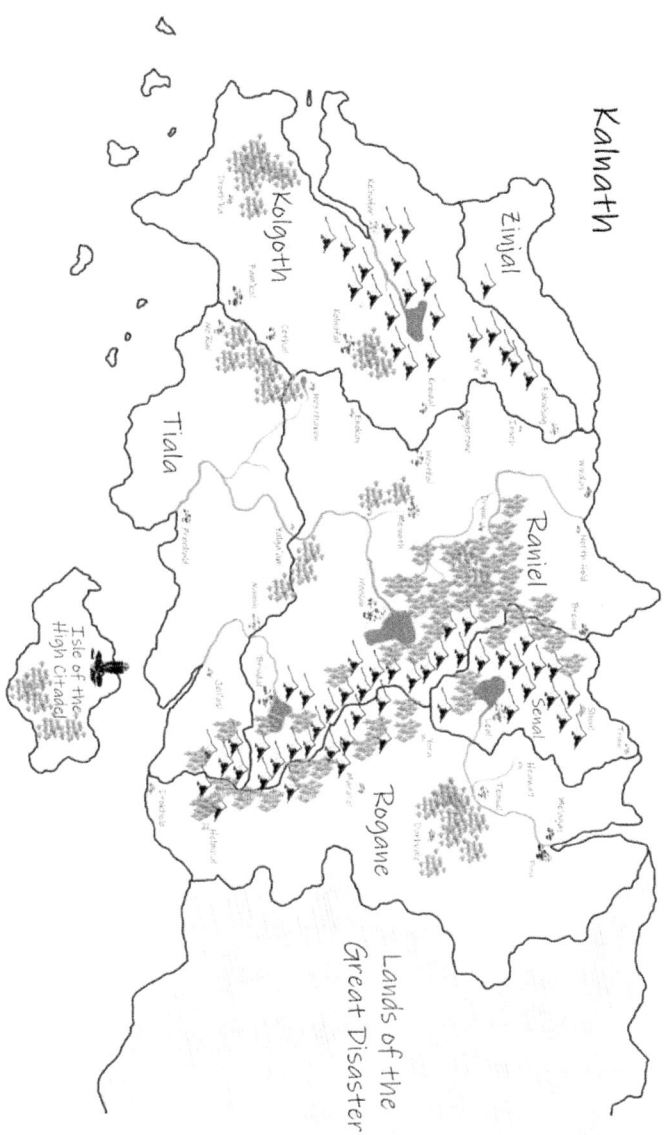

The Emerald Knight - A Dark Divide

Prologue

Inscribed runes on the shackles glowed with pearlescent power. Mere iron could not hold back the wrath of such a being held within. One who had defied the laws of nature and held sway over the peoples of Kalnath with tyranny and servitude. His ego-filled reign now reduced to kneeling in a dark crypt, head bowed before those who would see him pay for his cruelties. Centuries before, corruption had settled in the hearts of the Zinjal mages. Like and infection, it spread and a yearning for power had seen civil war destroy the glory of that fine land. One above all had brought order by travelling a darker path. Millennia before the cities of Zinjal were no more than mud huts, an artefact had been crafted, imbued with the power to unleash demon kind upon the world. Along with dark teachings and darker tomes an astute mage wielded the Emerald Knight to bring that order. However, for the people of Zinjal that order came at a price. Everything had a price – even life.

Raising his head, the Dark Mage stared coldly from inky, depthless eyes. A sneer of contempt graced his face, showing stained teeth. Saliva, mixed with the blood oozing from his nose, dripped onto the sandy floor.

A figure stood solemn and unyielding at the captive's attempt to intimidate. 'If you truly are ever-living, then this sentence will befit your deeds.' Her armour dented and scraped. Grime and filth more common than steel. 'The Brovan Order will see the end of dark magic.'

'You think your trinkets and artefacts can save you? I'm the darkness and the nightmare. These chains will rust and your flesh will fade. All things succumb to death. The bonds of life hold no confines for me.' The captive lurched, stopping a foot away from his accuser. His foul breath causing protective gems, worked into the Brovan warrior's helm, to glow.

The muttering of priests, elders and chieftains echoed from outside the poorly lit stone chamber. In the distance, through tunnels and catacombs, shouts and muffled screams could be heard. The warrior stood emotionless; eyes fixed on the captive. A man of late years, clad in a fine blue robe entered the room. No armour or weapons. The enchained spat at the ground where the newcomer stopped.

'Citadel rat!' Came the contemptuous welcome, as the moist jelly-like fluid fizzled and melted into the earth.

'Indeed, Talgameth, Lord of Zinjal. For your crimes against the peoples of Kalnath, you will be but a memory for years to come, then fade to myth. You will not see the light nor feel the air – buried by the earth that you so lorded over.' Scanning the resting place of a long-forgotten king the mage was satisfied that there was no escape. An ornate throne of carved granite and gold, some broken pots spewing forth gold and jewels, sat under the vaulted ceiling. No door, only an archway into the corridor. That wouldn't matter as an army of labourers would soon backfill any space. 'Are these all his possessions?'

'Yes, my lord,' replied the warrior.

'Ah, the Emerald Knight. Such an unassuming artefact, rough as if made by a child, yet this is what strikes fear in your victims.' Picking up the green precious stone, the robed man turned slowly and pondered the lines hewn into the smooth surfaces. Whispers of fate and power hissed at the edge of hearing.

'I remember that feeling, drawn to the power. Give in, Mage. All it needs is kings' blood,' taunted Talgameth.

The citadel mage began swaying slightly. With a battle-taught swiftness the Brovan warrior threw a leather wrapping over the mage's hands and covered the artefact. Released from the daze and gathering his composure.

'I saw it. I saw the darkness that awaits,' said the mage.

'And I'll enjoy the terror it brings.' The captive laughed at his adversary's insight. 'You cannot destroy it. You saw what happened in the east when you tried to destroy another artefact of such power. Hundreds of thousands of people from many races wiped out. Even I could not comprehend the hurt and suffering your citadel caused. All in the name of righteous virtue.'

The mage bowed his head in sorrowful remorse. 'Yet you blame it on me,' said Talgameth.

'Enough of this horror.' The mage, clearly shocked at the ease with which the artefact had affected him, turned to the Brovan warrior. 'Your last task is to bury this corruption. Travel far and tell no one of your mission. Do not fail in this or it will be the end of us all. By the gods, I hope and pray that it is never found.'

'Despair in the silence of your gods, mage,' mocked Talgameth.

Wrapping another layer of supple leather around the Emerald Knight, the warrior bound it tight.

'Wait!' said the mage. Placing his palm over the wrappings and mumbling in archaic tones, imbuing the wraps with a talisman. 'That should keep it safe for your journey. Now go. Speed be with you.' Placing the Emerald Knight in a bag under her robe, the warrior bowed to the mage and left the underground chamber heading for the surface.

Acolytes were ushered into the crypt, bound hand and feet. Afraid that their master was in chains or afraid of his wrath, their eyes wide and unblinking revealed thoughts of the cruelty that might befall them. The first shovels of earth were thrown into the chamber. 'In the darkness as black as your heart, eternity take you, Talgameth, and be that the last time you hear your name by free people of Kalnath. You will never threaten these lands again. Nor will the Emerald Knight.'

The mage turned his back. The Dark Lord of Zinjal gave a threatening growl. 'I will return bringing the fall of the citadel.'

Allowing his shoulders to drop he let go of a breath. Uncertainty crept into his heart. Although, there was some hope that the stoic warrior would fulfil her quest and hide the instrument of Talgameth's power knowing that, indeed, it could not be destroyed.

'Fill it in,' shouted the mage.

The next thousand years would see the great cities of Zinjal buried and the atrocities fade to stories told to scare children. The Brovan order and the Citadel would watch from their cowls for any stir or mention of his return or indeed the surfacing of the Emerald Knight. Rumours and myths trickle along whispered highways. Most were lies; however, one rumour was louder than the others. Talgameth may well walk among the streets again. Dismissed as nonsense. Believed or not, his name was spoken in hushed tones for fear of some truth. Others said his acolytes still practised the dark arts knowing that he was ever-living, willing him back.

Chapter One

As the arcane mist left Maleth's eyes the cobbled street raced up to meet him. Darkness followed, however before blacking out, he witnessed the aftermath of what he'd done – and the still body of the plucky little girl.

Sometime later, unsure whether it was real or not, the Brovan adept turned in his prone position, bringing a wave of heat and discomfort. The ringing in his ears and pain when breathing overwhelmed his consciousness and he sank back into his oblivion. Once again, as it had done for countless nights, it would bring on his nightmare.

The vivid recollection as clear as melt water off the mountains. The main plaza of the city thronged with people. Every vision was the same. *What did people need to buy*? Maleth wondered. The mid-morning chill had gone and the sun was making itself known. The stallholders rolled down their awnings to shade their valuable produce and keep their customers cool when parting with their pennies. Shoulder to shoulder, strangers walked past one another, each on their own mission to purchase food or clothing. Even the elite were here buying trinkets that had no purpose other than to make them stand out from the next lord or lady.

Maleth recalled standing next to a wall at the edge of the square, leaning gently on the sandstone, watching the dance of life play out. He took an interest in a young, slim girl moving fluidly between buyers and stalls. She was light on her feet: a quick step to the left, dropping slightly and a pirouette, never stopping to consider the next move – like smoke in the wind. Then he saw it: a lightning-fast movement of her hands. With a small blade, she cut the purse from a Highborn and melted into the crowd. It impressed Maleth, and the foolish Highborn only realised the theft after concluding a bargain with a spice salesman. It was his own fault really – if you left scraps out for the imps, they would eat it, and your hand if you weren't quick enough. A belt was not the place to carry coin in Weelan.

The smell of fresh bread, spices and cut flowers filled the air alongside a dampness in the grass and shop drapes after last night's mist had receded. Hiding his contentment behind an unfocused smile Maleth smoothed off his adept's robes. A feeling of freedom with no real ties. He was in Weelan for a reason, however that could wait. There hadn't been a sighting of the Dark Lord for over a thousand years, not much chance of him popping up now. The trip, for him was a jolly. Glad to be getting out of the chores back in Senal.

He had a gift and could steal whatever he needed. This didn't sit well with his mentors, not becoming of a Brovan warrior apparently. Since he was a boy all he'd done was, well what he wanted. Those dusty old farts would try and get him to conform and take a calling. Either help the sick, diplomatic errands, building maintenance or, what most of his fellow adepts gushed over, archaic history. The study of long forgotten heroes and tales of the worlds doom. Nope, for Maleth, it was looking after himself.

Long ago he found that, if he wanted something, all he needed to do was to focus his mind on it and it would happen. Of course, everything came at a price: changing stones to gold for twenty minutes required the same effort as walking up a flight of stairs; other things took far greater effort – and Maleth didn't believe in wasting too much energy. When he was younger, on one occasion he'd been caught stealing sweet buns and given a hiding. Knowing that he deserved it didn't make the pain go away, and unsure if his first attempt at healing magic would actually work, he had focused hard, concentrating on the pain and the bruises, willing the swelling to fade and getting rid of any soreness. Blacking out he had woken two days later with his parents by his bed. Still badly bruised, the process had left him more tired than he'd ever been.

Maleth would regularly use regeneration and sustaining techniques, which didn't take any effort these days. He found that the more he used them, the easier the focusing became and needed less recovery time. Practice was the key. With a small green flash in his eyes, unnoticeable to anyone not looking directly at him, he felt well fed. He could be rich – the plaza was hot for picking – and if this young girl could weave her way through the crowd with a bit skill and a stubby knife to earn a wage, then Maleth could fleece the lot of them. But truth be told, he couldn't be bothered. He was happy to watch the world happen … over there.

Two of the City Watch brushed past with a slight tinkling of their interlinked plate armour. The familiarity of the sound made his dream fade ever darker. The dullness and unkempt nature of the plate did not bring any form of leadership to mind. A black cloak hung off their shoulders with the city's emblem in white silk stitching revealing an open palm to show openness and justice. But over the past couple of years, the Watch had been filled with a distinct class of soldier: mainly opportunists with vendettas against previous acquaintances, their positions guaranteed as the foray in the west took experienced officers away.

Maleth spied the little girl again. She was getting brazen, her hand under a woman's shawl, trying to unclasp a pendant which hung around her neck. He felt uneasy. The girl was being foolish. *Give it up*, he thought. *You're going to get caught*. There was a scream and the woman turned. Stunned that her luck had run out, the girl looked at the woman and froze.

'Thief, thief! Call the Watch!'

Maleth remembered glancing over as one of the watchmen snapped his head round with fly-like precision to where the shout had come from. His helm made the move look even more sinister. *Shit! The silly bitch is going to get a hiding. Stay out of this, Mal*, he thought to himself. Getting wrapped up with the Watch was not a good life choice, but something made him stay.

'That little monster tried to steal my jewellery.' The woman hollered.

The two guards were now shoving their way through the crowd with vivid purpose. More people had started to take notice of the altercation. One man tried to grab the girl. She spun round and dodged the attempt.

'Thief!' was shouted again.

Quickly coming to her senses, the girl made a run for a gap in the crowd, she was tripped up by another bystander and landed hard, elbows bloodied, with a burst lip. She was hauled to her feet and held by a burly stallholder. 'Thieving little bitch!'

There was a terror in her face. Before, when Maleth had noticed her, she'd had a carefree confidence about her. His own stomach was knotting. He should have walked away. She wasn't his problem. Thieves got caught all the time; their own fault for getting too cocky. This was a kid though. At worst she'd get a slap or two, be taken to the Watch House, left in a cell overnight, given a good breakfast and released in the morning.

Without warning, the watchman's boot landed square on the little thief's face. This brought a change in the stallholders' understanding of the situation. Once-upstanding members of the community were now unwillingly accomplices to something unimaginable.

'Officer, it's a little girl,' the stallholder pleaded, still holding her.

The crowd edged back, shock changing into disgust at the actions of the Watch officer. Sensing the change in mood, the other watchman drew his sword. The scrape of metal on the scabbard, along with the sight of the unsheathed blade, let the crowd know that no one interfered with Watch duty. The smaller of the two guards, the one with the heavy right foot, grasped the girl up by her throat. 'Well, little one, theft is not tolerated in this city.'

The girl was sobbing, her face too sore to cry. Maleth shifted uneasily, a heavy heart getting heavier. This was not how he'd planned the day unfolding. Cautiously he whispered, 'Hold in there.' Looking around for the woman who'd been the target of the theft, the guilt on her face spoke a thousand words. The gaze that Maleth gave her begged her to intervene and say it was a mistake. After all, she still had the pendant. She turned and looked away. 'Coward!' he mouthed.

With a spirit sharpened from years on the streets, the little girl lashed out with a flurry of misplaced strikes. What happened though, was her wriggling made the officer lose his grip and drop the little pickpocket. Realising, he grabbed her wrist and rotated her arm, applying immense pressure to her shoulder, almost dislocating it. Maleth's heart pounded. He had to stop it, but this wasn't his fight. The girl's face was now pressed into the ground, her sobs turning to screams. The watchman used his boot once again, this time to the side of her head. Her screams were silenced.

'Let that be a lesson to thieves.' The officer proclaimed.

Maleth could contain himself no longer. He focused on the two watchmen, pulling untapped rage from deep within him. Gritting his teeth and staring at the officers paid to protect the people – *all* of them, not just the rich – a red mist obscured his eyes. Those closest sensed the hatred engulfing him. The guards looked at the crowd, ready to answer and questions with the same violence. The onlookers remained frozen, powerless to break free. Every face looked at the girl – all but one. The watchmen fixed their gaze on the slender man in blue, unable to work out what was happening. They both clawed at their armour, desperately trying to remove their helms. Panic set about them as steam escaped from small gaps in the plate. The guards fell to the ground screaming and writhing in pain.

There was a different silence, one of sleep interspersed with the hiss and ticking of hot metal. Would there ever be respite from the pain or the memory of the little thief?

Maleth woke to the screech and clonk of the cell door latch. Recoiling through the pain to the corner of his bunk, he waited. The familiar damp odour from the guard wafted ahead of him and into Maleth's cell. With partial sight in one eye the wiry figure could be seen removing his thick leather belt.

'Best keep you under control, scum. Too weak to use magic, eh?' The guard struck out with the buckle at Maleth. All he could do was raise his arms to protect his head from the onslaught. Again, and again with feverish intent, lash after lash was aimed at the broken magic user.

'P, please. Stop.' It took all he had left to speak.

'Stop?' The guard raised his voice. 'Oh, did you stop when you poached the two innocent Watch guards?' His lips pulling back to reveal saliva coated rotten teeth. Another figure entered the cell at hearing the commotion.

'Think you've done enough on him today; the other bastards will be getting jealous.'

With a heady rush of supremacy, the final blow knocked Maleth out. 'See you tomorrow.' The guard said with some satisfaction.

There was no joy in his dreams, only the events leading up to him being in jail. They were taught in the Brovan order that, *'nothing good comes of using magic, that's for the Citadel. How right they were.'* He'd kept his abilities to himself for near forty years. Letting go of his disappointment in himself was difficult. He would obsess over what happened numerous times. If only he said no to the assignment. There were rumours of Talgameth being in the Ranielian capitol. Maleth was sent to watch and listen, no more. He'd heard nothing, then again it was difficult to strike up a conversation about a fabled dark mage returning to seek revenge. It was all nonsense to him anyway.

Awaking a short time later and wincing as he opened his good eye. A bloated rat tucked into his meal, stale bread and some kind of fatty meat.

'Have at it my little friend, I'm not going to last much longer.'

Chapter Two

The resident imps darted between legs and tables alike, sniffing out scraps and trinkets. They were a pest, but a necessary one, as they kept the mice and cat population to a minimum. Imps were a strange breed, no bigger than a hefty cat, with large muscular hind legs and short front legs ending in what could only be classed as *hands with sharp claws*. They had a language that, to most, sounded like crackling logs, and when communicating with one another they seemed to be a scheming lot.

The tavern was bleak to say the least. A heavy curtain of smoke hung from the old oak rafters. Candleholders decorated the bar area, whereas others, hanging from the roof, seemed to float in the smog. The life and death of past candles was evident in the dripped wax on the floor and soot marks on the wall. Like any tavern in the city, small groups had gathered in the booths to discuss the state of the country, city and society in general, but hadn't come up with any solutions. Stories endured in a fashion, repeated to new listeners, with the tales sometimes being retold with different endings. The clothes on their backs suggested that they were working folk, getting by, paying their dues and tipping their hats to the City Watch. Not that the Watch came into Croft's Alehouse. There was no actual need. Suffice to say Croft, a respected barkeep, didn't stand for too much rowdiness. As long as customers put their pennies across the thick oak bar, he'd keep filling their mug. When the time came and he thought someone might be heading south towards the floor, his two sons helped them happily on to the street.

For those who felt aggrieved by this method, Croft had a lengthy piece of western heartwood from Darkvale Forest, which made compliance much easier. In general, the clientele of Croft's were decent people.

At this point in the night around twenty locals were quaffing liquids of varying colours and potency. The sun had gone down about an hour earlier and the usual mist had started to roll through the streets of Weelan.

In one booth, a solitary man sat nursing a mug of ale, wallowing in his own company, his features covered by unkempt, wavy brown hair. A short beard covered his square-set jaw. He wore a brown leather overcoat which, by its look, had maybe served as bedding on a few occasions. With callused fingers he turned the mug, lifted it and took a small mouthful. The ale was either of the cheaper persuasion or he had glass in this throat.

Inhaling and closing his eyes with a slight shake of his head he lashed out with his foot. Connecting with something soft. The response was a squeal and a scuttling of claws on the wooden floor. *Damn imps*, he thought. This common interaction was not helping his mood.

'Bloody horse piss!' This wasn't said with any malice or intention, but enough of a bite to make Croft take note.

'If you don't like the ale, Marin, you know where the door is. If you don't, my boys will remind you.' This too did not contain any malice, but it was indeed a threat.

Croft, once a Corporal in the Watch and like most retirees of that persuasion, they didn't take any shit. Not even from a loyal customer like Marin.

Smirking and eyeing the barman through half shut lids. 'I remember the last time Jack thought he could throw me out.'

Croft's knuckles whitened round the bottle he was carrying. 'You're lucky to be back in here after breaking his arm. Just settle down, have your ale, then bugger off.'

Marin emptied the mug, spilling some on his tunic, gave a moan of achievement and wiped his face. 'You don't appreciate me, you old goat. I'm going home to where I'm king, lord of my castle —a he who must be obeyed.' Stumbling a little, he made it to the bar and placed the mug down gently, and turned it slightly for dramatic effect. He looked up at Croft with his piercing green eyes, a little bloodshot after eight mugs of sewer runoff and grinned.

'Are you still staying in Simpson's barn then?' Croft asked.

'Aye. Lord of the Straw,' Marin replied.

'You certainly smell like it.'

Marin deftly picked up the mug and threw it towards an array of bottles. He didn't wait for the chorus of exploding glass. Instead, he turned on the balls of his feet, feeling the traction on the wooden floor through his thin leather soles. Aiming for the door, and hoping no imps were in the way, he bolted. He was a strong man, not like the barbarians in the south, but strong enough from days of hard labour in the fields. He was at full speed when Jack's now-mended arm connected across his neck. The meeting of these two forces meant that something had to give. Jack, being of good breeding and even better eating, was six-foot tall and the same shape as the barrels that lined the cellar. Marin's feet were no longer anywhere near the floor, although his back and head were approaching it quickly. As Marin landed, he had barely enough sense to keep his head from smashing against the floor. His body compressed with the impact and all the air left his lungs. Jack lifted him up to eye level. Marin saw it coming, but didn't have the voice to plead for any viable escape option. Jack's fist made contact and the lights went out.

The regulars had seen it all before: Marin tossed out into the gutter, followed by threats and profanities. He would be back tomorrow pleading to get in and apologising for the night before. One of Croft's best customers would not be turned way over a few broken bottles.

Cleaning up the broken glass, Croft felt a dullness in his chest. 'Go check on him, Jack, just to make sure you didn't kill the little bugger.' Everyone continued with their conversations, taking little heed of what had just happened.

Jack stepped out into the half-baked mud. 'Well, horse boy, at least it's not raining.' Jack gave Marin a friendly kick to see if he was awake. The incumbent Marin gave a moan. Picking him up with ease Jack carried Marin home. Simpson's barn wasn't far away and he felt a little bad at not giving him the opportunity to defend himself. He wouldn't see his friend stuck, arsehole or not.

There was a familiar smell – comforting. In that brief moment everything was fine. Marin was warm and the straw was soft on the side of his face. Then the pounding started in his head. *Holy shit! How much did I have to drink this time?*

The ache felt like the constant pressure of a thumb onto his temple. He dared not move, but he would never get to work with that attitude. Slowly, he opened his eyes, squinting, ready for the onslaught of pain he knew was coming. The shard of sunlight that came through the barn door attacked him like hot needles. He let out a cry and quickly shut his eyes again. Marin didn't like the mornings: more often than not, he was hungover and, on this occasion, battered and bruised. He sat up from where he lay and propped himself against the stall. He felt a gust of hot, oaty, moist air on his neck followed by a curious tongue.

'Morning, Treen.' Treen was a milking cow that the Simpsons took great care of: a prize beast that produced large quantities of quality milk. Mrs Simpson made wonderful cheese and butter and that's what Marin was hoping to tuck into for breakfast. If only he could stand.

Marin pulled himself up the stall until he was balancing on his feet, still clinging to the post like the mast of a boat in a storm. The room spun. He knew to ride it; it would be over soon. Treen's water trough was only four or five steps away, but his legs and head had fallen out and were not talking to each other. Snaking his way round the post and crawling along the gate, all the while watched by the other inhabitants of the barn.

Lowering himself to his knees, grabbing both sides of the trough he submerged his head in the chilly water. The shock brought him round, seconds later lifting his head out. Water cascaded down his tunic and onto his lap, beads of water dripping from his hair. *'Well, that's a wake-up and no mistake.'* It took Marin a few minutes to gather his thoughts. Recollections from the night before started to muster themselves.

Best go apologise to Croft later. Unsure whether it was the guilt or the hunger making his stomach tense.

'You in here, ya lazy bastard? Where are you? Drunk again?' Mr Simpson's tone was angry, but with an undertone of acceptance; the same tone used on a family pet when asking who shredded the bedding, knowing full well who it was and that he would not get an answer.

'The cart has left for the fields, so you'll have to earn your keep here today. The gods know why I keep you around, but I'm yet to see it. If Talgameth returns I'll hand you over and no mistake.' He threw some stale bread and cheese down wrapped in cloth.

The reason for Marin receiving the Simpsons' hospitality was straightforward. He was a good hand to have around the place in case of trouble. There had been a couple of attempted thefts of tools and livestock from the barn. Marin was quite able with his fists and made sure that the thieving bastards took something away with them that didn't belong to the Simpsons.

'Morning, sir. Don't mean to be a burden,' said Marin

'Eat your food and get this place mucked out.'

Sometime later, after his chores were complete, the barn was as fresh as it would get, the tools all sharp and oiled. Marin took a walk, in which he spent most of it talking to himself, arriving at the ale-house door he took a few more seconds before entering. Either for courage or to convince himself that he was going to be welcome, he pushed the heavy door inward.

'Well, fist me. I didn't think you would be back so soon. The blood on the floor isn't dry yet.' Croft was tempted to bar Marin on principle and the fact that he'd wrecked the bottle shelf.

'I've come to apologise.'

'Okay then, let's hear it. The imps pissed you off again?'

This wasn't the first time Croft stood, arms crossed, waiting for the same bullshit to spew forth.

'I am sorry this time. You and the Simpsons are the only people that give me the time of day and I don't mean to be such a dick.' Croft offered him a seat at the bar. As he pulled the stool out, Jack and his brother came up from the cellar.

'What's this shitbag doing in here? You have some nerve. You want us to throw him out, Dad?' Said Jack.

'No, leave him be.' Croft could see that this time Marin was a little different, not the same arrogant shit he usually was. 'But don't go too far in case the bugger needs to be reminded of what he did last night.'

Marin sat at the bar with his head bowed. Croft poured him a mug of ale and placed it between his hands. 'That will be two coppers.'

As Marin handed over the coin, he spoke half to himself and half to Croft. 'What am I doing with my life? This isn't what I'd planned. I wanted to be a blacksmith and make swords that would defend this country from her enemies.' The great trades took young lads to train them, usually following a large payment from the boys' families. They wouldn't even let

Marin near their forge knowing that he was skint and living in a barn. 'I'm no use to anyone. Would I be missed if I weren't around?'

'Everyone has worth, lad.' Croft had seen many people in this state. 'You just don't see it at the moment.' Croft moved off to serve another customer.

At this point Jack came and sat with him. Nudging him with a huge shoulder to break his musing.

'Sorry for all the grief that I've given you in the past,' said Marin.

'Well, I ain't sorry for all the times I've hit you.' Marin looked at Jack and smiled.

The two were the best of enemies. For the rest of the night, they shared ale and stories. Jack even suggested heading west and going treasure-hunting in the old haunted ruins of Zinjal.

'Those are myths, kids' stories and bait for the gullible,' Marin retorted.

'I want to see them someday and come back here with diamonds and rubies as big as your ugly head. Buy Dad a new pub, then me and my brother will work the bar.'

'Ha, it's nice to dream. Let's just say for argument – and you like an argument – that there was such a place. Surely, it would have been looted way before now.'

'But what if it wasn't,' said Jack excitedly.

'Well, if we came back stinking rich, I'd buy the Simpsons a new farm, twice as big and with 100 hands to do all the labour. Pay them back proper.'

'Listen to the pair of you. Like children.' Croft took an interest in the conversation and moved back along the bar. 'Look, I've been far and wide and I've never heard of such a place. It's all nonsense, boys. If you want to get rich, you have to graft and earn it.'

Croft knew full well the place they were talking about and also the dangers that lurked in the shadows of that cursed land. He didn't want his son getting any adventuring ideas.

The thoughts of adventure and stories of the old Brovan Order heroes filled their conversations. Marin walked home this time. Swooshing an imaginary sword and ducking to the side of invisible foes. Oblivious to the late evening shadows that seemed to move with him, he was in his own fuzzy world. In the depths of the alleyways though, watchers lurked and passed whispers.

Chapter Three

'What do you mean my father is dead?' The words resounded from pillar to pillar. An echo, questioning every intricately carved line and marble tile in the great hall. Lord Hal straightened and filled his barrel chest with a calming breath. Closing his eyes to the sombre news he allowed his brow to furrow. The hollow grip of loss holding him in place. The second thought to that of the loss of his friend was the grief that would now flood the heart of his charge, the king's daughter. 'No! It's not right. It's more propaganda from Kolgoth.'

The court was silent, the news sinking in with the royal aids and advisers. The runner who had delivered the letter bowed his head, reluctant to make eye contact. There were rumours of the ruthless sentences the princess handed out in her father's absence, and it didn't take much to lose your head these days. He had travelled for weeks, with little sleep and even less food. He too was feeling the loss of the man who'd inspired a nation to war.

'Who brings this nonsense?' There was madness in the question's delivery.

'It was I, your highness.' The tired, dishevelled young man took a step forward and knelt before his Queen. 'I served with the Red Lances.' His mouth was dry. Keeping his head down, he could smell the stale sweat from the horse, which came as some comfort to him in a room filled with perfumes and scents from around the kingdom and beyond. His heart beat faster, threatening to trip his breathing and give away his fear. 'I was given the task twenty-eight days ago this morning.'

Lord Hal scanned the crowd, taking in what he could. A venomous lot. Some stood with hard eyes eager to see the act play out. Either numb or uninterested in the loss of their king, they watched with voyeuristic intent at the heir to the throne's every move.

The young princess ambled down from the throne. Her dress showed off her curves as it clung to her thighs, azure blue made from the finest Ranielian cloth. Those around her saw her breathing change, slow. As each step made contact with the polished marble floor it rang through the throne room, like a death knell. A nervous twitch surged from the messenger on each toll.

'You seem a little tense,' she said. 'Tell me, lancer, have you met my father?'

'No, your highness.' His heart pounded and sweat run down his temple.

'Where are you from?' Her tone softened. He looked at her, searching for a clue to the correct answer.

'Where are you from? Why did you sign up to serve?'

'Sorry, your highness, I ...' His mind raced, praying to the gods that he would survive this questioning. 'I'm from Westhaven, a small fishing town on the banks of Lake Las.'

'Ah, a border town. Go on.'

'I joined to do my duty to the Crown.'

'Cut the bullshit!' The change in the princess's tone was abrupt. By now she was a pace away from the messenger. 'Border towns are synonymous with being sympathetic to Kolgoth. Were you sent by those evil child-eaters to scare me and disrupt our campaign?'

'No, your highness, I am true to the Crown. I would have given my life for the king.' As soon as the words left his dry chapped lips, he knew that the executioner was getting ready.

'Would you indeed! Then tell me why you are here and your king is not.' The messenger was silent. 'I know little about military things, but are soldiers not supposed to protect their king? Speak!' The last word was a shout with all the anger that had been building up since her father had left a year before.

His entire body convulsed at the outburst. He tried to speak in response to the question. No words came. He gave a cough, swallowing what little moisture he had left in his mouth. 'On my honour, your highness, my part in the battle was to chase down the routed Kolgothians, but the gods were not in our favour and they overran the main battle lines. Our task was then to rescue the survivors. We were five miles from the border and ferrying terrified soldiers to safety. They stopped at the border and allowed us to gather our dead. We lost over 10,000 souls.'

He was interrupted. 'I only care about *one* soul.'

Lord Hal witnessed the tear that the messenger had been holding back. 'Among that 10,000, your highness, was the king. His body was returned to us by a chieftain, with full battlefield honours. His household guard fought to the last man.'

'How could an army of 15,000, well-trained, heavily armoured soldiers be overrun by those guttural beasts?'

No one offered an answer, still in shock at finding out that their king was dead. The princess turned her back on the messenger and walked towards the throne, stopping before the first step, and looked over her shoulder.

'Your oath is fulfilled. Hang him!'

Sinking to both knees he sobbed. 'Please, your highness ...' Two guards lifted the man to his feet, turned him slowly and escorted him from the throne room. Lord Hal stopped them and laid a hand on the messenger's shoulder and whispered in his ear.

'Keep it together, lad. You have done your king and country proud. May the gods keep you.'

'I'm sorry for your loss, your highness,' Lord Hal gave solemn bow. 'I understand that this is an extremely difficult time, but I'm not sure that sending that soldier to the gallows was a good political move.'

'Be careful, Lord Hal. Today is not the day to cross me. There is room on the gallows for you too.'

'I mean no disrespect. He did his duty. Some would say that he did more than he signed up for, and he lost his commander and king. Your opposition will see this as you going too far.'

Sitting on the throne she stared into the empty space where the soldier had knelt.

'My Lords, your king is dead.'

A chorus rose from the lords and advisers: 'Long live the Queen.' And one by one they knelt with heads bowed. The new ruler of Raniel looked at the scene, all eyes were to the floor. With that, she marched her way to her private chambers, passing palace staff and handmaids with blank disdain.

The great and worthy of Raniel were milling in the throne room. Murmured discussions were taking place. Alliances were reaffirmed as the future was now a far riskier place. Losses in the west would bolster the argument for further diplomacy. However, some viewed those losses as a need for revenge.

'Lord Hal, we must seek a peace treaty.' The shout came from within the knot of gentry framing the main chamber. The gravity of the situation was becoming apparent to most in the room. Raniel had just lost a major battle in the war and their king to boot. Would Kolgoth stage a counterattack? Would the other races see this as weakness and try to exploit her borders?

'It is for our Queen to decide our next action, and may the gods have mercy on us.' Said Lord Hal.

A small-framed man stood out to address Lord Hal. 'You are her adviser. I suggest you advise. Maybe your advice has been poor. After all, you were in King Thomas's council that sent legion after legion west. Few have returned.'

'You have your opinion, my lord.' Lord Hal's response was caged. The room became restless.

'I speak for the people. This war has crippled us and left us open to influences beyond our control. With all the mistakes you have been involved in, maybe it's time to step aside as Chief Adviser.'

'For you?' asked Lord Hal.

'Sir, it would go to a vote within the court.' The outspoken noble looked around and saw some approving nods. This bolstered his attack on the chief adviser. 'I think we agree that a man of your past should not hold office.'

Most of those gathered welcomed this altercation, someone standing up to the Crown. But for those who knew Lord Hal, they were very aware of the temper that came with his calmness.

'My past?'

Confidence left his accuser in that simple question, but he was too far in to stop. 'Well, let's say that your temper and the need to prove yourself should not have the Queen's ear. Maybe if you'd held your temper your wife would still be here today.' All sympathy for the challenge evaporated in an instant. Lord Hal bowed his head and sighed.

'You see, my–' The nobleman's sentence was cut short as the chief adviser drove his sword hilt into his rival's face. Lord Hal gritted his teeth slightly as they locked eyes.

'I atone for my sins every day.' There was a hush around the room broken only by the sound of whimpering. 'Guards! Get him out of here.' The general hubbub of the room rose again, this time with immense nervousness among the gathered lords. Lord Hal stood deep in thought.

The return of the Queen brought lord Hal from his daydream and set a chatter among the nobles. 'Lord Hal. I trust that you are still able to advise your Queen?' She saw the blood stain on the floor and sensed the nervousness of the gathered crowd.

'I can still advise as long as I still have the Queen's ear.'

'You do my lord. You were a friend to my father and are my most trusted adviser. What of your fellow advisers?' Gesturing to the smear on the flagstones.

'I believe that I have the full confidence of the court. He misjudged his attempt to undermine me and now understands his mistake.' Lord Hal showed no emotion.

The assembled advisers stood. Nervous at how would this young woman would handle the position thrust upon her? Sure, she had kept the throne warm when the king was away, but all decisions had continued to be relayed from the west. Minor issues were one thing, but what now with the war in the west? How would other nations take to the new Queen? There was a clear change in her character, and the apple now fell far from the tree. They had to find out where they stood.

The Queen surveyed the room, noting each face that stared back at her.

'Lord Hal, you are my chief adviser. Would you say that all here today have my best interests at heart?'

'No, my Queen.' There was a gasp and murmurs of disapproval. A few of the gathered elite looked at each other, searching for comprehension to the statement just given.

'My lord, how dare you. We have all pledged allegiance to the Crown and are patriotic towards this great land.' This came from a well-dressed woman whose need to prove herself outweighed her fear of Lord Hal.

'If I may finish ...?' He kept his gaze on the Queen. She gave a curt nod. 'The people gathered are Raniel. They all have a vested interest in the success and prosperity of the Crown. They are – my apologies, *were* – your father's advisers. He felt the need to keep such individuals close so he could understand the needs and wants of the public. For the most part, they were happy to manipulate the king for their own agenda, although never to the detriment of Raniel. I believe that some may now feel that the monarchy is coming to an end. Be wary of those who offer everything and have a lot to lose, for they will do all that it takes to keep it.'

'And what of you, my lord?'

'I have nothing.' He walked forward and drew his sword. The guards on either side of the throne drew theirs at the same instant. Aware that in a duel, the chief adviser could best them. As they stepped forward to intercept the threat, the Queen motioned for them to halt and lower their weapons. Lord Hal stood in front of the throne steps, dropped to his knees and placed his blade ceremonially in front of him. With both hands on the floor, he bowed his head. As he came back up, he looked at the Queen. 'It was my honour to serve King Thomas. I now pledge my life to you, my Queen. May I protect and advise you, by the grace of all the gods.'

This show of fealty only heightened the others' nervousness. 'Guards!' As one the guards in the throne room stood to attention, their heads snapping round to face the Queen. A couple of sobs were heard and an unfortunate trickle of water appeared from the leg of one particular gentleman.

'Understand this: I rule, I command and I demand loyalty. Those who disagree can discuss it with my father when they see him.'

'Lord Hal, I am in need of a general. I believe you have military experience?' Her tone was one of determination.

'Yes, your highness.'

'Those bastards killed my father. They destroy our assets in the west, going back on a treaty they agreed to. Some of you here would see us treat or bargain with the savages from Kolgoth. This would make us look weak to the other races, who may feel that this is the time to make advances on our borders. I tell you now that I will kill every Kol runt that crawls out of Kolgoth. Any objections?' There was a pause. She would still listen to their concerns before hanging them for treason.

'I thought not. *General* Hal, I charge you with strengthening the army. Empty the prisons, bars and whorehouses. Anyone able to hold a sword is now in the service of the Crown. Make examples of protesters if you feel the need. Drill them day and night. They must be battle-ready. Send a message to the mages' citadel. We may have a few more magic-users coming their way.'

The Queen scanned the crowd and her gaze fell on a petite woman in a fine green cape

'My lady, you are in charge of the Treasury?'

'Yes, my Queen.'

'I need funds.'

'Taxes are already high. I'm not sure that we can raise any more revenue.' She said, clasping her hands together to stop them shaking.

'You misunderstand my request, my lady. Get me the funds I require! I'm sure there are some very persuasive techniques that can be employed to aid in this task. We have agents abroad, and maybe some of their skills could be put to better use to relieve our good neighbours of some coin.

'This court is adjourned. There is a funeral to organise.'

Chapter Four

Not much remained in the great cities of Zinjal. Weather-beaten stone and piles of earth were the main features of this land. Nothing stopped the wind howling over the makeshift villages of souls eking out a survival. They had all come for different reasons. Fortune and adventure, freedom from justice and for some, the call was far stronger – a belief in a thousand-year-old myth. The followers of Talgameth were a sinister cult praying on the vulnerable and weak through faithful rituals, willing their master to return. They carved inscriptions of fealty and signalled to all that the ever-living stalked the places honest folk feared to tread. Some said they had seen him, clothed in flayed skin. Others said he could change his appearance. All agreed that his coming would mark the end of the realms that they had been chased from.

A tall heavy-set woman led a dozen ragged figures from an encampment. Shovels and buckets slung over shoulders. Dusk had fallen and a light dew caressed the less than fertile soil. Sandals offered little protection from the chill ground. The only protection they needed was from the whip of their masters. That came from the hard toil through hours of digging and scraping in the unforgiving earth. Those not deemed to be putting in the effort were made examples of. Their lifeless, bleached bodies hung at the entrance to the dig sites for all to witness.

These work parties had one task; to find the Emerald Knight. It is said the power held within the artefact would unleash a plague on the world that Talgameth would use to raze the great houses of the citadel and the

Brovan order. In truth no one knew what it looked like or if it even existed. The lashings of their overseers were testament to a faith that it did exist and they would find it. If their lord should return, he would surely bequeath such a gift as life ever living on the one who brought him his greatest weapon.

The same was happening all over Zinjal. The cult had grown in numbers over the years, strengthened by mages who walked a darker path, shunned from the citadel and persecuted for attempting to use dark magic. They had taken to raiding and capturing slaves to work the tombs and dungeons that they uncovered. Every city, town and building were now being mined. For a century the pace was picking up. The overseers lusting ever more over the progress towards their goal.

'Move.' The whip snapped sharply overhead. Sobs and moans were muffled by the rotten cloths that covered the slaves' faces. The harsh wind blew dust that tore at any exposed skin. The woman was deft with her skill. Many had been on the receiving end of the lash. Sometimes just for cruel pleasure. Lacerations would fester and rot. The slaves would hide such things from their captors for fear of more punishment. Many who entered the tombs would not return. Succumbing to the rigors brought on by disease or getting lost within the miles of tunnels, the slave's days were dark indeed. There was always a hope in their minds that the sun would bless them one day with an end to the misery.

'If you won't move for me, maybe you'd prefer my master's demons to devour your pitiful husks.' Another crack of the overseer's whip added to the torment, driving them on to their restless labours. The artefact must be found.

The train of shuffling sandals snaked its way through the dunes. Stopping at a crooked bell tower. The rotting stone protruding from the earth like a great sea beast taking its final breath before a dive to the ocean depths. A dozen corpses tied to stakes, evidence of past failures, lined a slope heading towards an opening. Heads down, each slave accepting the fact they were not the only ones in this situation.

'Your kinfolk chose their fate. You need but say and I'll deliver you to the gods. There are plenty of villages and towns to reap more labour.' She said rather self-indulgent.

Those assembled had learned long before this day to stay quiet and let her have her moment of torment.

A voice rang out from the chiselled opening. The overseer drew her sword and faced the challenge.

'Another runaway finally found the surface, eh? Should have stayed in the darkness. I'm going to run you through.'

The voice, shrieking and breaking as it came closer. An emaciated figure with barely a cloth covering his dignity burst forth from the bleak hollow entrance.

'I have it.' His eyes wide with a feverish grin. He held aloft a cloth wrapping. Stumbling in his elation he caught his balance and faced the overseer. 'I have it.'

The man's excitement lifted the hearts of those tasked to go search the depths of the city. A murmur started, which in any other situation would cause the whip to quell any talk. The slaves looked at one and other and a bright hope manifested in each face.

Like a jester bouncing on the balls of his feet, eyes darting between the overseer and what he held. 'I have it, I've found the artefact.' He held it out in both hands offering the package.

Her heart thumped and a dryness grew within her mouth. Hands trembling slightly as she took the offering. The man fell to his knees with a joyous cry. The overseer's thoughts turned to her own glory. Her finger tips tingling she gently unwrapped the cloth bindings. Her breathing had stopped, held to somehow alleviate the shaking of her hands.

'I found it.' Another cry came from below.

The last wrap was tentatively removed. The overseer let out a controlled breath. And the cloth wrappings fell to the ground.

Looking up, the man had hoped to see the gratified features on the one who he'd worked so tirelessly for. Instead, what he saw last was a rock about to connect with his face.

There was a deafening roar as the overseer bludgeoned the waif of a man with the very gift that he'd brought. As if possessed, with barred teeth and flaring nostrils, she continued her violence. Panic now ripped through the huddled slaves. Very little of the man's features were left as she stood lording over the corps. In her hand she held the gift. A bloodied stone. No carving, no powers and no offering to the ever living. Her chest still heaving she gently uncurled her fingers and let the rock fall to the ground. The thud as it landed was like a monastery bell to the slaves, breaking them from their awe at the violence delt to one of their own.

Turning to the quivering workforce. The calmness of her voice adding to a wordless threat.

'Find *me* the artefact.'

Chapter Five

A small commotion grew to shouting. 'What do you mean release them? They are for the gallows in the morning – criminals undeserving of sympathy.'

Lord Hal stepped between the guards. 'Where is the soldier who was brought in yesterday?'

Thinking he had more authority; the jail guard made a stand. 'My lord, I don't understand. This is unheard off.'

Lord Hal spun round with piercing eyes. 'Do not waste my time, you wretch. All prisoners are to be turned over to the army, and seeing as there will be no prisoners, that means you too.' The guard stood in dumb silence. 'Now, where is the soldier?'

The guard skulked down the corridor with a ring of keys in his shaking hand. Reaching the cell door, staring sheepishly at the two inhabitants. Maleth, curled up in bloodstained sheets, was barely conscious and unable to fully concentrate on what was happening. The soldier, however, struggled to his feet. The cell door screeched open. Maleth winced at the high-pitched attack on his ears.

'Get out of my way!' Lord Hal pushed past the guard and into the cell. He saw the mess that the messenger was in. Staying as calm as he could, the newly appointed general approached the soldier. There was a less than distinct hand gesture. It was all the soldier could muster as a salute. 'You were not to endure such things as this. Guard, who told you to beat this man?'

The guard stood sharply. With a quivering voice pleaded. 'No one, my lord. They are all criminals and due to be hung tomorrow. I ... I ... We weren't to know that he would be freed. Please, my lord, I was only doing my job.'

'Is your job to humiliate and beat a man in his final days on this earth? If every man were not needed, I would kill you where you stand and feed you to the rats.'

'Thank you, my lord.' Lord Hal noted release in tension in the guard's voice.

'Do not thank me, for you will have to stand beside these men on the front line in battles to come. Your actions may catch up with you. Release the other prisoners.'

Lord Hal's spoke softly to the soldier. 'The Queen is overcome with grief. You have done a great service to Raniel. Either by luck or ill fortune you have been given a second chance,'

'Yes, my lord.' And with that, the pain came like a wave and the messenger collapsed. Lord Hal made no attempt to catch him. 'Get the healers in here. Clean up this mess. Sergeant, how many do we have?'

'Twenty, sir. One dead in the end cell; looks like he's done a few rounds with an ogre.'

'Just the facts, please, Sergeant.'

'Sir! All seem able. A couple need healing, but nothing too severe.'

At the edge of the room there was a scraping. Lord Hal fixed his gaze on the noise and waited. Vermin were not to be tolerated in the jails. A quick flash of orange scale confirmed his thoughts. *Damn imps*! Shaking his head at the state of the place it was no wonder creatures like that thrived in the city.

'Get them ready for the carts. Count them in and sound off their names. Every wretch in here is now a member of Her Majesty's Army and will be treated as such.' Lord Hal was about to go through the personal effects in the tight little room used as an office when the jailer crept up.

'My lord, what of the magic-user?' His nervousness was plain to see.

'Who?' came Lord Hal's curt reply.

'Your friend's cell mate.'

'What of him? Looks like you took care of him too.'

'He's very dangerous; he killed two of the City Watch using magic – boiled them in their armour, unprovoked, while they were helping a young street kid off the ground.' Lord Hal thought for a minute and bellowed to the sergeant.

'Sergeant, restrain the man in cell four. He may be an interesting character.'

Trade was going well for Croft. He could handle Marin being the pain in the arse as long as he put coin in the jar. A few hours had gone by and Marin and Jack were passed out on the bar. A handful of customers lingered in the booths.

Croft's other son, a simple lad same height as his brother, but only half as wide, got on with his tasks around the alehouse. He wasn't strong – that was what Jack was for. Just about able to string a sentence together, he didn't have many dealings with the customers. He was sweeping up when the door opened. Four of the City Guard stood in the dim light of the sconces. The younger brother stopped and looked in wonder at their armour and weapons. First in the door was a well-built man with a stern expression on his face. He had a rolled-up parchment in his left hand. The three other guards fanned out and started looking in the booths. Frowning at the intrusion, Croft gave a false smile. The Watch, on occasion, would pop their noses in but rarely did the City Guard come down this way and certainly not to enter any of the businesses.

'Can I help you, sir?'

The officer looked at Croft with the disdain of a person of higher breeding and station. He unfolded the parchment. 'Can you read, barkeep?'

Croft was in a tough position. In his years of service, he had seen and given many beatings to jumped-up shits like this; they had authority and went to town on it. However, there were four of them and all he had was two sons, one of whom was in a drunken stupor. The other was standing idly, holding onto his broom. The way the guards were armed, they probably weren't for messing with, but he still fancied himself having a go, kicking the first one in the balls, which would even the odds a little. He awoke from his daydream.

'I can re–' He was interrupted by the ranking officer.

'All able-bodied persons shall be, without notice, impressed into the Ranielian Army. The authority has been given to me by the commander of Her Majesty's Army to carry out this mandate. Any force, as deemed necessary, shall be employed in order to complete this duty.'

'Her majesty?'

'Word has arrived that the king was killed in battle across the border from Longstone. There will be a state funeral before the end of autumn. The Queen has decreed that the army be brought up to full capacity for a counterattack on Kolgoth.' The officer left Croft in a state of disbelief to look round the bar area. His men were ushering people out of the booths and into the main saloon. Some struggles ensued, but they were overpowered by the soldiers.

Croft looked round in a panic. With dread he saw Jack. 'Please, sir, I run this alehouse with the help of my sons. My wife died some years back and I need their help. Can you spare them so I can make a living?'

'If those guttural beasts come east across the fens, there will be no city and no folk to sell your gruel to. You said *sons*. How many do you have? I guess that streak of piss with the brush is one?'

Croft took a sideways glance, too subtle for most to notice. The officer turned straightaway and narrowing in on the lads hunched over their mugs. 'Sir, I need my boys. I can't lift the barrels, clean and serve. They're simple lads; they would be no use to the army.'

'You are somewhat right, barkeep. I think your lad by the door couldn't lift a shield to save his own life.' With that, the realisation came to Jack that something was happening. He stood to his full height, wobbled a little and cracked his knuckles. 'But this bastard's been well fed.'

'You alright, Dad? Who're this lot?' Jack gave Marin a nudge. Marin now stood side by side with Jack. There was an uneasy tension in the air. The two eyed up their odds, scoping for an easy target or, in Marin's case, the exit.

'Looks like it's got nothing to do with me, Jack.' Marin made a move for the gap between the officer and the bar.

'Not so fast. You are hereby enrolled into the Ranielian Army. Wait here for transport to the military training grounds.'

'What? Piss off! I'm no soldier. I'm just a farmhand that stayed a little late in the pub.' With that there was a crash of chairs and a struggle of sorts. Two of the guard had pinned down a punter who, by all accounts, knew their parentage by calling the soldiers all the bastards under the sun. Marin and Jack were frozen as a guard punched the man repeatedly in the head. 'Guess he was right about him being a bastard then.' This comment earned

Marin a sword hilt to the gut from the officer. Marin doubled over coughing. 'Guess you're his brother, ya shitbag.'

A heavy leather gloved fist came across his jaw and burst his lip. Jack attempted to block the next blow, but was stopped by his father.

'Sir.' Croft stepped in. 'I am still the owner of this alehouse and, as far as I am aware, it is an offence to use your powers of office to intimidate law-abiding citizens.'

'Be careful, old man, I do not discriminate when educating the lower classes, young or *old*.' There was a bite to his comment that showed that he meant what he said.

'Enough!' The shout was loud enough to be heard across the scuffles and protests of the bar's patrons. 'Guards, round them up. Knock them out if you have to. Barkeep, your age has saved you from the rigours of military service. As for your sons, you can keep the simple one. If the war goes in our favour, and he serves his country well enough, your other son will return the better for it.'

It took three of the guards to control Jack, who was tied at the wrists and dragged outside, while Croft pleaded with the officer to leave him be. Marin was also escorted outside unceremoniously. Ten new recruits were press-ganged with a few minor injuries. Croft was left sobbing in a chair, watching his remaining son who continued to sweep up. 'If any gods are watching, please look after my son. If not, curses on you all, and Talgameth take you.'

Chapter Six

Lord Hal, dressed in the raiment of his newly appointed office; steel-plate armour with a black cloak draped over his shoulders, watched on as the Queen sat on the throne. It had been over a month since her father's death and the letters of condolence had been a constant reminder to her that she was wasting time sitting here. She was eager to be on the road heading to war. King Thomas had sent support to the border towns against raids. Diplomacy had broken down after emissaries had not returned. What did come back were frightened tales of brutality and murder at the hands of mounted raiders. The king could not sit idle and had raised his banners and led his army against Kolgoth. An ill-advised folly in the west which now left his daughter with a kingdom to rule.

The next hour dragged on. Lord Hal made pleasantries with some of the emissaries. He could see the lack of interest in the Queen's face. Listening in to some of the conversations between messengers was also tedious. Virtue signalling so as not to raise any question of their fealty to the crown. Lord Hal shook his head, content that nothing more sinister was afoot. He took notice of one unfortunate fellow, gangly and awkward. The messenger was ringing his cap in callused hands. He leapt when the chief adviser reached him.

'Apologies, I didn't mean to startle you.'

The messenger swallowed hard, 'beg your pardon my lord, I dint see you approach.' His wide eyes trying to soak up all the information assailing them.

Lord Hal gave a muted laugh. 'Ha, first time in the great hall?'

'First time out of my village. My father is the magistrate although he is too poorly to attend.' His voice trailing off.

'I wish your father a speedy recovery, sir.' Lord Hal bowed and went to turn. He was stopped by the young messenger.

'S'cuse me my lord.' His voice quivering a little. 'Which one is the Queen?'

A light hearted smile grew on Lord Hal's grim features. 'That will be her sitting, looking bored on the throne. She's been listening to the same drivel all day. Hope your speech is better.'

Struck by what he saw, his response was less than the decorum required in the great hall. Stifling his enthusiasm, he measured his next sentence. 'My, she's beautiful.'

'Reign it in lad, she's not for you. With the way things are going, she'd have you locked up and sent to the front lines with a snap of her finger. Don't let your village down by making a fool of yourself.'

'Thank you, my lord. I'm sorry for any disrespect.' Lord Hal locked eyes for a little more time than was required to make sure the message got across. He continued on to mingle and keep an eye on proceedings having the odd chuckle to himself over the young messenger.

A tall, slim-framed Tialan stepped forward to address the Queen. Tiala was a nation of engineers, problem-solvers and thinkers. King Thomas had gone to great lengths to ally Raniel to the logic schools of the southern lands. They were also sympathetic to the need to gather resources. After all, if you had no raw materials then all the thinking in the world could not make a self-loading crossbow. The emissary had a slight purple hue to his skin, which was tight across high cheekbones. Long ears were his most noticeable feature and this somehow made people question a Tialan's honesty. The people of Weelan were a mixed bunch, but the greater population of Raniel didn't like change, or anyone who happened to be different from them.

'I offer my condolences on your bereavement. The king was respected among our people. He is a loss to us all. I trust that our nations will continue to prosper in friendship.' He gave a slow, shallow bow.

'I am in need of friends. These are troubled times.' The Queen did not reciprocate any diplomatic gestures. Her guest noticed this subtle omission with a little annoyance. 'I trust that you will be comfortable in the time that you are with us. It may interest me to hear some of your views on Kolgoth.'

'You have my counsel.' He bowed again and left with an elegant stride.

As the last of the messengers and emissaries finally left the Great Hall, Lord Hal let his shoulders drop and took a breath to help relax. The air was stuffy and warm, full of perfume and body odours.

Holding his black-plumed helmet under his right arm, he walked purposefully to the throne. He was unarmed. The Queen had deemed it unnecessary for anyone in the court to carry a weapon. That didn't sit well with him. She had nothing to defend herself with.

'I am weary, my lord. Make it quick.'

Lord Hal reached the throne steps, and took a moment to survey the room. 'Your Majesty. I have an update on preparations. We have mustered over 12,000 soldiers and the training camps are drilling them 10 hours a day. Five hundred offi–' He was abruptly cut off.

'Drill them for twelve.'

'As you wish. Five hundred officers have been commissioned. They will be ready to take office in two months. However, I must add that as the plans go it will be winter when your army is ready to march.'

'Then double your efforts.'

'You misunderstand my point, your highness. We will be ready in the winter. Anything before that would mean the suicide of our forces, not only in the field, but also, our journey west will have the weather against us and make the movement of supplies difficult. Food will be short and poor morale will lead to some desertion.'

'What affects us will also affect Kolgoth. Any desertion will be dealt with, I'm sure.' The Queen had made her point clear and Lord Hal gave a courteous nod. 'What of magic-users? Did we find many lurking with the low life?'

'We found just under forty, but none powerful enough for battle. I will use them as healers for the wounded.'

'I do not see the need for healers. These soldiers are fighting for Raniel and the only way is forward. Send them to the mages' college. I will give you the extra time you need, but get them battle-ready.'

'May I speak freely?'

'No. You will do as I command and act in the manner of your station. You have until the end of winter. Now leave.'

She always was stubborn and difficult but she's changed. She's no longer her father's daughter, Lord Hal thought to himself. 'Your highness.' He made a bow and started to move, then stopped and turned, thinking this might be his chance to give uninterrupted advice. 'I hope that you do this for the right reasons. We all grieve for those we have lost. I will be with you at the very end and my counsel has your best interests before all else.' There was no reply from the Queen. 'Your army will be ready, but in order for them to fight, they must understand the reason. That reason cannot solely be for your revenge, as that could spell the end of Raniel.'

'Take your leave.' This was level and calm. 'You have advisers in this court who would say that you are unfit to command my army.' She let that hang in the air. Lord Hal lowered his gaze and headed for the door. Before he made it, the huge door opened and another emissary strode in. Lord Hal placed a hand on his shoulder and was instantly struck by fear and doubt. In a split second his terrors filled every space in his mind. His nostrils were even filled with the stench of past battles, crafting the memories more vividly. Staring at the newcomer with furrowed brows, searching for answers. All that came was a face, not of the man before him but of a more sinister being with empty lidless eyes. A voice spoke to his very consciousness. A tone between a scream and a lullaby, only heard by lord Hal.

'Raniel will fall, as will the citadel and Brovan order. None shall stand in my way once I have the Emerald Knight.' The words came from lips unmoving. Lord Hal winced at every syllable unable to let go.

'Fear me, I have returned to reap the souls from this land.'

The brief encounter made Lord Hal stumble back. Looking around, he fixed his attention on the emissary. He was unsure what had happened or even if it happened.

'My lord, forgive me for my entrance, could I speak with the Queen?'

Lord Hal's daze receded allowing for a little more clarity. Standing aside, he let the emissary approach the Queen. Keeping his distance, the adviser watched the two speak in hushed tones. Once their discussions were finished lord Hal escorted the emissary out of the great hall. Lord Hal bid the emissary good day as the memory of the interaction faded and the Queen sat motionless, with a hollow gaze.

Chapter Seven

Labouring on four iron-rimmed, wooden wheels, the cart made its advance along Raniel's dirt tracks, pulled by four large horses and driven by soldiers of Her Majesty's Royal Ranielian Army. The soldiers were lightly armoured; iron-mail shirts with leather pauldrons, shin guards and studded bracers. Both were wrapped in rough-spun cotton cloaks. The weather wasn't bad for the start of autumn, but sitting up on the front of the cart all day could drain a man of the will to live. Inside the cart were twenty-four citizens of Weelan conscripted to the army *for the protection of her majesty and the realm of Raniel*.

This statement was going over and over in Marin's mind.

Every bump, stone and hole in the road made its human cargo bounce off the wooden benches and collide with the poor bastard next to them. This did two things: piss off the person they landed on; and drag them from their thoughts into the present nightmare.

Marin took a minute to look around. No smile or acknowledgement came from any of the faces. Most heads were bowed, some covered with long unkempt hair, whereas others hid their glazed eyes beneath the hoods of their cloaks. But no hood or hair could disguise their despair. The only recognisable frame was Jack, hunched over, taking up almost two spaces on the bench. Marin did not envy the two passengers squashed on either side of him.

'Jack! You, okay?' There was no response. Jack sat, silent. Marin went back to trying to understand how recent events had unfolded. He had been sober for almost eight hours. The very day that he'd thought about getting his life together and making something of himself, the crazy bitch Queen had robbed him of any opportunity to sort his shit out.

The train of carts continued to meander through the Ranielian countryside, ten strong, with two mounted outriders for each. The occupants thought that this was for their safety in case of ambush on the way to the training camps. In reality, it was in case any of the new conscripts decided that army life was not for them and tried to escape. Then they would be chased down and persuaded that returning to the cart was the best option for their general health and well-being.

Two carts to the rear of Marin held Maleth. The twenty-three other inhabitants of that cart regarded him with nervous fascination. His face was scarred and bruised, with eyes barely open. His hands were bound with tight leather thongs. One thought, shared with a few of the other conscripts was, how could he be so dangerous? Another thing that set Maleth apart was that he wore a steel gorget around his throat inscribed with runes, to stop him using magic.

There were murmurs around the cart, but every one kept themselves to themselves. No one knew what was to come; all they knew was that their old life was now far behind them, as they wound their way east to the training camps. There had also been an attempt by a couple of fools to self-discharge themselves from her majesty's service, which had been met with a swift interception from a well-drilled and capable mounted guard, who didn't really care if the poor sod ended up with broken bones because of being run down by their horse. Watching the event unfold did not inspire any more efforts.

Maleth meditated on his recovery. He couldn't use magic, so his restoration had to be left to Mother Nature. The uneven road for him was a sentence in itself. Multiple rib fractures had rendered any position uncomfortable, let alone the constant shaking and bouncing of the cart. His thoughts drifted back to Senal and the life he'd had. How hard would it have been to pick up a brush and clean his mentor's study? Longing for his bunk in the dormitory and the sweet smells of meadow grasses in the forecourt. He remembered getting caught. Sneaking out into the city, his over confidence didn't take into account that his mentor had been keeping a close eye on him for many months. His hands were full of bread and cheese. He sensed the disappointment in the guards faces even through their elaborate helms. Nothing was said on the march back to the grand master, his fate surely sealed to slop duty or helping the stable hands. He cursed the morning he'd got his orders to head south to Weelan.

The cart came to an abrupt halt, its sudden stop leaving those inside a little disorientated and still feeling the vibrations through their feet and backsides. Orders were shouted outside. When the doors opened, white light bathed the conscripts. Each one shielded their eyes from the glare.

'Everyone out! Stand in line next to the cart.' Shuffling towards the rear, they climbed out one by one onto the hard-packed earth. Marin looked around and saw the training camp for the first time.

'Holy shit buckets!'

'Get in line. Move.' The impatient guard gave Marin a less than friendly nudge.

The rest of the carts were emptying and the full extent of the camp became apparent. A 10-foot-high wall of earth and wood enclosed over 500 tents, with a large area in the centre and some wooden buildings off to the right. Groups of soldiers were running around the perimeter in formation. Others were being drilled in weapons. *Looks like this is it then*, Marin thought.

Looking along the lines of the other conscripts, Marin noticed one who stood out with hands tied and a severely beaten face. 'Shit! He clearly put up some struggle to get in a mess like that,' he muttered to the world in general.

'Quiet! Sound off your names.' The officer went down the line asking each person their name and occupation and if they had any military experience. It was Marin's turn.

'Your name?'

'Your mum.' Marin was not the brightest and Jack, having heard his response, shook his head.

'I don't have time for this cocky bullshit.' The officer motioned to the guard, who moved behind Marin and pushed him to the ground.

'Lesson number one.' The officer was abrupt but unfazed by Marin's response. 'We are all here for the same reason and I'm sure you would all like to go back to the hole they dragged you from. But I assure you that our land and way of life is under threat. We must all step up to defeat the enemy. Keep your heads down, get on with the training, do as you are told and you will be on the front line soon enough. If you survive, then that hole will be waiting for you on your return.' The officer bent down level within an inch of Marin's face. 'And it's, 'your mum', *sir*!'

The conscripts were ushered off to the quartermaster for uniforms and effects. Each recruit received a set of cotton breeches and undershirt, a leather lobster-plate set of body armour, boots, gloves and a full-length cloak. Along with the military attire, they were also provided with personal grooming paraphernalia.

'If you lose anything, you'll be paying for a new set.' The quartermaster was not to be argued with. He was a very stout man with a large beard tied in plaits about four inches long. His arms were enormous and he was covered in tattoos and the odd scar. It was clear that he had seen action. His eyes were full of experience and stories he was unwilling to recount.

One recruit piped up, 'We aren't getting paid for this shit!'

'Better not lose it then, or you'll pay for it in fingers.' With that, he took his knife and sliced off the end of a cigar before lighting it. The recruit made no further comment.

After getting their things, they were marched off to their assigned tents. Each tent had ten bunks, a small stove and a lockbox for their personal gear. It was cramped, with barely enough space to stand and get changed. Marin gave a slight chuckle at the unfortunate reality for those who were sharing with Jack.

A guard pulled back the tent flap. 'You have thirty minutes to gather your thoughts and acquaint yourselves with your new surroundings. When the bugle sounds, you will be on the parade ground in two rows with your tent mates.' Marin looked at his bunk and thought it beat sleeping in straw and smelling of horseshit. A woman next to the tent entrance started the introductions and eventually came round to Maleth.

'Well, if you wish me to speak ...' – this was difficult as Maleth's broken jaw was still healing – '... I guess I was in the wrong place at the wrong time and I witnessed the *honour* of the City Watch.' The vision that haunted his thoughts came freely to the front of his mind. 'A young girl should have just been given a telling off and a skelp across the arse. But no, those bastards beat her and stamped her face into the ground. She's stealing off the gods now.' There was silence in the tent. A young lad didn't know where to look. 'How old are you, boy?'

'Sixteen, sir ... well, I will be soon. Don't tell the guards.'

'This doesn't seem to be a game children should be playing. That little girl was half your age and look what they did to her. And there's no need to call me *sir*. I'm just arrow-fodder, like you.' Maleth's hands were unbound and he sat staring at them. They were clenched into fists. 'I killed the two guards. I set fire to them, roasted them in their armour. After that I fell unconscious and woke up in jail.' The occupants of the tent darted looks at each other.

Marin took an interest. 'That was you? I heard a different set of events.'

'I wish it were different. I never intended to kill anyone. Rage took over and here I am.'

'What's with that fancy thing round your neck?' Marin asked.

'It's a Tialan magic gorget. It stops me from using my *talents* as they put it. It's a curse in my opinion.' There was a tangible release of nervous tension in the tent. 'According to the guards, I'm very dangerous.'

There was an awkward moment as if Maleth was interrupted from his train of thought. 'I still see that little girl's face,' he said quietly.

Marin sat down on the end of his bunk, thinking of the story he'd just heard. 'What's your name, friend?'

'Maleth.'

'Well, Maleth, if the temperature in here gets too hot, too fast, I'm going to stab you in the balls, but you might be handy for drying off the socks.' There was a pause and the rest of the folk in the tent took a breath, not knowing which way that comment could be taken. Maleth laughed until it became too sore.

'I'll take that.'

Chapter Eight

The Queen paced the old oak floor of her bedroom. She felt adrift in the wind, her loyal protector had gone mad. Drunk on spirits or position. Whatever it was, he was gone. Her own thoughts were confused and jumbled. Anger boiled then it was washed away with compassion. Fear bled into panic and she would end up with knuckles white as the first snow of winter.

Looking out her window on the city, she clutched her arms around her chest. The city was not what it used to be. Her days of sneaking out and ambling though the markets were a distant memory. There was a heavy shroud hanging over the streets and she could feel it. Shutting her eyes, a vision flashed. It was the face of an emissary but however she looked the skin slewed off to reveal the horror that lay behind. Rust-stained teeth, glistening with moisture. A black tongue licking purple lips. The hoarse whisper of a desert breeze called out

'Raniel will crumble, you are the key. Your father's disappointment will cling to you like leaches on your heart.'

Stumbling she fell to the floor just catching the edge of the bed. With a heaving chest she wailed, letting all the emotions that had kept her strong flood out. Tears fell onto her now trembling hands. The salty water stinging. Turning to see her palms, she saw the blackness of burnt meat and cracks of oozing blood. Screaming for the world to hear.

A knock at the door preceded the guard bursting through. Behind him was a maid who ran to the Queens aid.

'Your Majesty, what is it?

'Ahh, the visions and the horror, is he here?' The maid motioned to the guard to leave and close the door.

'It is only the two of us my Queen.' Pulling her hands down the maid gave a gracious smile. 'You are safe from whatever vexes you. Shall I recall the guards to check the room?'

'No, thank you, I am a mess. Please fetch me a towel.' The maid curtsied, and returned with some water and towelling. Calmer, the Queen scanned the room and checked her hands. 'They were burnt, the pain felt real.' Gasping she remembered the face, disfigured and foul. Struggling to dry her face with shaking hands, the maid gently dabbed the fine cotton cloth on the Queens face. The maid's smile never left her face.

'Thank you, I don't recall seeing you before. What is your name?'

'My name is Freya, your Majesty, and I've not been here long.' Studying her face the Queen saw only kindness in Freya's eyes and a youthfulness like her own.

'Well Freya, you should not see me in this state. I have had the most unpleasant time and think that I should retire. I will need my strength for tomorrow and the days to come. Would you turn down my bed and draw the drapes.' Freya curtsied again then paused.

'If I may? I could help you with your weariness.'

'Are you a magic user?' The Queen said cautiously.

'Not as such, I have a gift to make people feel better. I used to use it on my sisters before.' She broke off stifling the rest of her sentence. The Queen now eager to hear the rest of her story motioned her to go on.

'They enlisted and went west with your father. They have not returned.'

The Queen's own anger at the loss of her father bubbled to the surface. 'Then we both have need to feel better. Please help me.' She smiled and witnessed Freya's eyes glow a feint green. Dropping her shoulders and rolling her neck the Queen let out a giggle. 'Well, that hit the spot. I feel like a child again, safe, and that my parents are in the next room waiting for me to jump onto their bed for a hug. Freya you have entered my life at the lowest point. What can I give you as thanks?'

'I am here to serve. I would ask nothing of my Queen.'

'A woman with your talents should not be a mere maid. I am in need of someone to whom I can talk with.' The Queen and her newest adviser talked late into the night. Something that she never had, a person of the same age to chat and gossip about court life. Freya's own life was far different.

In the centre of a large stone and wooden structure, a brazier smouldered. The embers were still glowing, but no flame showed its prowess to the onlookers. Twelve there were, all in solemn contemplation, the light from the brazier creating deep shadows on their faces and armour. One muscular figure stood out from the rest, adorned with tattoos and scars. He rubbed his temple pulling the creases tighter around his furrowed brow. Guldr was first and foremost a warrior and through many trials he'd become the protector of the Kolgothian way of life.

His low voice reverberating around the sacred space. 'Dark has the news been of late. War is upon us and the reason is clouded. Brothers, as High Chief and Guardian of Kolgoth, I ask the great tribes to meet this adversity as one. I have consulted with the Shaman and the spirits show great pain and misery for our people. The lands will burn. Our way of life will change, but the great Kolgothian race will endure.' This brought a murmur of agreement among the rest of the Tribes' Council.

Silence fell once more on the group. As a mark of respect, time was given for the speaker's words to sink in before any more debate. An old warrior raised his hand.

'If I may speak, Guardian?'

'With my respect, Great Chief.' Guldr gave a slow bow. The new speaker had pale, almost grey, skin. A long mohawk of silvery white hair cascaded over his shoulders. The lines on the speaker's face told of worry, and scars told stories of a thousand trials of his own. His beard was as white as his hair, pleated with many rings, each a symbol of authority.

'For almost 400 years have I walked among the grasses of the northern lands and been blessed by the light of the stars. Peace bathed our lands for centuries before my time. Ever since the fall of Zinjal, all peoples of Kalnath shared wisdom and knowledge. Of late the skies in the north have been veiled, crops have failed on fertile land, there has been talk of animals giving birth to abominations and brother killing brother. It saddens me that I have to witness these times, but I cannot long for the past. They will not come back. I have sought wisdom from our Shamans and I have taken several journeys with our ancestors. My dreams bring me back to the same conclusion: I know not what ails these lands, but it is dark. Rumours cast to the wind suggest a return of a long-forgotten evil.' This time, the pause was a little longer. The old chief was much esteemed among the Council.

'Take comfort from your memories, great friend.' The High Chief had heard rumblings of similar stories. Looking around the gathering, Guldr stopped at a younger chief, no less adorned by scars and braid rings. 'How do the southern lands fair?'

'Guardian, my lands have seen no change. Our trade with Tiala is prospering. The sun rises on the birth of the next generation of my family and we have mastered the construction of large ships to sail. With the permission of the Council, we would like to explore west in search of other lands. We have also heard rumours from our Shaman of the ills that befall our neighbours.'

A low, deep sneer, almost a growl, came from opposite the High Chief. 'I'll tell you what ails this land – the treacherous Ranielian swine; those who used to be allies against the threat of the Zinjal mages. I am Golth of the Noidal Tribe.'

The High Chief, breaking with common etiquette, interrupted. 'I knew your father well. This is your first council meet and you are welcome to speak freely. Do not dishonour him with ill-chosen words.'

Golth gave the High Chief a withering look, which was ignored. 'My lands have been ravaged by these rats. Peaceful logging and mining villages have been burnt, kith and kin murdered. One year ago, my father sat at this council and spoke of such atrocities. It was the Great Council's decision to let be the misguidance of rogue Ranielian criminals; let the eastern tribes deal with the insertions themselves.'

Golth stood to his full height. He was seven feet tall, with broad muscular shoulders. Scars were evident across his chest and face and alluded to the challenges he'd confronted to hold the chief's position after his father's death.

'My father died protecting these lands, when you would give no help. We faced them as they defiled our farms ready for harvest. Their golden hero sat mounted, commanding an army of thousands. They did not come to find peace; they came to murder and destroy. Many Kol brothers returned to the earth that day to rest with the ancestors. We were victorious. Word came to me as I knelt in the bloody mud, holding my dying father, that the Golden Knight was dead and that it had been the King of Raniel. I was enraged, but my father spoke to me and beseeched me to give the king an honourable exit from the battlefield. He insisted that the king knew not what he did. This was his last wish before his soul left him. Out of love for my father we let the survivors live and allowed them to cross the border back to Longstone.' Golth sat back down and awaited a reply. When the response came, it was not what Golth had expected.

As he stood Guldr looked around at the eleven tribal chiefs from all over Kolgoth. 'Our wisdom was misplaced. Your father is an immense loss to this council and to the lands that he protected. May our actions be judged by the Mother Shaman and our ancestors.' He took a braiding ring from his long, plaited beard. 'I owe a debt of gratitude to your house. Accept this ring as payment, to honour that which was given by your father.'

Golth took the ring and nodded. Each of the other tribal chiefs took a braiding ring from their beards and gave them to Golth.

'We may not know the reason behind King Thomas's course of action. The death of such a man will lead to revenge. I ask you all to speak to the ancestors and look inside yourselves for guidance on the right path. We are heading towards the inevitable, but how we get there may decide the outcome. We will meet again as the winter gives way to spring.'

As one, the tribal chiefs got up, bowed to the Guardian and left the hut. Guldr steadied his thoughts. Stretching out his hands to the brazier, letting his focus pass by and into the inviting glow. Moments passed or maybe hours before a thought came. *Head east now and crush their weakened army.* He would certainly get the support of the tribes. Bloodlust made his fingers tingle. Too long had he sat as guardian, getting weak and longing for battle. Concentrating again trying not to let his thoughts run away, he took a few more shallow breaths. *Send a messenger, look for peace.* The muted growl was testament to what he thought of that idea.

A sharp pain as ice on skin borrowed deep into his head. Reeling he cried out in silence. Like the drowning, gasping for air. His heart thump against his chest. *What is this madness?* he thought.

The voice was neither in the future or in the past. It didn't exist where ever he looked for it. It was familiar yet unknown.

'Kolgoth falls with you Guardian.'

'Who are you spirit? The night plain does not belong to the dammed.' Guldr searched inside his mind for the source but found only shadows. The walls within were getting further away, the space opened up to visions of cavorting shapes, none of which he recognised. Laughing and screeching forms exploding into reality then gone as quick.

'I am the forgotten. Lay bare your soul to be reaped.'

He awoke, panting next to the cold and lifeless brazier. The embers had long since died and the smoke replaced by his own breath. With fists clenched as tight as his jaw, slowly releasing the strain on his muscles he came too from his vision. Soaked through and shivering, Guldr could not place what had happened. He would need to find someone to make sense of his dream.

Chapter Nine

The ground was solid with rime and the trees that surrounded the outer balustrade of the training camp bare of foliage. Dark fractal lines against the azure of the winter sky gave the only glimpse of the boughs that once formed the tree. The view of nature's death added to the misery in the camp. Marin's arm was twisted tight from his shoulder to his wrist, his face driven firmly into the hard ground and a knee on his shoulder blade. He was pinned for a second, then released. Maleth gave a smile and took a couple of steps back.

'You're really getting the hang of this shit, Maleth.' It was now Maleth's turn to attack Marin. Close-combat training had been going on for a couple of weeks and the recruits were slowly building up an immunity to sore and aching muscles. Maleth took a swing at Marin. Marin had driven both forearms into the punch, connecting with his partner's bicep and wrist. There was no power left in his attack and Maleth thought he had broken his arm.

With lightning speed Marin swept at his friend's legs. He hit the ground hard. Rolling over onto his back he looked up at Marin, silhouetted against the bright sky.

'No need to go in so hard. You near broke my arm, ya bastard.' Maleth began to rub some life back into his arm. 'That'll bruise.'

'Sorry, pal.'

'No, you're not.'

'Your right. C'mon, get up.' Marin grabbed his good arm and hauled Maleth to his feet. 'We need to get this set of moves nailed before moving on to weapons.'

'I'm done in. I've been on the ground about a thousand times this morning already and I ache all over. The only saving grace is this bloody collar. At least you can't put any chokes on.'

'Don't give up, Mal. Those Kolgothian bastards aren't going to give you a rest.'

Maleth lowered his voice, beckoning Marin in closer. 'I need out.' He rubbed his muscles whilst keeping an eye on the trainer. 'I shouldn't be here. My job was to find information on a 1000-year-old ghost and report back. I'm not even Ranielian.'

Their conversation was getting some attention from the other recruits. Marin grabbed his arm and dragged him over his shoulder.

'Keep talking,' said Marin.

'A little hard when you're thrown to the ground.'

'I did it gently and it will keep the rubber lugs from listening in.' The two rolled about a bit and made the odd screech and tap out. Marin noticed there was no fight left in his friend.

'Let's do it then. We can make a run for it on guard duty. Or, I guess we could take on a couple of the guards and have a fair chance,' said Marin raising his voice slightly.

'I wouldn't get far with this round my neck. I don't want to hurt anyone else.'

'Apart from me, eh?'

No smile cracked Maleth's face. Muddy and bruised he sat with a crushing weight on his chest. 'If we run, the rest of the group will get the lashes.'

'Bugger them.'

'If we get caught, we'll all get lashes.'

'Let's ride it out, when were on the march west we can make a go then. Shit, we won't be the only ones. If we keep our heads down no one will notice two more ugly bastards missing.' Marin gave a nod and helped Maleth up again.

The horn blew for the end of the session. There was a sigh from Maleth. They fell in line in front of the Sergeant. The rest of the recruits were in no great shape either. A quick scan of the line revealed bleeding noses and burst lips. One unfortunate trainee had been taken to the healers with a broken arm after a rather overenthusiastic attack. The Sergeant unrolled a parchment. Four names were called out and one by one they stepped out of line to the front. Maleth noticed something that he had not seen before. Each person wore a collar similar to his. The collar felt extremely tight now. Marin was oblivious to what was happening. The hairs on Maleth's neck stood up, he took a slight inhale, then it came, like a blow to the stomach.

'Maleth from Weelan.' Marin's head snapped round in recognition of his friend's name. This was no pairing-up drill for the next session. Marin's dread came when he realised that he had genuine feelings for Maleth. He had never really had a friend. Sure, there was Jack, but he'd just kicked the shit out of him now and again. And come to think about it, Marin had paid his father for the privilege.

Maleth stepped forward. It was about now that the old Marin would have stepped in and given the sergeant some lip, but a little wiser now, he stayed in line. He fought his rolling stomach and the instinct to fight. Why were these people being singled out?

'You five have been identified as magic-users and as such are to be transferred, immediately. There is a coach waiting. You have twenty minutes to get your things together and fall in at the gate.' There were confused murmurs from the ranks and a great deal of relief that they hadn't been dragged out for punishment. Maleth slowly turned to face the ranks and his eyes met Marin's. There was an empty, hollow air to his gaze, almost stunned. Within a minute, Maleth's tent mates were around him.

'You're leaving us?' came a question. 'You'll be missed.' Like Marin, Maleth had a connection with all the tent mates.

'Hope the gods look after you, Mal,' said Marin.

'They cursed me the day they gave me magic. Can't see them changing now,' he said.

'Just keep your head down. Looks like you'll be going to the High Citadel. You might get to be a healer. You'll sleep in a proper bed, in your own room no doubt.' Marin tried to smile. 'With any luck you'll get a maid to empty your chamber pot and she might even keep your fresh cotton sheets warm.'

Maleth smiled back. 'I'll be thinking of you, freezing your arse off in the tent.'

'Better not be thinking of me when you're with your maid.' Marin extended his hand. Maleth clasped it and pulled him in for an embrace.

'Thank you, Marin. You've kept my spirits up when I was low, kept us entertained and have always been honest – sometimes brutally so. I'm honoured to have known you, friend.'

'Piss off! You'll be wanting to bang me next.' They broke off the embrace, but kept their hands clasped.

'You couldn't afford me,' Maleth said with a smile. They shared a brief laugh.

Marin took on a more serious tone in his voice. 'I'll see you on the battlefield.'

'And if hell comes first, I'll make sure they stoke the fires for your arrival,' Maleth replied.

The sergeant bellowed an order to get back to training.

'I'm going to miss that bastard,' Marin said as they walked away, leaving Maleth in the tent.

'We all are,' said the trainee next to him.

The last few miles were on foot – a welcome break from being rattled about in a wooden cart. Trying to straighten up and clicking things back into place was painful. They had regular stops for camp, but walking upright in the fresh air was tantamount to a form of freedom. Maleth kept his thoughts to the here and now, not wishing to fantasise about potential scenarios towards which they might be heading. There were no large gates or guardhouses, just sprawling homesteads and fields, which merged slowly into one another, becoming more and more populated. Thirty of them ambled along in two rows, everyone soaking in what they saw. Each had many questions, knowing no one would answer any of them.

A few hours passed and Maleth and his companions were deep in the merchant city of Jeil'asl. The air was heavy and stale, caused mainly by the huge buildings overhanging the street. Tightly-packed shop fronts with stalls on the street stopped any form of breeze. The streets had their own climate, with the only wind that which blew out of the back end of a horse. Little of the sky could be seen. Maleth thought of the streets back home – this place had none of the graces. The inhabitants were not much better and wore heavy leather cloaks mud-caked around the bottom, and multi-strapped boots up to their knees. Most had a large dagger fixed to one boot, secured in a scabbard. The grizzled and angry looks on most of the faces told of hard bargains and a mistrust of all.

They walked a little further and the buildings opened up to the sun splitting the sky. Maleth took time to adjust his eyes to this sensation. When the white spots abated, the vista he encountered was of sailing vessels and pontoons filled with crates, barrels and bustling men lifting and carrying goods. Slowly, sounds crept into his ears. The enclosed nature of the streets had deafened him but now a vivid symphony of tolling bells, shouting merchants and boat-rigging dancing in the wind was a wonder to behold. The group was herded onto the quayside. No one paid any attention to the assembly of weary travellers. To most, they were just another commodity left on the wharf. Maleth listened to the lapping of the waves against the hulls of grand ships. The vessel in front of them was the *Dying Siren*.

'Cheery sort of name for a boat,' Maleth whispered to the man next to him. 'I would have preferred *Swift Wave Rider* or *Mighty Unsinkable*.'

'Yeah, and I'll hazard a guess that were getting on it. If there's a jolly fat man with a wooden leg and eye patch, I'll end myself.' Maleth chuckled at his companion's response.

They watched the man in charge of their party animatedly discussing something with an officious-looking woman. She had a small satchel by her side containing a few rolled-up scrolls. She wore a fine cape, a tight leather jerkin and trousers of loose-fitting cotton. Her attire set her apart from other people on the quayside. *Probably one of the harbour master's assistants*, Maleth thought. She gave a curt nod and walked to where the group was milling about.

'Ladies and gentlemen, I will be your captain for your voyage aboard the *Dying Siren* to the Isle of the High Citadel. I have been told that payment will only be granted when you arrive safely at your destination. Should you choose to die before making landfall, a very talented member of my crew will resurrect you. Then you'll wish that you had never set foot aboard my ship. This is no pleasure cruise and I will expect you to help when you can.'

Maleth's companion tilted his head towards him. 'If that's the type of pirate you get around here, I might brace my mainsail and try a life at sea.'

This is it, he thought. He had to go through with whatever gods forsaken plan Raniel had lined up for him. He supposed that the citadel might offer him something. He didn't know what exactly. If he spoke to someone who wasn't barking orders, they might see the mistake and send him back to Senal.

'This way.' She gestured to them to follow. 'We leave at high tide.'

Chapter Ten

The emissary De'sal was in an alcove reading a parchment under a sconce. He looked up without moving his head and saw Freya walk towards him. He had noticed her in the Great Hall, a beautiful woman by Ranielian standards, but her ears were too short and her pale skin tone did nothing for him. On his wrist he wore a silver bracelet with engraved runes and a small precious stone. Again, without moving his head, he noticed that one of the runes was glowing slightly.

'Emissary? I'm glad that I have caught you.'

'My lady, we have not been introduced.' De'sal folded the note and placed it in his inside robe pocket and simply raised his head to give this newcomer attention.

'I am Freya, the Queen's adviser.' As she spoke a white haze came across her eyes, so faint it was barely noticeable. The stone on De'sal's bracelet radiated a little light. He hid it quickly under his sleeve. Freya was trying to read what was written in the note, but could not make out the fuzzy letters. She was fluent in Tialan script but unable to put the shapes together. 'The Queen would like us to discuss terms of an arms trade.'

'You do not seem like a military person or, for that matter, a politician.'

'Looks should not lead you to a conclusion which you may regret.' *Ah, a barbed threat so soon into our discussion*, De'sal thought.

'My apologies. I am not familiar with the Ranielian Court.'

'May we talk in private?'

De'sal looked around. There was no one nearby. He'd found a nice quiet spot to read his notes. 'As you wish. Please lead the way.'

Freya escorted De'sal along a couple of corridors and into a small courtyard. Off to the left there was a door. She pressed the latch and looked inside. 'Perfect! This is the maid's study and is sometimes in use, but it's free at the moment. Please, take a seat. I'll get some wine. We water it down so that the taste is there without the hangover in the morning.'

'Indeed.' He gave an acknowledging nod. 'You wish to discuss arms?' When her back was turned, De'sal checked his bracelet. There was no shine from the stone, but a rune was still glowing.

Freya sat opposite him and took a small sip of the blood-red liquid. She crossed her legs, giving De'sal the slightest glimpse of her thigh. She saw him look for a split second. *This is too easy,* she thought. 'Yes, we are in need of your more technical advances in warfare and, as we are protecting your borders as well, I feel ...' She stopped herself. 'Sorry, the Queen feels that the price of these goods should be lowered out of good faith.' She gave a small curt smile.

De'sal had played many a game and lost a few, which had cost him a pretty penny and a little reputation. He had learned from his mistakes and this little whore would not get the better of him. 'I'm sorry, my lady, but everything has a price, whether it be for a friend or foe. The ability for us to speak freely cost the lives of missionaries and diplomats many years ago. I commend your forwardness, but bankrolling your Queen's adventure to Kolgoth is not in our best interest. Selling arms and supplies is however.'

'I understand, emissary. When we take the western lands—'

'If.'

'*When* we take the western lands, there will be free trade throughout Raniel and the Queen will look favourably on those friends closest to her.'

'I believe that this would be a toxic deal for Tiala. The risks are too high. We also share a border with Kolgoth and it has been peaceful for many hundreds of years. War is not a solution to all problems, but a means to make money from the blood of others.'

'For a country that sells arms that is a misplaced comment.' She said.

'We see prosperity in both outcomes, but are unwilling to fund such a cause.'

Freya was losing patience. She looked up from her glass and a dark mist covered her eyes. The stone in De'sal's bracelet shone again. Freya gave a stern command. 'You will relinquish all military artefacts to us and pray that we do not turn our attention to Tiala.'

De'sal remained unfazed by what had just happened. 'Ah, you are a magic-user. I regret to inform you that I have about my person a device that dissipates any activity of that sort. Therefore, your tricks will not work on me.' He stood up and made to leave. Freya grabbed a brush handle that was propped next to the dresser and took a swing at De'sal. Quick as lightning, De'sal engaged a blade concealed in a device on his wrist. Freya stopped as the blade neared her throat. 'You do a grave dishonour to your Queen. Pray that our dance here does not escalate.' Freya backed off, now in a panic as to what to do. *Magic does not work and he is clearly capable in a struggle.* Her thoughts brought her to another conclusion.

'Help!' she cried out. De'sal stood, confused. 'Help, guards!' With a flash of red in her eyes, her appearance changed so she had a torn dress and cuts to her face and body. She lay down slowly and revealed her breast. 'Help, please.' She started to cry.

'You stupid bitch! What do you think you're doing?' A guard burst into the room to find De'sal standing over her, his concealed blade outstretched. Another guard was quickly on his heels. Protesting, De'sal was dragged into the courtyard. 'She's a magic-user. She manipulated this situation. Let go of me.'

Freya hobbled out of the room trying to cover her dignity, tears rolling down her face. 'Are you okay, my lady?' Another guard had now entered the courtyard.

'Thank you, I'll be fine. I'm just a little shaken. I must get back to the palace and inform her majesty that the emissary attacked me.' She carried on the act, as the third guard turned to assist his colleagues and gave a grin that only the emissary saw, which made De'sal struggle even more. It was futile to resist three guards.

As Freya rounded the corner a wisp of red mist returned her appearance to normal. She dusted off her dress and flattened her hair, convinced that De'sal would no longer be a problem.

With a determined stride and keeping her head looking forward, Freya locked eyes with the Queen. Not paying any attention to what was happening in the hall, she reached her recently acquired friend.

'Your majesty, I request an audience. It is of the utmost urgency.'

Stunned by the intrusion, the ruler of Raniel stopped her conversation. She was discussing funeral arrangements with two of her other advisers. She rounded on Freya. 'How dare you intrude!' Her anger was clearly visible to those unfortunate enough to be in the vicinity. 'You may be my adviser, but you shall not disrespect the etiquette of your station.' The two advisers agreed that if it had been anyone else other than Freya, they would have been dragged out and beaten for the lack of decorum, let alone interrupting the Queen. Freya also knew that this was a show and she had to play along with it. Their friendship had grown. They were playing the games that most children grew out of, however the Queen grew up with no friends, and Freya, well, had nothing.

'My apologies. I would not impose if it were not serious.' Freya kept her eyes on the Queen, completely ignoring the other advisers.

'Very well.' Looking at the two advisers. 'Leave us. Prepare your plans,' said the Queen. She waited a short time for the advisers to bow and leave, then give them enough distance so as not to hear any discussion. 'What is it?' There was sisterly concern in her voice.

'Our strategy must change. My meeting with De'sal did not go to plan.'

'He refused? What happened?' Her friend was at a loss as Freya seemed to have a gift for manipulating men to her own way of thinking: which had been put to more humorous ends with the errand boys within the palace.

'He attacked me.' Freya said this with all the proficiency of a seasoned liar.

'*What?*' she exclaimed, loud enough for the entire hall to hear. Those who looked round went back to what they were involved with, just in case they got the blame, which was becoming more common these days.

'Wait. Listen to me.' The Queen was growing in anger. She was listening to Freya, but also making up events in her head, which included a couple of unpleasant ends for the emissary. 'I tried to persuade De'sal, as we discussed. The Tialan was unmoved by the normal route to a man's brain. I overstepped my confidence and he pulled a concealed blade on me. He then grabbed me, saying that he had really enjoyed the Queen's hospitality, but this far exceeded his expectations.'

The Queen's jaw was clenched and her knuckles were going white. The notion of anyone laying a hand on Freya sickened her.

'Are you hurt? I'll stretch him and send his pointy ears to his family.'

'I'm fine. I was able to call for help and some guards came to my aid just in time. We can't look to Tiala to aid us. He was clear in that. I'm sorry I failed.'

Taking a moment to think about where this left her. 'No, you have not failed. You could never fail in my eyes. Tiala has a lot to answer for. One of their emissaries attacked a member of the Royal Court. He also disrespected me at our meeting by not showing the correct etiquette on leaving my presence.' The Queen thought a little more. Freya went to speak, but she was stopped with a flourishing hand gesture. 'They will respond to our request, considering recent events. We will return De'sal on the understanding that Tiala will supply us with the military weapons and armour we require.'

Freya looked worried. 'It's your decision. This monster tried to molest me and I don't believe that he should live past the morning.' Freya's thoughts turned to a vision of her being found out. Putting this to the back of her mind, she trusted the Queen was making the right decision.

'If they do not comply, then the option left to us is to execute him. Lessons need to be learned. Raniel is not weak and any trespass against her will be met with severe consequences.' She took a couple of paces then turned to Freya. 'I will see De'sal myself and discuss my terms.'

'Is that wise? He's a Tialan and not to be trusted.'

'And I am not a woman to shy away from an aggressor to the Crown.'

Making their way to the guardhouse which held De'sal, the vision of the Queen and her adviser walking towards them surprised the two guards on duty outside the jail. They swiftly snapped to attention, eyes straight ahead and halberd tucked tightly into their left shoulders. One guard felt compelled to inform those inside of the approaching visitor, but nerves go the better of him. When the Queen was within a couple of paces of the door the two guards broke rank and opened it. Those inside, once registering the visitors' identities, stood to attention.

'Captain, where is the Tialan?'

The captain bowed and led the two visitors down a set of steps to the holding cells. As cells went these were kept for those of special importance. There was no dampness or mould on the whitewashed walls and no imps stealing food from the prisoners. The cells were clean, and fresh bedding was given on request. This part of the prison was in better condition than most of the homes in Weelan and the inmates better fed. The smell of lavender rose from an incense stick smoking away on the wall. Some prisoners' bowels gave up before their will during questioning and the guards thought it would be unfair for others to put up with the smell of shit … until their turn, at least.

De'sal was sitting on a stool next to a small wooden desk. Parchment and an inkwell were the only effects that De'sal had in the room. He felt the approach of someone to his cell door. He finished the sentence he was writing, slowly placed the pen back in the inkwell and turned to the door. Instantly his rage rose. De'sal swiftly got to his feet.

'This is your hospitality? Sending this whore to manipulate an emissary by using magic? You have made a grave mistake, your highness.' In his rage, some saliva had built up around his teeth and he spat his words. 'This is an outrage, accusing me of attacking this bitch. Get me out of here! I demand diplomatic immunity.'

The Queen stayed calm. 'I feel that the mistake is on your part. You attacked one of my advisers, who, in my service, was requesting a deal that would benefit both countries. I guess you felt, having a woman alone, that you would take advantage of the situation. You are correct in the assumption that she has magic, but I assure you, it is only for healing.'

'You have your version of events, which is somewhat different from what happened. Maybe her manipulation has tilted your own views.' This did not go down well with the Queen.

'You suggest that I am of weak mind and can be controlled!' De'sal did not respond, but kept his eyes fixed on his accuser. Freya placed a hand on her friend's back, to reassure her and calm her down a little. It was also supposed to go unnoticed, but the captain saw the gesture. Freya quickly made him avert his questioning stare by giving him a razor-sharp look.

'Well, you will get your diplomatic immunity – of sorts, at least. You will be expelled.' De'sal gave a small, thin smile. 'Oh, I wouldn't smirk. If Tiala does not agree to our terms, you will be executed and sent home, a piece at a time.' The Queen was grave in her threat. 'If they agree, you may leave, but minus an ear or two, so that every time you look at your reflection you will be reminded you that you broke the diplomatic relationship between Raniel and Tiala.'

'Your highness, she has fabricated this story because her cheap petty tricks did not work on me. I am innocent. What reason would I have to throw away 200 years of friendship and trade? And, it would seem, my life?'

'I would ask the same of my aid.' As the two turned and went to leave, De'sal bellowed, 'Be wary who you lie with. The love of the rose can make you blind to the thorns in any garden.' The Queen paused for a moment, then carried on up the steps. When they reached the office area, Freya relaxed a little. That had gone better than she'd hoped. She went to speak to the captain, to reinforce the message that he had seen nothing of the caress she had given the Queen. Any rumours that would arise would lead straight to his door and the consequences could be fatal.

At this point, The Queen had spoken to one of the guards and asked to see the Tialan's belongings. She searched casually through his things. She found a note, some money, the weapon and a bracelet. The note she took and the bracelet intrigued her. *De'sal said that tricks did not work on him*, she thought. Running the bracelet between her finger and thumb, she felt the inscribed runes and the small stone set into the silver. She placed it in a pocket within her dress.

By this time Freya had ensured that the captain would hold his tongue or she would have it pulled out.

They returned to the palace in silence. The Queen was deep in thought over the meeting.

Freya gave her a questioning look, but received no response. Maybe it hadn't gone so well after all.

Chapter Eleven

Maleth sat with his back against a beam in one of the holds. There was plenty of space on the deck of the *Dying Siren*, but he wanted some time without chatter and sea tales. He had found a spot where the creaking and drone of the giant timbers was bearable and, more importantly, he was on his own. A week had passed, pissing and shitting in a bucket, with only a cloth curtain to hide his dignity. Meal times were a little cramped. The ship's cook either had a poor aim or just didn't care if you ate his food or wore it. Once you had your bowl of what passed as food, reaching your bench could be very tricky, given the heave of the ship, not to mention sitting down, squeezing between the other diners. All in all, it was not a pleasant experience. The hold was not designed for live freight: benches had been packed in tightly, and given that there were over thirty people in a small section of cargo space, tempers could fray. Each person still had a gorget clamped around their neck. Just as well really; the way things were going, thirty magic-users could either turn the place into a farmyard or a fire ball.

Something caught Maleth's eye. He didn't move or make a noise, just gazed toward the slight gap between a few sacks of vegetables and a crate. A short time passed and he saw it again – two small glistening black orbs about the size of his thumbnail. The flickering light of the candle above his head was reflected in them. Fear embraced him. His heart knocked on the wall of his chest. He had nothing to defend himself with apart from panic and violence. His throat had dried up. Paralysed, he sat, waiting for the next event. He didn't have to wait long. The orbs disappeared for a split second, then returned, seeming to fix on Maleth. A small bead of sweat formed on his temple. There was a crack like the flexing of knuckles, a purr, then out of the gloom, along with the glassy orbs, came the tip of a leathery nose, with a blueish hue to the skin. It sniffed the air and gave another crack. The orbs blinked once more.

With a little more confidence, the form ventured forward, looking from side to side, then back at Maleth. More quiet crackling, this time just on the edge of hearing, and another sniff. A couple more steps and the creature emerged in full candlelight.

'Seven shits! An Imp!' Maleth's relief sent a tingle all over his body. 'Well, little fella, you had me there.'

The Imp sat on its hind legs, shaped to some extent like a rabbit. It sniffed the air and cocked its head at Maleth. Taking this to be a sign that the small individual wanted food, and hoping that it wasn't some form of mating ritual, Maleth took a small wrap of leather out of his pouch and unfolded it. A more intense set of clicks came from Maleth's new companion. He offered the Imp a small dry biscuit, which was received by a dainty pair of hands with deceptively sharp claws. A fine line of blood appeared on Maleth's thumb. He looked at the cut, then back at the Imp. What he saw in its face could honestly be understood as *sorry*. More clacks and crackles. With one last sniff, the Imp moved over and sat resting against Maleth's leg.

'Looks like I have a friend for the journey.'

'Click.'

'You're right. I shouldn't be here either.' He didn't understand the crude form of noises, but he felt he understood the meaning.

Standing on the prow of the ship, Maleth watched as the hulking beast was gently steered into the harbour. There was one mooring on a short pier. He noticed that there were about a dozen figures milling around the dockside, waiting for them to berth. Garbled shouts went in both directions. Maleth only recognised a couple of them as Ranielian and a crude form of Tialan. One thing that he picked out clear as day was the captain's request that no one got off until these dead men had been paid for. *Odd choice of words*, he thought. The great hull of the ship swung gracefully into the large beams that protected the side of the pier. With a slight lurch their voyage was over, somewhat to his relief. Once the gangplank had been lowered, the captain strutted onto the quayside.

Maleth was holding a small bag that began to move. 'Settle down.' He gave the bag a comforting rub. 'We'll be on dry land soon and I'm sure that I can let you out without anyone noticing. Just have a little patience.' The bag gave a grunt, then stilled. The air on deck was salty, with a sweet scent blowing off the land. The long winter was ending and the vegetation was coming alive. After being at sea for two weeks, Maleth was happy to see anything green that wasn't vomit or the colour of the meat, depending how the light hit it. He was a city lad and wanted nothing to do with ... well, anyone. Now he was at the High Citadel to learn and hone his craft for the glory of Raniel. He gave a nasal laugh, shook his head and headed for the gangway with the rest of the poor bastards singled out as *magic-users*.

'Would you all kindly line up?' The welcoming party consisted of one middle-aged gentleman in a long grey coat. As requested, they lined up in no real order and were counted by one of the crew.

'One missing, cap'n.'

'Yeah, shame about that. Clearly thought that life in the sea was better than on board. That's revenue lost. Here is the consignment of thirty, sorry, twenty-nine able bodies from the Ranielian Army, safe and healthy with no apparent issues from their journey, apart from the missing female.'

The waiting mage gave a concerned look, then handed over a bag of what Maleth assumed was gold – unless the old goat knew a pebble-to-gold trick. He didn't think the captain would be a good person to try it on though. Walking back to the ship she strode passed the lined-up merchandise that she had just unloaded and grabbed the crotch of a young male. 'Hope it heals up soon.' The young lad was shocked and embarrassed. He turned bright red and tried not to make eye contact with any of his fellow passengers or, for that matter, the captain.

After clearing his throat, the mage spoke. 'Well, you are to be the next generation of mages. Some would say that it's an honourable trade, using such a special gift to help those in need. Alas, those people are few and far between. Today, we are shunned and disliked by the general population. However, in times of need, such as they are, we are pivotal to the success of the army. These are unfortunate times because there is so much to learn of our craft, and we have been given but a month to get you battle-ready. Ordinarily a youth would be handed to us because their parent could not cope with the games that youngsters play. From there we would school them in several disciplines, including healing, shape-shifting, conjuring and augments. We have the history of the world in our library and every spell imaginable to learn. Yet, her majesty only wants you to destroy life – such a waste.'

Maleth's heart sank a little deeper. He had hoped to be a healer and not use his abilities to hurt others. Well, he didn't have to use them, he supposed. He was hoping this war wouldn't happen. Surely the advisers of both nations would come to an agreement. He started thinking about this more now that he was here.

They were led into the citadel through great oak and steel doors. The thick walls were at least four times the height of a person, and made of what looked like solid rock rather than blocks. Once in the main square, they halted. Maleth looked around. There were stalls with all imaginable things: clothes, food, weapons, armour, books, scrolls and maps, not to mention devices which Maleth did not recognise. A stall even sold small ornaments. *Odd*, he thought, *that mages would be interested in decorating their dorms*. There was a stable at one end with an array of destriers; big powerful-looking animals. Even from a distance they were intimidating.

A procession of mages entered the courtyard. Each approached an individual and led them away. A heavily set woman approached Maleth. She had a motherly air to her and a reassuring smile when she spoke, as if she was cradling him in a cotton towel. He felt a weight lifted from him.

'Hello, Maleth. I hope that your journey was agreeable.'

'Yes, thank you. Eh, how did you know my name, if you don't mind me asking,'

'No, I don't mind you asking.' Maleth waited for an answer, but none came.

'Please, come with me. I am to take you to your mentor. I see that you have a friend with you. The blue ones are rather more daring, don't you think?' Instinctively, Maleth put his hand on the bag he was carrying. He didn't understand how she knew he had a companion. The imp hadn't moved or made a noise since they'd got off the ship.

The woman started speaking in clicks and crackles and the little imp popped its head out of the bag and started clicking back.

'You can speak to imps? I didn't know that was possible. I didn't mean to bring it ashore, but I couldn't leave it on board.'

The woman stopped and turned to Maleth. 'Do you realise where you are, young man? No, you don't know what's going on here, do you?' Maleth stood blank-faced. 'The imp that you carry is male and his name is Tep. He is thankful for your company and has enjoyed listening to you speak to yourself and sometimes on his behalf. Tep is a wonderful judge of character and sees something in you. I sent him aboard to find a unique person. For your information, I can read your mind, and no, I do not wish to be your mother.'

They started walking again. 'Shit indeed, young Maleth!'

Tep sprang out of the bag and scurried off under a stall. Maleth's mind was racing too fast to take anything in. He was wondering how much the woman could actually hear of his thoughts.

'That's a good question,' she replied. The next words out of his mouth were of a sort that children and young adults should never hear.

'My word, you certainly have a colourful vocabulary,' she said.' To put your mind at ease, I can only mind-join over a short distance of a few feet or so. I've been working on it for about twelve years now, but more practice and study will allow me to use it over greater distances.'

They arrived at a small wooden door with two candles hanging on the wall on either side, which helped a little with the gloom of the corridor. On entering they found themselves in a study full of books and paperwork. Maleth was fascinated to see light balls hanging in mid-air at random points throughout the room. He then thought of the pointlessness of the two candles outside the door.

'Yes, they're just for decoration,' his guide said.

'Stop that!' he said, then interjected with 'please', apologetically.

Sitting in a high-backed chair was an old man, with long thin grey hair and a wispy beard. A book lay open on a small table next to him. The pages seemed blank, but Maleth noticed that words were floating above the book and changing as if the old man was reading the text. Maleth had seen many things – strange things – since landing on the Isle of the High Citadel. This, however, was a whole new chapter.

'Would you please refrain from using that kind of language, young man! And I don't care if you didn't *say* it, I still *heard* it.' The chaperone was, at this stage, quite upset. She made her way closer to the old man's chair and spoke softly to him. There was the odd grumble and some hand gestures.

Maleth stared at a fixed point on the wall, trying to keep his thoughts from running wild. He was beckoned over to the chair.

'May I introduce the High Mage, Master Falvor. He will be your mentor for the duration of your stay. Master? This is Maleth. He's from Senal.' The woman smiled at Maleth. 'Ah, I see you're getting the hang of emptying your mind. Well done. Now, if you will excuse me, I have errands.' She bowed to Master Falvor and left, leaving the two alone.

'Young man, come closer.' Maleth obliged and moved close enough to get a faint aroma of urine. 'I have a job for you. If you fulfil the task, I will train you.' Maleth kept gazing at the wall. 'What are you looking at, boy?'

'With all due respect, sir, I am trying to keep my mind clear.'

'Ah, well don't bother. I've not done cheap parlour tricks like that for over a hundred years. I don't care what you think.' Maleth relaxed and instantly his mind flooded with thoughts, although some he felt were not his own.

Well, if I am to be involved in this foolish adventure, I suppose I'd best get trained, he thought. Master Falvor gave him a curious look. 'What is the task you require me to do, sir?' Maleth asked.

'I am old and frail. I struggle with attending to myself.' *Well, this is going south quickly*, Maleth thought. 'I would ask that you give me a bed bath. Due to my age, I have a tendency to have a few accidents and it gets uncomfortable.' Maleth was a little repulsed by this and was trying to plan a response when the Grand Master began to snore.

'Sir?'

Another heave of air was taken into the old man's body. Maleth waited. There was a pause and silence, for longer than Maleth supposed it should be.

'Sir?' There was still no response. Maleth took a blanket from another chair and placed it over the Grand Master's legs and body. 'I will return later, sir, and we can discuss your bathing. Hopefully someone else will come in before me and help you out.' As he turned to leave, Maleth felt there was someone else in the room. He looked back to see the old man standing next to his chair with a wry grin on his now less wrinkled face.

'Well, my boy, the look on your face. I don't know which was better; the one after being asked to give an old piss-ridden man a bed bath; or the one you are presenting me with now. I am not an old man – well, technically I am – but I've aged very well here on the island. Well done, you passed my task. You did not mindlessly carry out what I asked you to do, yet you left me in a dignified manner, even though I may not have heard you. That shows something about your character. Do you know that I had one student try to take my trousers off? The little bugger nearly soiled himself when I woke up. I am indeed the Grand Master here in the Citadel. And welcome, Maleth. I hope that you can fulfil your potential in such an insufficient space of time.'

Maleth stood in silence and awe, waiting for his brain to process what was happening. 'Are you still staring at the wall, boy?'

'My apologies. That was the test?'

'Yes. Now, let's get started with your training.'

Chapter Twelve

'Guard!' De'sal's voice boomed through the jail hallway. A short time later a young guard presented herself at the cell door. She was well aware of the protocol for dealing with the prisoners in this section.

'Yes, my lord?'

'I have a task for you and it is of very high importance. Are you a loyal Ranielian?'

'With all due respect, my lord, I am not the one in the cell. My loyalty is unquestionable.'

'I am glad to hear it. Will you deliver a message? And please do not tell of it to anyone. You may read it first so that your conscience is clear.' De'sal handed her a note.

Dearest friend,

Unfortunately, I have found myself in a spot of bother. I have run up arrears in a few bills that need paying as soon as possible. Therefore, have I been incarcerated in the palace jail. As a guest in this city, I do not wish to insult my hosts at this difficult time.

De'sal

The guard scanned the note and handed it back to De'sal. 'The contents seem fine. I'll deliver the note.' Such requests were nothing new. They were usually begging letters to wives asking for forgiveness – *This is the last time I'll visit whores* – or it was just a *big misunderstanding* that all the family savings had disappeared.

'Excellent! Could you pass me wax to seal it, please?' There was a pause from the guard. 'It's quite embarrassing that I'm in here and I don't wish my peers to know what difficulty I'm in. Therefore, I'd rather seal my note.' As she turned away, De'sal took another note from his pocket and folded it into a tight square. On the return of the guard, he heated the wax over the candle and dripped it onto the note, sealing it shut. 'I thank you for your trust and, please, you must give it to my friend as quickly as possible and tell them to hurry in their response. I am in dire need.'

The guard took the note and looked at the name on the note. Recognising the name and giving a sharp inhale of breath, she left swiftly. De'sal was only slightly confident his plan would work, but he needed to try something. He liked his ears, and his life for that matter. He pulled a note from his pocket, opened it and gave a slight chuckle. 'Money worries?' Holding the message over the candle, he burnt it without a trace.

'My lord!' The wheezing messenger arrived at the Generals office. The run was only five minutes however court life did nothing for her fitness. Composing herself she stood to attention.

'Yes?'

'I have a note from Emissary De'sal. He was explicit that you should act with the utmost haste, sir!' She gave another rasp.

'Breathe.' Motioning for the guard to take some water from the jug on the office sideboard. He broke the wax seal and unravelled the note. Mindful that the soldier was still in the room sipping the water, he stopped. Waiting until she had finished, he quietly said, 'That is all. You are dismissed.' Aware that she had overstayed her welcome, she saluted nervously and left, closing the door behind her.

Lord Hal continued to open up the note.

My Lord Hal,

I spoke to you briefly after my audience with the Queen. I took you to be an honourable man with sound judgement. I ask for your help, not for me, but for the future of Raniel. There have been false allegations made against me and I am being held in the palace jail. My fate may be sealed, but I implore you to meet with me, as I have a matter of great concern to discuss. As you will understand, I cannot scribe such matters on this note.

Emissary De'sal.

Lord Hal thought a while about the request and then about their meeting. De'sal seemed genuine enough. Why would he risk getting caught sending notes from prison? He had been positive about the trade between Raniel and Tiala. Lord Hal had enough on his plate. Were these just ramblings of an enthusiastic diplomat or as suggested, was there something that he needed to look into?

'Sergeant!'

'Yes, sir?'

'I'm heading to the palace jail.'

'Sir!'

When Lord Hal reached the steps to the palace jail. A remnant of the dying winter blew through the streets and chilled the night air. Street lamps had already been lit and the darkness that they chased away retreated into the corners and alleyways. Shadows brought fear, but these days there were more sinister things afoot, talk of muggings and beatings, which was nothing new in any large city, but now there were fewer watchmen on duty, which gave some individuals the confidence to mete out their own style of depravity on the locals. Murders and mutilations were becoming more and more common. There were also rumours of darker things hunting in the shades. Before he entered, Lord Hal mused over better times, before the king had gone west.

There'd been a guard on every corner and an understanding with the gangs that they would keep their feuds to themselves. There had also been some respect for the Watch, albeit in very loose terms. Since then, the city seemed to have lost control and was now eating itself. What did De'sal need to say that affected the future of Raniel?

The desk guard was leaning back in his chair with his feet on the desk, using a dagger to hook out the dirt from under his nails. Lord Hal's boots touched the wooden floorboards. The Sergeant panicked and, in the commotion, kicked some paperwork on to the floor. He also sliced his finger with his dagger. Lord Hal felt his rage building.

'Is this the professionalism required of an officer of the palace guard? Get yourself sorted out, before I put you on slop-out duty in the northern camps. And there better not be any bloody imps running about.' On hearing the commotion, another guard came rushing up the stairs and drew to a sudden halt on seeing Lord Hal. Snapping to attention, the guard saluted.

'My lord!'

'You have the Emissary De'sal in your custody?' enquired Lord Hal.

'Yes, my lord. This way.' The guard led the commander down the stairs into the holding cells. A figure sat at a table next to a flickering candle. Both light and darkness frolicked across the wall. De'sal composed himself, stood up from the chair and acknowledged his visitor.

'My lord, I thank you for attending my request.' He gave a small bow of respect.

'Emissary, you have matters you wish to discuss?' Lord Hal's response was cold. He noticed De'sal's eyes shift to the guard standing off to the left and then back to meet his own.

'Guard, you may leave us.'

'My lord, I am to accompany all visitors.'

'That is my understanding. However, I am giving you an order to leave. I don't care what you do or where you go. Just leave.' The guard gave an inquisitive look and a pause. The pause was long enough for Lord Hal to straighten up and fix his eyes squarely on the guard. A sudden acknowledgement of understanding washed over the guard.

'Sir!' The guard retreated briskly up the stairs.

'Once again, I thank you for coming. You are truly the man I thought you were.'

'Cut the shit! Why are you in here? And what's with sending me a note? If you killed a whore or took a boy instead, *that* isn't my concern.'

'My lord, I was attacked by that bitch plaything your Queen has.'

'Nonsense!' Lord Hal gave a weighted sigh. 'You expect me to believe that she got the better of you?'

'She is a magic-user.' At that point, things suddenly became serious from Lord Hal's perspective. De'sal continued. 'I have been travelling these lands for many, many years and I have come into contact with countless communities and tribes. This is not the first time I've seen magic. With that in mind, I carry upon my person an artefact that dispels magic. When her seductive magic didn't work on me, she lost her composure and attacked me.'

Lord Hal leaned back against a desk in the hallway and folded his arms, as De'sal continued. 'Her skills as a conjurer are deceptive. And therefore, here I am, under threat of having my ears cut off.'

Lord Hal rubbed his chin. Without speaking, he turned and headed for the stairs.

'My lord, wait. Please, hear what I have to say.' It was too late – the hall was empty. De'sal was at a loss. He had not envisaged Lord Hal's departure. He had to think what his next move would be. Stroking his ear unknowingly, an uneasy feeling came over him. Maybe this was his fate.

Lord Hal pulled a chair closer to the sergeant's desk, which made the other guard a little nervous.

'Why is the emissary in here? And before you answer, know that I am not a man to play games, listen to lies or gossip.'

'The emissary was brought in by the Queen's guards. When I processed him, I was told not to put him in the register and informed that he was not allowed visitors. But I suppose you are an exception, sir! The Queen and her adviser also paid a visit not long after he came in.'

'What of his personal effects?'

'Everything is in the lockbox, but nothing has been registered.' The Sergeant went over to the cabinet and took out the box with De'sal's cell number on it. 'This is all, my lord.'

As Lord Hal looked through the box, he quizzed the Sergeant. 'Is that it, as you remember?'

'Yes, sir!'

'Very well, Sergeant, carry on.' Lord Hal stood at the top of the stairs, then turned to the guards with a concerned look on his face. 'I want to know if anyone comes in here. And *nothing* happens to the emissary without me knowing.' The undertone of threat in Lord Hal's voice was clear. Without a word, both guards saluted and went about cleaning the office.

Placing his palm on his chest, De'sal let out a sigh 'You have returned, my lord.'

'What if I don't believe you and suspect that you have taken against Lady Freya? Maybe you chanced your hand. After all she's a good-looking woman, even for Tialan eyes. What if you were trying to undermine Raniel's preparations for war. We are in troublesome times, Emissary: we bleed our population dry of sons and daughters; taxes are rising to pay for the war. In the Watch's absence, the streets are a haven for bastards without morals, who see it as an opportunity to terrorise the public. Why would Lady Freya try to seduce you? My understanding is that she has an appetite for the softer parts of the human anatomy.'

'There are things happening in the west that you are not privy to, my lord. Kolgoth is strong. If the tribes rally, Raniel will be broken and those sons and daughters will be given no quarter. Lady Freya tried to arrange a deal that would see Tiala bankroll your war. We are unwilling to pick sides. I'm sure that if I'd not had my bracelet, I would have sold all of Tiala's weapons for a kiss on the cheek. As things stand, Kolgoth will still be victorious. The Kolgothian Guardian will not look kindly on Tiala for its choice of allies. Understand this, my lord, the *only* race that wants this war is Raniel.' He paused. 'There is something else.'

'Go on.'

'There is a darkness in Weelan. I have seen the creeping shadows. There are few people in this world aware of such things. Let's call it *anti-magic*. Some can sense magic, whereas I have to use a bracelet. Others are immune to its effects. Again, the bracelet helps. I am sure of what I have seen and I saw it in Lady Freya.'

Lord Hal thought about De'sal's response, then about Freya. He didn't warm to her, but the Queen was quick to trust which was a little strange. He found it difficult to imagine her as a magic-user. The dark arts were a thing of the past, from way before the Great Disaster. Some said the Dark Mages had caused the destruction of the lands to the east, by trying to control death and become immortal. Lord Hal's shoulders were heavy now. This information, whether true or false, changed the path of his decisions.

'Are you looked after well enough, Emissary?' De'sal was surprised by this question. *Was all that he had said for naught*?

'Yes, my lord.'

'Good. I would not like to think our hospitality is lacking.' Lord Hal stood straight and flattened out his tunic. He searched to find something else to say. 'I was unsure of what I knew when I woke this morning. I am sure, however, that this conversation never happened.'

'As you wish, my lord.'

On leaving the office and bracing himself against the chill of the winter wind, Lord Hal looked intently at the shadows. He had never felt uneasy walking the streets, but De'sal's account made him take a second glance at the gloom, which sat like a veil over the city. Shaking the nonsense from his mind he headed out onto the street. A figure approached, hooded and cloaked; female by the shape and walk. Under the cloak he could make out fine clothes. At this time of night, a woman would usually be the type plying for affection, but this was no commoner. He approached the woman cautiously. 'My lady, these are not the times to be wandering alone in the streets.'

'Get away from me before I flay the skin from your back.' As she spoke, she folded back her hood and a dark mist bathed the stranger's face. On realising that it was Lord Hal, Freya composed herself and apologised.

'My lord, I'm sorry. You gave me a fright.'

'Dark words, my lady. Should you be out at this hour?'

'I may choose to walk whenever and wherever I wish, Lord Hal. And sometimes a lady has to defend herself and all she has is harsh language.'

'I believe that the Emissary De'sal has been on the receiving end of that harsh tongue.' Freya sensed Lord Hal knew much of what was going on – too much for her liking. It would be all too easy to end him here and make it look like he had been bested in a fight, but she thought he might still be of use. The same dark mist shrouded her eyes.

'My dealings with De'sal are none of your concern. I bid you goodnight, my lord.'

As if coming out of a trance, Lord Hal acknowledged the statement and continued on his way, with just the faintest recollection of their meeting, but unsure where or when.

Freya was at the entrance to the jail and stopped to think. *Had Lord Hal been to see De'sal? He clearly knew about the altercation. Did he know about her magic?* Maybe this was not the best time to visit the emissary. She would have to be more cautious with the Queen's General.

Chapter Thirteen

The figure lifted their head to acknowledge the approaching messenger. Although it was a dry winter's day, there was a dank moisture in the air. The alleyway was full of crates and barrels of all shapes and sizes. The cargo that they had once held gave a confused aroma. This had helped in the past as the Watch's dogs could not pick up the scent of those hiding. That, along with the laziness of their handlers, meant that the alleys of Weelan were open for business.

'Master, he requests that our plans should hasten.' The messenger cowered in a low bow. An old-looking, blue-grey hand reached out from a sleeve in the figure's cloak. A string of small bones was visible through long thin fingers.

'Come closer, my child.' The figure's voice was old and raspy. 'I am poor of hearing.' This confused the messenger. He had been told to meet an agent and had assumed that … Well, he hadn't expected this shell of an old man. He stepped forward tentatively to repeat his message. In a heartbeat the old man's other hand was lodged in the messenger's chest. A shroud of darkness smothered them both. The messenger's body shrivelled to a husk; the look of surprise still visible on his face.

'Thank you, my lord, for your offering.' The figure's voice now seemed to have more life and power. Within the mist, the outline of a shapeless face appeared. A hiss just on the edge of hearing became faint words and sentences.

'Kill the general and the emissary. None must know of your involvement. The artefact will be found and the Queen will go to war.'

A vacuum of silence. Only the phantom's voice lingered in the chill air. A vision of the face disappeared and reappeared in waves that retained the figures attention.

'I shall see it done, Master.' More energy flowed 'Our presence in the city has grown by your design. Raniel will be on her knees soon and the Queen's host will march west.'

'Good. Freya, prove yourself and earn the gift I gave you; fail and all your years will pass as a day.' The acolyte felt the threat. For years she had been in the service of the Dark Lord. Duty came at a price: the longer she stayed, the higher the consequence of failure.

The messenger's carcass was dry and beginning to fall apart, his body void of any life, no moisture and no possibility of being brought back from the dead. Freya had seen untold atrocities in the long years. There were many ways to die, including having your soul ripped from your living body to live as a ghost and a shell for eternity. But what most frightened her was eternal darkness and the demons. Thinking once again about the gift that her master had given.

Looking at her hands, she opened and closed them a few times, happy she was back to normal. There were many benefits to his service too: a life extended and the strength to wield the dark magic bestowed upon her.

Freya pulled down her hood, letting the pale winter sun, bathe her face. Walking out of the alleyway, she looked at the old and frail citizens of Weelan: not strong enough to go to war and not strong enough to defend themselves against what was to come. *The fields are ripe for the harvest*, she thought to herself and headed to the palace.

Guldr, High Chief of Kolgoth, walked through the knee-high grass. The weak light from the sun suffused his face. There was no warmth in the rays – it was perfect. The cool wind moved his hair and the yellow grass alike. An ocean of grass separated him from the Mother Shaman's village. He had chosen not to ride the three-day journey but do it on foot, and alone. Many of his counsel thought this a foolish move, fraught with the danger of attacks from rival tribal leaders, who might use it as an opportunity to supplant the High Chief, not to mention the added risk of Ranielian assassins. But Guldr was stubborn and more than capable of looking after himself. You did not become Guardian of Kolgoth by birth right. Every challenge was a brutal fight to submission or death. More often than not, it was death. The shame of losing had no place in Kolgothian culture.

Another day would see him at Fethal, on the eastern coast, where he belonged, and free from counsel, tribal chiefs and the drudgery of ruling Kolgoth. Even more so, with the war looming, he wanted to be twelve years old again and running away from his father's form of education.

'You need to be strong. Use the pain and discomfort to your advantage.' Guldr's memory was all too vivid. He could hear his father's powerful yet caring voice. He flinched from an imaginary fist from his father.

Reminiscing, he followed a goat trail. 'You were right, Father. Your lessons were harsh and painful but look where I am now. All I hope is that you are proud and that I've earned your respect.' Taking a deep breath and clearing his thoughts, he spied a small outcrop with a few shrubs and sorry-looking trees. *As safe a place as any to camp*, he thought. When he got there, he had lost the light of day. A fire would attract unwanted attention, so he unrolled his bedding and sat down under the bough of a barbed shrub. The thick spines might deter investigation from hungry predators. He meditated for a short time, eyes closed, focusing on his shallow breathing. Satisfied he was at peace with himself, he lay down and hoped that he'd see the morning.

Morning came with the grassland's chorus of birds and insects. In the distance, he heard larger animals bellowing and howling. They may have picked up his scent overnight. He would not hang about too long to find out. In his pack he had various fungi and berries, enough to sustain him at least as far as Fethal. After a meagre breakfast, Guldr was up and away.

By late afternoon, he entered the village of Fethal and was greeted with much respect and offered food and lodgings from a host of village folk.

'Thank you, but I need to speak with the Mother Shaman and an old friend.' A large male stood in front of Guldr, dressed in leather armour plates with a few pieces of dented iron strapped to his legs and shoulders. His face was devoid of wrinkles and had too few scars to be a contender. However, he had a unique tattoo across the right side of his face: three lines, as if scratched by a wild animal.

The young Kol dropped to one knee and bowed his head.

'Guardian, it is with pride and honour that–' Guldr put out his hand to stop the pleasantries. Sokal regarded Guldr apologetically.

'Get up, Sokal.' The young male rose confused that the Guardian knew his name, although a little proud too. The feats of the High Chief were renowned in Kolgoth.

'My Chief, how is it you know my name?'

'We shall have that discussion over an ale, but where is your aunt?' Sokal was trying to piece things together. However, each question opened his mind to many more. 'Sokal! Where is your aunt?'

'Helda?'

'Yes, boy. Are you sure you're from the Minal tribe? By Mother Earth, I'll need a word with your father.' Sokal was not keeping up but mustered enough brain power to offer his lead.

'This way, please.' They walked a cart trail between wood and mud-clad huts. There were no streets as such, just areas of occupation and manufacture. Clearly, they were heading through tanning yards, given the smell. Some minutes later they arrived at a herb stall with an array of jars and bouquets of fresh plants. The scent was overwhelming. Hunched over a pestle and mortar, a woman was grinding seeds and leaves together. She wore cotton clothes of no real fashion and a leather apron. Her black hair was tied back with plaits and was a little unkempt, with a few herb twigs sticking out of it. She looked up and took a few seconds to register who was in front of her. The joy that welled up inside of her was plain to see. Tears showed as she tried awkwardly to get out from behind her stall.

'Run along, boy and tell your father I'm here.' Still swamped in confusion, Sokal thumped his chest and did what he was told.

Helda ran to Guldr with her arms outstretched. When they met, their embrace was one of instant comfort. Helda sobbed in sheer joy. She wanted to see his face up close but was afraid to let him go.

'I take it you are happy to see me, Helda.' She didn't move.

'I've missed you so much, you big brute. I curse the day you became Guardian.'

'Do you curse the day we were bound together?'

'That's all that's keeping me stable and from not running after you to Droth'Ka. Tell me that a younger chief bested you and that you are back home.'

'If I had been bested, you know I would not be here with you. I'd be adrift on the night plains with our ancestors, waiting patiently for your arrival. And if you had come to the Great Hall, you would be the one waiting for me. The wife of the Guardian must be kept a secret.' She broke away and looked for a cloth to wipe her face. Guldr offered his hand and rubbed away her tears with his thick thumb.

'If this is official, where is the rest of your counsel?'

'Let's not talk out here. I've been walking for five days.'

Chapter Fourteen

The fire in the hall crackled. The splitting pine logs making a familiar snap and hiss. The Queen sat close to the hearth in an upright chair. Her advisers had left, and the night was her own, apart from her personal guard. She had even made Freya take her leave. Wrapped in a wolf pelt, her bare feet resting on a giant deer hide rug, she looked into the dancing flames, the reflection playing out in her brown eyes. The heat bathed her, helping with the solitude she craved. She held De'sal's bracelet and studied the runes. She did not understand what they meant, but she knew enough of the world to know that there were magical items powerful enough to grant every desire.

All she would ask for was to be ten years old again, being lifted and hugged by her father. Her eyes glazed over, giving more brilliance to the flames mirrored there. She let the bracelet fall to the rug, touching her foot. She had thought of throwing it in the fire for what De'sal had done. However, something stopped her. *Could such a piece bring back someone to life? Could it take a life?*

For all she knew, it was nothing more than a family heirloom, the inscription from his children saying, 'Stay safe'. With this, her thoughts went straight back to her own father and the time he'd left to go west. *I could be robbing a family of their father.*

'Foolish thoughts,' she whispered. 'The bastard tried to hurt Freya. I'll be doing them a favour.' She snapped back to the moment and took out the note. As a member of the royal household, she had been schooled in the neighbouring countries' languages. She may not have been able to speak Tialan fluently, but she could decipher some of their writings.

My Lord Orator,
I have been given lodgings and treated well. I mourn for the death of King Thomas, as do most of the visiting emissaries. His daughter and heir to the throne is a strong-willed and ambitious woman. Her character is that of a child thrust into the political void left by her father's demise. She seeks revenge, as any son or daughter would, but she lacks guidance, or at least appropriate counsel. I have spoken to Lord Hal who commands Raniel's army. He seems to be a man of integrity and I hope one who can be trusted. I see no reason to deny the Queen's request for arms. This will benefit Tiala, but we have to be very aware of Kolgoth. If the great southern tribes rally to the north, then Raniel will surely fall. Our part in that would not go unnoticed and the chiefs may come looking for answers. I wander in my thoughts a little. If Raniel becomes the victor, the north-western lands will be open to mining and harvesting. If the rumours are true, then this could open Zinjal in the far north. That land is infused with magic and artefacts that we no longer possess the skills to make or wield. I aim to stay for a few more weeks and pay my respects at King Thomas's funeral.
Your humble servant,
De'sal.

Reading the note by firelight and holding it delicately as if it would turn to dust, she found it difficult to grasp every sentence and it took over an hour to read. On finishing, she got the impression that De'sal was interested in trade. 'Why would he attack a royal adviser?' She tried to make sense of his motives. *Too long away from home and needed to release some male urges? Freya clearly outsmarted his advances*, she thought. Freya was a beautiful woman; all races and genders were drawn to her. This made her the perfect adviser, but it hadn't worked on De'sal.

The Queen noticed that one rune on the bracelet was glowing slightly, which hadn't been evident before. Faint footsteps echoed on the stone floor. Without looking up, she gently slid the bracelet under the rug. She also threw the note into the fire, something convinced her that no one else needed to see De'sal's note. The information she would keep to herself.

She sat back in the chair and Freya lay down on the deer hide and shared the warmth of the fire with her friend.

'Guards, you may go.' They turned ceremoniously and left, thankful not to be privy to any awkward situations.

The sun was popping up over the balustrade and a heavy dew rested on the short grass. The camp was about three days' ride east of Weelan. There were low fields for miles and huge ominous mountain ranges in the far distance. Marin's watch duty was coming to an end. He had been bored shitless for the last five hours and had seen more people trying to break out than get into the camp. But he had his orders: there were reports of Kol raiding parties disrupting supply trains and causing havoc in the camps. He'd never seen a Kolgothian. Quietly he hoped some dumb brute would try to have a go on his watch, just for some excitement.

'Alright, Marin?' Every hour or so an old soldier would make a round of the camp, checking in with the towers and gates. He was as fed up as Marin, but at least he got to walk it off. He had a big build from too many pies rather than good breeding; a jolly soul who cheered you up just by his company.

'Heard four hundred Kols' broke in on the west side and ate all our porridge. Didn't leave a spoonful,' Marin said.

'The bastards! If I had been a little quicker on my rounds, I would have caught them and asked them to leave quietly and not wake anyone up.' They chuckled. 'What's the next story going to be, Marin? You have an hour to sort it out.'

'A dolphin falling out of the Camp Commander's arse dressed as the Queen,' said Marin impatiently

'Steady there, lad. You can't be calling her majesty out like that.' The old goat was a loyal subject and more than happy to serve in this stupid campaign.

'Sorry. I know you fancy the pants off her.'

'Hey!' He was getting a little flustered. 'Just get back to watching the approach.'

'This is horse piss!' Marin said. 'There haven't been any Kolgothians this far east since ... well, forever. I've never even seen one and I've been in the city for years – mostly in the alehouses, I'll grant you. Have you ever seen one?'

Looking over his shoulders, he crept up to Marin, his cheeks a little rosy from the early morning cool air. 'Yeah!' he said in the hushed tone of the keeper of a secret. 'I was running errands for my father outside Drynn, when an immense figure pushed me off my horse.' Marin was intrigued. This didn't sound like the normal nonsense stories that they passed between each other. 'I was shitting myself. He punched my horse on the side of its head and knocked it clean out. I'll tell you Marin, I thought I was a goner that day.'

'Well, you lived clearly. What happened?'

'I'm scared now just thinking about it. He stood over me. I was still on the ground at this point.'

'Yeah, I kind of got that,' said Marin. 'Go on.'

'Next thing he bellowed out an ear-splitting roar: spit, phlegm and all sorts of shit came out of his maw.' He made a face to emulate the encounter. 'He then sniffed the air around me and with a massive finger prodded my chest. "ME TAKE 'ORSE," he said. Well, I couldn't speak, I just nodded.'

'Shit! What did it look like?'

'Huge; almost nine feet tall; arms like tree trunks.'

'And?'

'Eh? Well, he was green with long, dark, messy hair. Big teeth too. Tattoos over his face. Can't remember much else. I know another guy who said that he saw one climbing out of a window with a couple of kids under its arm.'

'What ... goals?'

'No, you fool. I'm serious. They're nasty beasts.'

'Not sure if I believe you, but it passed a bit of time.'

'It's true, Marin. Plenty of other folk have had run-ins with them and even worse things have happened.' The old soldier carried on his round, happy that he'd told his little story. Marin turned back to staring down the road. No change: just bushes, grass, gravel, grass, rocks and more grass, but he had a picture of a Kol in his head now. The sun was up and his watch was at an end. He was about to turn in for his handover with another recruit, when he noticed a figure – a dark, cloaked, tall apparition just on the edge of a set of bushes. He was sure it hadn't been there a second ago. It wasn't moving. He felt goosebumps appear on his legs and arms. After listening to the old boy's yarn, he was a little jumpy. The shape was just too far away to get a detailed look at it and there was no point in shouting.

'Marin?' came a shout from down below and he near let go of his bladder. He beckoned to his replacement.

'Come here! Quickly.'

'This better not be another knob joke,' she said.

'Quick!' As he turned back, the figure was closer, but didn't seem to have moved. Marin was now fully on alert. The other guard came up and pushed him aside. Marin didn't move but motioned with his eyes.

'Do you see that creepy bastard out there to the right of the track?'

'Nowt there but the same shit we've been looking at for weeks.'

'What? There! Look! About a quarter of a mile away.' He pointed. She looked at his face and saw that he was sweating, and his pupils were dilated to the point that almost none of his eye colour was showing. As he focused more, a basket was knocked over beside him and crashed against some ale mugs. Once again, Marin's bodily functions were put under strain. He gave out a cry and a tingling sensation coursed through his body, ending at his extremities.

'By the gods, Marin you're a bit highly strung this morning.' When he regained his composure, he couldn't see the shape. He looked at his hands and they were shaking.

'You didn't see it? There was a figure; a shape in the gloom.' His voice broke slightly.

'Shit! You look terrible, even for you. Think you might need to get your head down. You'll be seeing the return of Talgameth yet.'

Chapter Fifteen

Lord Hal paced the throne-room flagstones, his armour making a distinctive tap as the small plate sections brushed against one and other. It had taken him an hour to get ready. *Why was he so nervous*? he wondered. He had gone over the route many times and drilled it with the palace guard and the Queen's guard. Everything had been inspected in the previous weeks. But something was eating away at him; the Queen would be exposed, a soft target for any assassin. She was his responsibility, not just for his job, but for the promise he had made to the king. He had watched her grow up, fall, laugh, cry and get angry. She was very good at the angry bit. Today would be hard on everyone. He was not only mourning the loss of a king, but a friend.

Checking his armour once more, he straightened out his cloak. The other advisers began to shuffle in.

He gave a shallow bow to each individually, which was duly reciprocated. One old adviser stopped. 'You are punctual as ever. I trust you are well?'

'Quite fine, Lord Hal. However, the fact that you carry a weapon unnerves me.'

'It is ceremonial. Nothing to fear.'

'I'm sure our colleague had nothing to fear. We stand very close to where you used your sword hilt to decorate the floor with our friends' teeth.'

'He had nothing to fear until he got above his station. And for your information, a sword does not make a man dangerous. It's the arm that wields the weapon.' His eyes were fixed on the nobleman to meet any other concerns he may have. Today was already turning out to be difficult. Exchanges like this just plied the fire with wood. After a brief, awkward moment, the adviser gave a nod and left an agitated Lord Hal on his own. His memory was now flooding with past experiences, not least the assault of a lord of the court.

He rubbed his temple and took a deep breath to steady his thoughts and save them for another time. Civic duty awaited and he mingled with the other advisers.

The horns blew, a few hundred at least. From behind the enormous oak door the fanfare was muted, but not diminished. The Queen's advisers lined up behind her, with Lord Hal at her side. Freya avoided contact with Lord Hal, keeping her gaze on the door ahead.

'My father was a kind man. He loved his people. He was trusting and compassionate. I am *not* my father!' With that, the door opened onto the cobbled main street. Crowds of people lined the path that the procession would take. The Queen's comment hung on the air.

The walk was slow down the grand steps. Each part of the descent, a thoughtful step towards the awaiting carriage. Some of the gathered crowd were crying, sobbing for a man they had never met.

'How dare they show their self-pity in front of me.' She kept her voice low for only Lord Hal hear.

'The rows of people have genuine sadness for the loss of their King, my Queen,' Lord Hal said, trying to ease the situation. Most of the crowd were dressed in black and holding chrysanthemums. On reaching the carriage, the Queen stumbled and caught her breath. Lord Hal was quick to offer aid but was pushed away. He saw the grief catching up with her, although she was trying to fight it.

The carriage was pulled by two large pure-bred horses, their harnesses polished to a high shine. Two fully-armoured palace guards took charge of the reins, the black plumes on their helmets blowing in the wind. They were stoic in their duty. The coach was draped in black silk with the white hand of Raniel emblazoned on either side. On top lay the gold-leafed coffin of the king, the ornate filigree glistening. As the Queen arrived at the coffin, a quietness descended along the tree-lined boulevard. Lord Hal felt that even the birds stopped singing as a mark of respect.

Taking a moment to gather her thoughts, the Queen nodded. Lord Hal raised a hand, and the two guards led the horses along the cobbles in slow order. Flowers were thrown at the carriage and prayers offered to the gods for thanks and protection. Lord Hal's armour was well-polished, the weak sunshine of the morning reflecting off the plates with every step. His ceremonial sword hung on his left side. Under his right arm he carried his helmet. He was glad not to wear it, like the two guards upfront. It could be stifling and limit the view.

With eyes unblinking he searched for what gnawed at him causing acid to well up inside. What was it? A gap in his thoughts or a misplaced trinket. Checking his regiment once again for reassurance.

The boulevard was just short of a mile long and the processional pace had been slow. The young ruler of Raniel kept her composure as the crowd showed their respect by bowing their heads when the carriage passed. She seemed uninterested in her new subjects. Lord Hal, on the other hand, was scanning the mass of grieving city folk. The noise of the hooves and the trundle of the wheels was the only thing tethering him to the present moment.

He was aware of some individuals keeping pace with the procession on either side. He strained to get a better look, but they seemed to dart in between the trees and mourners. He could not leave the Queen's side and investigate further, and this frustrated him. A gap in the crowd was beginning to open. There, he would get an unobstructed view.

Fixing his gaze on a person to his right. The clearing appeared and suddenly the figure was no longer there. He froze with a tightening chest. Looking to his left to see if the other person was there. He was met by the confused stare of the Queen with a thin smile on her lips.

'Are you ok my lord?'

'Yes, your Majesty, my thoughts wandered slightly. Nothing to worry about.' He shook off the notion of being followed. However, the feeling lingered.

Before they reached the pyre, the funeral procession heard the crowds and smelt the oil that dowsed the gathered materials. Lord Hal took another glance at the Queen. It saddened him to see her show no emotion. She had loved her father deeply and Lord Hal had been very close to her as her protector. Of late though, she had been cold to her closest advisers and callous in her decisions of state, showing no real interest in the fate of her subjects. All he could do was to stay close and offer her a hand to pick her up when she fell.

Rounding the street corner into the main plaza, they were met with an incredible sight. The Urus, those that built the pyre and were tasked to keep it aflame for three days, stood at each corner of the pyre, dressed in long, black, heavy leather cloaks, leather masks covering their entire heads except for small slits for their eyes. They stood to attention when the king's coffin arrived. The only people allowed to touch the coffin from now on were the Urus.

Putting eight large poles through the bottom of the funeral cart and with great strength, sixteen men lifted the cart off the wheels along with the coffin, the remnants being pulled away by the horses. Walking slowly to the pyre, they placed the king's coffin on top of the intricately stacked wood and herb branches. The herbs were to lift the king to the spirit world, to meet the gods and live forever with the forefathers.

Once all eyes were on the movement of the coffin, Lord Hal tightened his grip on his sword, concerned for the safety of the Queen. He looked around to make eye contact with some of the guards. Beads of sweat began appearing on his face, despite the cool air. He was aware that none of the guards was watching the Queen and, more worryingly, the captains of each section were not looking to him for orders.

As they stood in sombre silence all that could be heard was the rush of the wind and the snap of the black-and-white pennants of Raniel. A moment would be observed before that pyre was lit; a time for contemplation on the life of King Thomas and the future. All who stood round the square paid their respects. Not a word was spoken, nor a movement made.

More and more sidelong glances from Lord Hal gave notice to the Queen of his agitation.

'Be still my lord. Remember your place.'

Something wasn't right. He broke the stillness of the gathered crowd. Those closest were shocked at his apparent display of disrespect. Murmurs started to trickle through to those who could barely see. What they could see was the look on the Queen's face. Rage was developing deep within her.

Lord Hal marched to the nearest guard, oblivious to the stir that he was causing in the gathered crowd. His armour chinked as he strutted. Each footfall hung in the air like the toll of a bell.

'Guard?' As Lord Hal got closer, the guard lifted his head. Staring straight at the General through liquid, jet-black eyes, the guard opened his mouth and a high-pitched shriek pierced Lord Hal's ears and made him wince and stumble. Struggling to regain his balance and compose himself, he instinctively went for his weapon. Sword now drawn an intense noise filled his head, he stood in a battle stance, both hands on his hilt, his blade raised above his head.

A space had grown around the two soldiers. All the crowd could see was a shocked and scared looking guard being confronted by Lord Hal. For the chief adviser it was very real. The same fear he'd felt from the emissary in the great hall. Some comments reached Lord Hal's ears, which added confusion to the scene. Some were saying that he was drunk; others that the darkness has taken him and he'd gone mad. The guard was reluctant to raise his own weapon, especially against his commander.

'Sir, please lower your weapon. There is no call for this.' There was a tremble in the guard's voice as he looked frantically to left and right, trying to get the attention of the other guards. Help was on its way, but the gathered throng made his liberation seem a long way off.

Lord Hal stepped closer. To his mind the apparition's eyes were bleeding black viscous fluid down its cheeks. To the crowd it was still a frightened young soldier. Words formulated inside Lord Hal's head. Their meaning felt like sorrow, as if all Lord Hal's worst memories had come flooding back in an instant.

'All hope dies today. Raniel's death will tear asunder families and friendship. The long dark will envelop the realms. The blood of Kalnath will be spent and the Emerald Knight will open the world to horror and pain.'

Trying to clear the miasma from his mind. Lord Hal searched for a question. 'Who are you?'

The guttural laugh that preceded the response was mocking. 'I am the corruption that runs in the veins of your Queen.' A silky tongue lashed out from between purple split lips. 'I am the ever-living.'

With a powerful lunge and lightning speed, Lord Hal brought down his sword on the right of the guard's neck. The force tore through the leather gorget and bit deep into the collarbone – a blow so ferocious that the guard was dead before he hit the ground.

The voice was silent in Lord Hal's mind, but he could still hear a cackle of laughter. Once the haze of rage cleared, Lord Hal saw before him the body of the guard near split in two. Stunned spectators were unsure where to look. What they had witnessed was a young lad pleading with his commander to put down his weapon. Lord Hal's own experience far more visceral.

The recognition of what he'd done hit him at the same time as three other guards rushed and pinned him to the ground. The struggle was intense. His well-polished armour now dented and scraped. As they rolled him over and began to tie his hands, the crowd parted. The Queen stood over Lord Hal. There was a tear in her eye – one that she had not expected to shed this day.

'My lord, no words can describe what this is. You disrespect my father's funeral. You were a close friend to him, and my family and I cannot comprehend your actions.'

'Your Majesty, we are being manipulated by a darker power. Magic is being used to corrupt Raniel.' Pausing to grasp what he was saying. 'Even you.' He relaxed a little, to the relief of the guards trying to hold him down.

'No, my lord, this is all you. I can see no reason for your actions. I thought you a robust man who would not succumb to such madness. Maybe the events of the day have been too much, and you have found solace in the bottle.' Lord Hal wrestled to break free. The three guards were just holding on to him and no more.

'Enough! That foul light went out 1,000 years ago.' The Queen glanced to the crowd then to the guards. After a brief pause, she looked into his eyes. 'You are no longer General nor an adviser to the Crown. From today, you are but a common peasant. It is fortunate that you don't have a family, as they would have suffered too. I don't yet know your fate.'

He noticed a softening, maybe there was some emotion within her. He needed to warn her of his visions. The Queens roar removed that hope.

'Take him away.'

Freya smirked and shook her head slightly. As the former General was dragged unceremoniously, the crowd filtered slowly back to their spots to view the funeral. The Queen regained her composure and gave a nod for the Urus to light the pyre.

Chapter Sixteen

'Do you have to leave?' Helda lay on a bed of furs and cotton sheets. There was a quiver of despair in her voice after Guldr had told her of the impending war with Raniel. She hadn't seen him in three years and this visit was over too soon. She also knew that his rage would drive him into the heat of the battle. Only the gods could stop him. She had pleaded for him to send another chief as an emissary and resolve their differences, but Guldr had laughed at the suggestion, saying that it would be a sign of weakness and a rival chief would use that to usurp him.

Her eyes were glassy, but she did not weep. Kolgothians were fierce in battle and many of the tribes had fought each other until Guldr united them. The truce between the tribes was a tenuous one, to say the least. Feuds went back hundreds of years: grudges set by fathers of fathers, now continued by sons and daughters, who didn't even recall the names of past elders. For good or ill, the tensions with Raniel had only made these truces stronger.

'I must speak with the Mother Shaman. And you know of my duty. I do it to protect my family, lands and future generations of Kolgoth. Losing this would see our culture torn asunder and our people enslaved to work the mines and quarries.' Guldr dipped his head into a bowl of cold water to wake himself a little. 'I shall return later and we shall speak more.' He gave her a loving smile and left the house.

The sun was beating down and the glare made it difficult to see as he travelled westward through the village. A large wooden cabin came into view and created a shadow across the walkway, which provided a brief respite to his screwed-up eyes. Taking a deep breath he entered the hut, into a great open space with fur rugs on the floor. A couple of well-fed braziers gave out a comforting heat on either side. The hunched shape of a woman busied itself with herbs and roots. A couple of attendants helped the old woman with her chores.

'Mighty Guardian, Protector of Kolgoth, Great Chief of the Minal tribe and a little whelp of a boy, who would steal baking from my ovens, even though it was only meant for adults.' She turned and scowled, followed by a light-hearted smile.

'Indeed, Mother Shaman, and I remember the sickness afterwards. The herbs did not agree with me at that age.' The two shared an embrace. Guldr was a clear three feet taller than the old Shaman and had to stoop low. He thought it would have been easier to have picked her up, but that would have been disrespectful.

'I have heard what comes to the peoples of Kolgoth and I have walked the night plains. Some of my dreams of late have been very dark. The earth is in balance and that balance is about to be altered. I fear for us all, Chief,' the Shaman said.

'I hope that, with guidance from our ancestors, we will meet the foe and return them to Raniel with bloodied faces and a wound to remember.' The Mother Shaman stopped what she was doing and looked curiously at Guldr.

'Raniel? They are but pawns in this game, pieces to be played. You must ally yourself with our neighbours. A far greater danger spreads across this land and does not recognise fickle borders.' She was stern in her tidings. 'Sit. We must start the ritual before nightfall.'

Guldr remembered what the old Chief had said at the council meeting: 'Dark skies in the north and unnatural things coming to pass.' He sat at a low table, cross-legged on the floor and removed his shirt. Tattoos covered most of his body: tribal effigies and knots. Scars covered the rest of this great canvas. Every one testament to a fight won. On his arm was a set of six lines, to remember the tribal chiefs he had killed in hand-to-hand combat. Tradition said that the scar should not be able to heal for a year: either through nerves or respect, Guldr was picking at one of the scars.

The Mother Shaman noticed this unconscious act. 'To become a Great Chief many souls must pass on to the night plains. Show your respect, Guardian, for you will meet them once again. They fell to make you great. Now steady your breathing and empty your thoughts.'

Guldr closed his eyes and focused on a point in his mind's eye. Taking large slow breaths, his chest heaved like the filling of a ship's sail before it unfurled. 'Before we start, Great Shaman, if this goes ill and I do not recover, tell my wife I love her – she is the cup that holds the water and the life in every breath.' He resumed his meditation.

The Mother Shaman looked towards a wicker screen, where a pair of eyes stared with silent composure. Helda gripped the edge of the screen and the Shaman gave her a nod to bring out the ingredients: a mixture of roots and bark to add to the boiling broth that was on the hearth. More assistants appeared and produced hide drums. A low rhythmic thump ensued. Incense burnt and gave off a musty, earthy aroma. Guldr was still slowing his breathing down and the drummer kept pace. The Shaman began mouthing words of archaic origins. She touched each of his tattoos individually, giving respect to the gods. Each tattoo was an offering to a part of their tradition: love, war, family, light and darkness. A fear rose in her as she touched darkness, glancing at one of her assistants. 'Quickly now!'

Helda, witnessing this reaction, questioned the Mother Shaman. 'What is it, Great Mother?'

'Silence, child. You knew this was coming. I told you of the dangers. You did well to keep your knowledge from him. Now, keep quiet!' This scolding made Helda uneasy. The Shaman returned to her chanting, but more cautiously than before. Helda sat back and remained with her thoughts.

The broth was ready. Two bowls were filled and brought to the table. The Shaman uttered more words over the brew. She cupped some of the steam in her hands and placed them near her mouth, inhaling the vapour with a deep breath. Holding it there for a moment, she slowly let go of the intoxicating smoke. Her eyes were now clouded, yet she could still see. The drummer started a low growl which reverberated from his throat, still keeping up a deep rhythmic beat and creating an enchanting echo within the hut.

'Guardian.' The Shaman presented the bowl in front of Guldr. He was in a deep meditative state, but able to take the offering. Drinking slowly of the draught, he emptied the bowl and relaxed back into meditation. The other bowl was offered to Helda. She was reluctant to take it after the Shaman's reaction to the darkness tattoo. 'Girl, if you want this, you must drink.' Plucking up courage, she accepted the bowl and drank deep of its contents. 'Now, take deep breaths, follow the beat, focus on your breath and let the mixture take you. Don't fight it. Relax. You will witness the past, the future and the present. Guide your husband: he will need your tether as he walks the plains. Do not fear what you see. It has already happened or is still to pass, in which case it can be changed.'

Helda felt the draught wash over and penetrate her at the same time. It scared her. Her racing heart, pounding against her chest. She heard the Shaman's voice telling her not to fight it as hands clawed at her and dragged her down through memories. She felt the heat from their grip. The tighter they got, the more she fought. Opening her eyes, she saw Guldr fall back slowly onto the fur-covered floor.

She feared his death, her heart thumping as if in an empty barrel. Closing her own eyes again, she couldn't fight it any more. Deeper now, with more hands clambering over her. She panicked at the thought of her own demise, seeing fleeting glimpses of friends and family in distress, some in the past and some in places she did not recognise. She felt the heartbreak of losing her mother over and over again. 'Mama!'

The scrabbling fingers reached her neck, searching for purchase. Almost as if drowning, she tried to keep her head above the sea of hands. Utter desperation took hold. A voice resonated in the distance, low and deep. She knew not who was speaking, but any words she focused on would maybe give her hope. 'Hello? Help. Mama?' Still wrestling in anguish, the voice became clearer.

'Helda.' Low, deep and predatory. 'Helda, you should not be here. You are right to despair.' Helda was transfixed by the voice. 'Shadows blanket the land. Hopelessness and misery have arrived and death will come to Kalnath. Feel the darkness and prepare for my arrival. I am the ever-living.' Helda screamed, but no noise came forth. The hands overwhelmed her. Suffocating, she gave in to the inevitable. With her last drop of consciousness, she felt a change. The grabbing and scratching ceased. All she felt now was a large hand clasping hers. Awaking from her dream within a dream, she realised that Guldr was standing in front of her. With only the sound of a slight wind, Guldr's voice was clear.

'Why are you here? How is it possible that you are in my awakening?' Seeing the condition that Helda was in, he pulled her close and held her until she relaxed.

'I am the Guardian Maiden and I am charged to protect you on your plain walk.'

'I married you for your beauty and because you had the soul of the ancestors within you. Strength of heart can now be added to that list. Few people can survive this ritual unchanged, and I never imagined that I could share it.' Guldr took a deep breath and surveyed his surroundings. 'Let us continue, Guardian Maiden. I am glad of the company.'

As they walked the night plain, each took comfort from the fact that they were not alone. Their footfalls were silent and they didn't feel the pressure of the surface through their feet. Moving further into their collective dream state, they noticed familiarity and a sense of new experience at the same time. If Guldr focused on a rock or blade of grass, it would disappear. The sky was a vibrant blue, almost shimmering. A red haze drifted effortlessly across the horizon. Fractal lines appeared and stayed fleetingly. Helda gripped his hand tightly. A feeling of falling came over her.

'Guldr, I'm falling, but going nowhere.'

'I'm here. I'm always here.' He pulled her into a close embrace that she hoped would last forever. 'We must continue. This place will show us what we need to see.'

'I see all that I need in you, Guldr. I am happy here. I don't want it to end. Let's sit a while. I have never felt so at peace. I understand who I am, and my purpose in being with you. The crystal walls are cracking and letting knowledge in. Can you see it, Guldr? It's amazing.' In her reverie Helda felt as though she was floating, weightless, with no attachment to herself.

'Please, Helda, let's move.' Helda was experiencing bliss like she had never felt before and it was difficult to separate her from that. 'I need you to help me, Helda. We must speak with the ancestors.' Guldr sat with her for a moment and repeated his request. As if waking from a nap, she looked at him. 'Guldr? You're here, you're home.'

'We are on the night plain and we are going to meet with the Great Father.' Realising that she had let herself succumb to the dream, she apologised.

'I'm sorry, Guldr. I didn't know it would be like this. Time has stood still, yet also passed so quickly. I feel part of everything and that I am everywhere. Can we return?' Guldr held her again and reassured her that the plain would always be open to those who embraced the old ways.'

Nearing a hut, alone on the side of the path, thin tendrils of smoke danced elegantly from a chimney on the roof. No feeling of trepidation came, no caution before entering. They were both at peace within the dream. Walking through the door, they were met by a council of elders, which represented every tribe, even those whose names had been carved in caves aeons before they were born.

'Welcome, Guardian and Maiden. Please, take your places near the fire.' As they moved between past guardians and maidens, all legends in their own times, respectful nods were bestowed towards them. They sat across from the Great Father, the first Guardian of Kolgoth.

'I come for guidance,' Guldr said. 'Our way of life is under threat. I do not know what the future holds for our people, but dark have been the dreams of our Shamans. Wise ancestors, guide me through the times ahead.' There was silence, as if all were in collective thought. Then only the Great Father spoke.

'What of your own feelings? Do you see a future?'

'I see pain, loss and darkness.'

'Then you see well. We cannot foresee the future, but our spirits still trace the land of which we were once a part. You know of what I speak. You have had moments of not being alone. We are always with you, Guardian; that is another burden that you must carry – that we all live in you. You are connected to the earth far more than you believe.'

'Am I to be the last Guardian?' Guldr asked. Helda turned to him with a frightened look.

'You will be the last Guardian if what you feel comes to pass. However, you have a choice to change that path.'

'Then the future is not written?'

'All paths are laid out before us, but it is our choice which one to take. Look at what you see with different eyes.'

'I see that Raniel will take to the field. I believe us to be strong and able, but there is a shadow across my thoughts. The battle will go ill for all, with no victors, but the shadow still lingers.'

'The truth you see is Talgameth – once a great mage, then corrupted by the darkness in his heart. He stalks these lands again. He hunts for his artefact of power, the Emerald Knight. This above all else should make all races uneasy as the dread which it holds is all encompassing. It was with fortitude that it was not used before. Talgameth was not strong enough to attack any kingdom for the catalyst.'

'What was the catalyst?' asked Guldr.

'King's blood, and now the only lineage left is Raniel and she is weak, easily duped. They have lost their way, forgotten to look up at the stars and know their place. They befoul the land for their own gain. Both Raniel and Kolgoth are linked to this doom and both are needed to survive.'

'Then it has befallen to me to either save both races or end my own. This is a heavy burden, Great Father.' Guldr lowered his head. 'I am to break bread with those who would cry war. Am I to ask that powerful warrior tribes stand idle while their ground is trodden by invaders?'

'Yes. Be strong, Guardian. Guardian Maiden, you also have a task. All must fight against what is coming, but not all must wield steel and iron. You and your kin are adept with plant medicine. Listen to what the earth is telling you. Use what is given freely and be a guide to those who have to leave the mortal plain. Help those whose time has not yet come. Help all that are in need.' Helda didn't speak, but she understood what her task was – it was simple.

She felt sorry for Guldr: he had to convince all the tribal leaders not to fight, and save themselves for a stronger enemy.

'Courage, Guardian. Do not falter from your path. Hope will come from an unexpected place. Know this: there is a seat for you here in the halls of your ancestors. You will sit with us and we will be honoured by your presence.'

As the occupants, and the hut itself faded, the Great Father's gaze locked on Helda and in her soul he asked her to protect Guldr.

Standing alone, the Guardian and Maiden knew their tasks. Sharing another embrace, it was now Guldr who didn't want to leave. 'Can we stay here, Helda?' She made to reply but no words came out and all around her began to wane into fine dust.

Opening his eyes, Guldr adjusted to the gloom of the Shaman's hut. He sat up.

'Not so fast, Guardian. Get the bowls ready! Quickly!' His head spun and his stomach heaved. 'That will be the poison leaving your body. It will be over quite soon.' The Mother Shaman looked over to see Helda waking. 'Ah, another bowl is required.' She too threw up the contents of her stomach.

'I know now. I understand the doom that we must face. Talgameth lives,' said Guldr.

Chapter Seventeen

De'sal had noticed that a smell was starting to cling to the place. He had been here for some time and learned the routine. There used to be regular cleaning once a day – after all, this was where the gentry were put, to dry out or reflect upon the night's activities – but the recent clientele had been of a very low standard. That didn't include his most recent neighbour; the former General had been a welcome conversationalist, unless you got him on to the subject of the Queen's newest adviser. Then a whole subsection of vocabulary was unleashed in a blue haze.

He had tried to make the best of the situation, knowing that they would release him, after the pitiful little game the Queen was playing came to an end. He also hoped that the threat of removing his ears was off the table. He kept his small cell tidy and was pleasant enough to the guards, who, he had noticed, were not as chatty as they used to be, nor, for that matter, came round as often.

'This place is going to the dogs, my lord.' He couldn't see his neighbour, but he knew by the pacing that he was in the middle of the cell between the bed and table. 'What do you say?'

'I'm going to kill that whore!' Hal's voice was calm and steady, the same tone he'd used in court to get his point across, or the odd threat. He'd never needed to raise his voice, as he'd found that doing the opposite of what his opponent thought would put them off-guard. 'I need to leave this place.'

'It's only been a week, my friend, and to be honest, you did kill an innocent man.'

'Do we have to go over this again? Said Hal

'No, sorry. You've told me the story many times and your nightmares are testament to the anguish that you're going through. My feeling is that you need patience. Once the army moves west, they will at least let me out. Then I may have enough of a standing to get you off the hook. Although crime and punishment and all that ...'

'Ha! You think they will let me out? No, De'sal, they will hang me in good time. And as I'm swinging, I'll be cursing that black-blooded fiend that has managed to work on the Queen. She's young and she needs guidance.'

'And, if I may say, a slap!' interjected De'sal.

'If you did, I'd cut your hand off.'

There was a noise in the guardroom. Footsteps were heard on the stone stairs. The chink of steel plate, Hal knew, was from a palace guard. 'Look lively, my long-eared associate, this is the business end. That's no jail guard.'

The messenger walked at a slow pace up to the first cell and looked in. De'sal was standing up straight. He'd just smoothed his robe. 'Ah, my good man, am I to guess that my situation's misunderstanding has come to a close?' The guard didn't say a word and passed on by with a grunt. He stopped at De'sal's neighbour.

'The infamous Lord Hal.' There was a short silence between the two men. 'The Great man himself and adviser to King and Queen alike.'

'Okay, you've made your point that you're a dick. What do you want? I'm busy.'

'I knew the guard you cut in two. He was just a young lad, proud to be asked to line the journey of the royal hearse.'

'I know, you sack of shit! It was me who asked him. What do you want, eh? To stand there and show the wicked man how disappointed you are in him? I'm not playing.'

'Some people may believe your story, but I think you are just an old washed-out drunk who snapped, chose an easy target.'

'Come in here and we'll see what *snapped* looks like.'

'I think not. I would get in a bit of bother if I killed you.'

Hal gave a hearty laugh. 'Piss off, man! I can feel the fear in you. The cell bars have given you balls, I'll grant you. What's your name?'

'You don't need my name.'

'I might. How else am I going to find you when I get out? And just to let you know, I'm going to open you up from top to bottom and leave you to the rats.'

'No, Hal.' This wound Hal up even more until he was almost frothing at the mouth. He no longer had a title but it bit that this guard thought he was better. 'My message is from Lady Freya.' Hal's focus rounded solely on the guard's eyes. 'You are to rot in here. I was to give you your last meal, but I dropped it getting off my horse. Maybe now it is you who will be left to the rats.' The guard gave a wry grin.

De'sal was at his cell bars. 'And what of me? I am an emissary of Tiala.'

Keeping his eyes fixed on Lord Hal, the guard answered, 'Well, old man, it looks like you will at least have some company.'

De'sal sank to his knees with a tightening of his chest. He started to weep. 'I have a son, a wife and a home. I've done nothing wrong. I'm not even interested in your stupid war.'

The guard turned and strode up the stair. The last thing they heard was the bolt being slotted into place and a chain wrapped around the handle.

'Well, that could have gone worse,' said Hal.

'How, you oaf? How in all the gods' names could have it gone worse?'

'We are still alive and we don't have to eat that shit food anymore.'

De'sal was at a loss for words.

Back on his horse and settled into his saddle, Hal's tormentor cantered alongside the other guard. 'I'm worried that crazy bastard will get out and kill me.'

'Nah! No need to worry about him.' In an instant there was a knife in his side. He looked round with inquisitive eyes to see a black shadow envelop the other guard's face. The blade was in deep. Dark energy radiated through his body and he sank slowly, slumped over his horse and then tumbled, hitting the cobbled street with a dull thump. Moments later, in a miasma of curling dust, all that lay on the ground were clothing and a few personal trinkets. The mist cleared from the guard's face and he trotted on through the quiet street whistling a cheerful tune.

Both inmates sat quietly in their cells, contemplating their situation in differing ways: one resigning himself to inevitable death by starvation; the other willing the bars to come off their hinges and memorising Freya's mocking grin.

More time passed without much being said. A sigh from Hal led to him opening up a conversation. 'I want to apologise for your treatment, De'sal, and I ask you not to blame the Queen.' There was silence from the other cell. 'De'sal? I know you are there.'

'Shh!'

'Look if we are going to die together—'

'Quiet! I think there's something in this cell with me.' De'sal's voice trembled. The candles had long gone out and he was huddled up at the bars near to where Hal was sitting. There was rustling from over by his bed, as if something was searching. De'sal's foot slipped, scraping sand across the flagstone floor, as he pushed up against the wall. Fear gripped the Tialan. The rustling stopped. Without seeing, De'sal knew something was watching him.

'Magnificent effort in keeping quiet,' Hal said.

They both heard the scrape of claws on the stone floor. In this darkness their minds tried to picture what creature could be lurking there. Both knew of the unimaginable horrors that could be unleashed if the Dark Lord had truly returned. The tales seemed real now, very real.

Hal lurched up and started to make a lot of noise. 'C'mon, you fiend. Come through here.' He was kicking the bars violently. 'Leave him be! Come on. I'll tear you apart, whatever realm you're from.' This display came a little from fear and from trying to protect De'sal.

Quivering slightly, De'sal had his eyes closed, waiting for whatever ruin might befall him. If he'd had the courage, he would have seen a red imp with a slight orange hue to its belly sitting on its haunches, its head tilted in a questioning way.

'Click.' At the noise De'sal opened his eyes to see a small snout an arm's length from his face. He could do nothing, but roar with laughter, all tension released at once. Hal could only sit and wonder what was going on.

'Never heard a man laughing as he was dying before!' Hal waited for De'sal to calm down.

'Oh, my friend, it's just an inquisitive imp. I thought I was about to be taken to the Ethereal Realm for an eternity of torture. Ha! It looks like we're stuck with each other for a little longer.' The new arrival scuttled through between the bars and stood outside Hal's cell, again with an inquisitive look. Standing in the same place as the palace guard, the little imp reared on its hind legs.

'If this bugger calls me Hal, I'll rip the bars off.' The imp started giving a series of clicks and gravelly noises. It was also making hand gestures, waving its clawed fingers back and forth.

'It could be calling you anything for all we know. He's an excitable chap.' The imp moved towards the bars and Hal took a cautious step back. It started to tap away at the bars and click with enthusiasm.

'Sorry! I don't understand.' With that, the imp stopped and slid through the bars. Hal was not so relaxed as he had been with the imp on the other side of the cell door. 'Can these buggers bite?'

'I believe they are very formidable opponents for their prey, such as cats, dogs, rats and the odd horse.'

'A horse?'

'So, I've been told.' De'sal said.

The imp came close to Hal and held out its hand. Hal, unsure what to do next, paused at the surreal moment.

'Click.' The response broke his thoughts and he reached out to touch the imp's hand. A small hand, very similar to a human, but with long and dangerously looking sharp claws, closed gently around a couple of Hal's fingers and pulled him toward the bars. The imp made it through, but clearly Hal could not.

'Another month with no food, little man, and I'll fit through quite easily. But for now, we're stuck. He made a show of using a key to unlock the door. The imp kept pulling. Hal wrestled free of its grip. 'I can't go through the bars. I need the door open.' A big wrinkle appeared on the imp's forehead and it looked back and forth between the keyhole and Hal. More clicks and cackles, then some hush.

'Clack!' With a startled bolt, it made for the stairs.

'Looks like we've been shafted twice today.'

A few moments later the imp reappeared with a huge bundle of keys.

'De'sal, my good man, you will not believe this. Our leathery friend here has just given us a ticket out of here.' The imp offered the keys to Hal and stood back. Without much difficulty, he found the correct key and let himself out. As soon as he did so, the imp was on him and pulling at his leg to follow him.

'Easy! I'm going to let my friend out.' There was elation on De'sal's face and it took a while for him to compose himself and get back to his normal demeanour.

'Well, we're free,' giving Hal a hug.

'Whoa! Enough with the hugging.'

'Sorry, I'm still a little overwhelmed. We'd best follow our saviour and see what he wants.' They followed the imp down to the room at the bottom of the cell corridor. The door was slightly ajar. Beyond it was dark with a very distinct aroma. 'My, this is getting interesting.' Hal pushed the door over. It made a shrill squeak and a series of quick echoing crackles. The imp led them over to a wooden toilet box where, to their surprise, they found an imp's arse looking at them.

'Okay, it's the least we could do. Grab a leg, De'sal!'

Chapter Eighteen

The Brovan and the High Citadel had interfered. The Dark Lord had been on the cusp of ruling the known world. The Emerald Knight would unlock powers that no mage would be able to stop. Talgameth himself had been buried in a crypt, never to be released; a sentence that would guarantee anyone went mad – eternal life, in eternal darkness. All witnesses sworn to silence so that his whereabouts would never be known. Over time, Talgameth's malice had grown and his hatred for all life had boiled within him.

Eventually, a lone scavenger seeking gold in the Zinjal capital had dug his way beneath the desolate wastelands above, into a dusty black cavern. On shining his candle through a small hole, he had caught glimpses of light reflected from coins. Digging deeper, further, into the crypt, he had found more gold and precious jewels – too much to carry. He knew he had hit the jackpot.

Curious to see what else the tomb held; he lit more candles. Turning to the back wall, he saw bodies with desiccated skin, the frames of the deceased covered in tattered robes and brittle leather sandals. One form sat on an elaborately carved chair inlaid with gemstones and fine gold filigree. The scavenger knew that he was the only person to have entered this crypt since the day it was buried.

Either through excitement or clumsiness, he tripped over the foot of one of the prostrate figures. His light source rolled and stopped a few yards away on a pile of gold. He lit a new flame and looked at what he'd tripped on. Then, he picked himself up, brushing off the fine dust that covered everything.

'A visitor, I see.' The gravelly voice came from the figure now leaning forward in the chair. The adventurer had been struck dumb, paralysed, unable to move or speak. Fear gripped his muscles, so startled by shock that his heart gave out its last beat. Before he could hit the ground, the occupant of the chair sprang to catch the body and drove its hand into the scavenger's chest, drawing the life force from the body and renewing its own vigour. Pleasureful groans rebounded off the stone walls. With a new lease of energy, the figure stood straight. He clicked his fingers to create some light, but none came – a slight frustration, although he knew that it would return.

'Thank you for your inquisitiveness, young adventurer. You have brought ruin to the world.'

He studied the husk that had been the interloper to his crypt. 'Strange are your garments and you do not look of this land.' Opening a satchel dropped by the adventurer, he unrolled a scroll with a crude map drawn on it to represent the city. Also, within the contents were vials of red liquid, some food in the form of hard bread and a pendant. Opening the pendant, he saw two miniature paintings of a male and female, both strange to his eyes. He pondered this for a short time, then picked up the skull of the unfortunate youth. Looking into the now-empty eye sockets he gave a thin smile and with his newly revived hand, using very little effort, crushed the skull to small fragments which fell into the dust.

'Now is my time once more.'

Talgameth, Lord of Zinjal, left the crypt.

Another few swings of his pick would see the slave allowed a break. The cramped conditions of the tunnels, the constant digging and hauling rock and earth, took its toll on every part of his body. Not that the overseers ever had any pity for them. If they fell over, more lashes were used to get them up. With a torturous heave of the pick, using what little energy he had, the slave made contact with the tunnel wall. The loose rock and earth gave way to reveal a wooden door. The discovery gave the slave a little more drive. The nightmare might be over if the artefact was found. Breaking dry panels with the haft of his pick the newly opened room offered him no more comfort than the tunnel. The musty air filled his nostrils and dried out his mouth further. As the candle picked up outlines of benches and shelves the light fell upon an armour-clad skeleton. In its hand was a package. With some excitement the slave called out, his voice echoing through the tunnels under this long-forgotten city.

'Master!'

'It has been found, my lord.' A cloaked figure stood with its back to the messenger. The air was dank and still. Gloom permeated the space surrounding the two inhabitants. The sound of the air whistling through the tunnels was the only evidence that there were walls. Moist, mould-covered earth deadened the sound even further.

'Are you sure? Do not fail me on this.'

'Yes, my lord. It was found among the remains of a warrior. As the master had said there was the sigil of the Brovan Order on the armour.' Their conversation made no echo. They were deep underground.

'Long have these cities been buried. Over the past thousand years, the great vaults have been looted by adventurers looking for wealth and glory,' the overseer said.

'Then it is by luck that it still remained.'

'Luck is a point of view. Bring it to the surface and fill in the vault.'

'What of those labouring still?'

'Congratulate them on their sacrifice to Talgameth. In their eternal slumber they may be called upon to serve once again.'

'Yes, my lord.' The messenger gave a bow and hurried off along the tunnel.

The overseer was very cautious. He knew that failure was not an outcome his master would accept. Finding the Emerald Knight, however, might lead to more gifts and praise for his service.

On reaching the surface, the overseer scanned the windblown ruins of Draden, a once-powerful city of Zinjal that had commanded trade and commerce. A well of magic was said to spring from its centre, so powerful that it could be seen as shimmering air and had given rise to the great mages of that age. He had heard of the magnificent place it had been. Shining marble arches, gold and bronze statues depicting glorious feats – all gone now. Dust and fractured stone were all that remained. They had been digging in these parts for nearly 100 years since the return of Talgameth.

'Maybe with this artefact, the power of Zinjal will return.' He spoke to the wind, almost reassuring the city it had not been forgotten. Spying a running figure heading his way he turned and waited with pleasure. It was one of his servants carrying a cloth bundle.

Out of breath, the thin female dropped to both knees and offered up the package.

'My lord. The artefact as requested.' The servant did not look at him but kept her stare on the ground.

He took the package. It was unnaturally heavy, almost lead-like. Trying hard to keep his nervousness from showing, he unwrapped the fragile leather carefully, one-fold at a time. The servant was still on her knees waiting to be dismissed. However, the overseer was now fascinated by the contents of the bundle and paid no attention to the woman in front of him. His eyes widened as, holding his breath, he peeled back the last flap to reveal the small crudely carved figure of a knight, made entirely from one solid piece of emerald. A glow given off by the sun's light traced through its core. In his mind, frolicking shadows weaved and chased. Memories and the fates to come mixed in a miasma of darkness. A small tear of black resin ran from the corner of his eye and scarred his cheek. Snapping out of the dream he recoiled from the burn.

He spoke softly to himself. 'This is what my master wants – a powerful relic. If this truly is the key to his plan, then the board is set.' He remembered that the woman was still kneeling in front of him. He lifted her chin tenderly and looked into her eyes. 'Soon our great lord will consume this land for the glory of Zinjal. You, my child, played a part in that.' He placed his hand on the side of her head and began to mumble an incantation. The woman struggled to release herself from his hold, as a searing pain now burst through her head. Screaming, she clawed at his hand. Her body evaporated into a grey smoky cloud that swirled round the two of them. A second more and there was nothing left of the woman's body. The cloud, the shade of darkness itself, continued to spin in a vortex around the overseer.

A voice, as if from a distant age, spoke. 'You have news, my acolyte?'

'Yes, master. What you covet has been found. I have the Emerald Knight.'

'Long has been my search for this artefact. In my slumber I recalled a memory of a device with such power. Bring it to me.'

'By your will, master.'

The cloud shrank and all that could be heard was the wind. Kicking the pile of clothes that graced the ground in front of him, he thought of a just reward for his efforts.

Chapter Nineteen

Two figures huddled in an alcove in one of the many corridors away from prying eyes. Whispers broke the snap of spitting candles.

'Mistress, you wish for me to deliver a message?'

'Yes, it's getting more difficult to influence the Queen. She seems to question what I do, as well as look for more reassurance that I am on her side. The Council of Advisers is slowly coming around to our methods. They are weak, only interested in money and status. They don't understand that purpose is far more rewarding.' Freya had done a lot of work to subdue the guards and staff. Easy mind tricks and false information worked extremely well on the cattle of Raniel. However, she still felt the need to hide. 'It is inevitable that people will talk. Things have been quite different around here. There is a palpable tension in the air, an almost fear of the dark.' She smirked. 'I must sow a little more of that fear and keep reassuring the Queen. I will be the only one that can comfort her. I serve you master and with your guidance I will see your plan to fruition.'

A shadow peeled itself away from a corner and hung like a scarf around the messenger's neck. A hissing sound just on the edge of hearing filled the alcove.

'Company is coming.' He said looking over Freya's shoulder. Bowing he pulled his cowl down further and walked out into the corridor and left Freya to compose herself before the Queen joined her.

'Freya? Who was that person you were speaking to?' The offhand question did not sound accusatory, although the Queen had been very paranoid of late. She felt that everyone was watching her and the only person who would stop and speak beyond their palace duties was Freya.

'That was my wicked master. He was giving me orders to turn the shadow demons on the palace staff.' Freya let the comment hang in the air for a short time. Then, she burst out laughing.

'That wasn't funny.' The Queen gave a brief smile, the first one she'd had all day. 'Do you know what they're saying about you? I heard the maids talking as they scurried outside my chamber. I should have them flayed.'

'Sorry. I'm only having a joke with you. You have been very uptight recently. Are you feeling, okay? I know what they say, but it's just nonsense. They're just silly little girls. If I was what they say, then surely you would know. I'll speak to the house steward and ask them to behave.' She gave the Queen a slight tap on her arm that made the Queen feel a little more in control of herself.

'I don't know what I would be like without you. You keep me sane and … well, you're my only friend.'

'I'll always be your friend, your Majesty. How else am I going to control this land with dark magic if I can't control you?' They laughed at the silliness and shared a smile. Letting the moment pass, they went their separate ways.

Stopping, the Queen turned. 'Who was he though?'

'A merchant from Freehold. I'm trying to acquire fresh food for our march west. I hear that all sorts of rotten garbage are being used to feed the staff and I don't fancy an arduous journey eating that.'

Content with the story and her mind at rest, the Queen continued on her way. Freya had a bit of business to attend to below stairs.

Two flights beneath the main palace, the maids and cooks hurried and darted between rooms carrying and shouting orders. The air was stuffy and the only light was from the odd set of candles suspended from the ceiling on chains. No one really noticed Freya and she was happy in that fact. She listened and took in all that was unfolding around her.

'Oh, I'm so sorry. I didn't see you there. May I help you?' A slight woman in a maid's uniform was towelling off her hands when she nearly bumped into Freya. On noticing who she was, the maid became quite nervous. At any other time, Freya would have relished the fact that she made people cautions. This was not her goal at this point.

'Please, no need to be sorry. I am in your domain, maybe even trespassing.' She smiled at the maid to put her at ease. 'We have a big journey coming up and most of the staff will be travelling with her highness. I wanted to speak to them and see if they are okay with what we are about to contend with.'

The maid was confused. 'Well, this is quite unusual. We never really get asked anything down here. But you will have to speak with the steward. Please, this way, my lady.' Freya was led through a rabbit warren of rooms and corridors, where linen was being pressed, while others contained large fires with pots and pans of all sizes hanging over them.

'It smells amazing down here.' Freya studied the layout, indulging her senses at the same time.

'After a while you don't notice it, my lady, but when we go upstairs, there is such a beautiful array of scents from all the fresh-cut flowers, it fair makes your eyes water.' Freya was shown into an office where a middle-aged gentleman at a desk was surrounded by paperwork, scrolls and packages. He looked to be under an immense strain. The maid gave a quiet cough, 'S'cuse me, sir!'

'Oh, what now? I don't get five minutes these days.'

Freya looked at the steward. 'Well, maybe we could alter your employment,' she said coolly.

The steward looked up sharply and his heart sank at seeing the Queen's adviser staring intently at him.

'My sincere apologies, my lady.' He stood and moved away from his desk. 'Thank you,' nodding to the maid. 'That will be all.' The maid curtseyed to Freya and left. 'What can I help you with? We rarely get visitors of your stature down here.'

'I wanted a word with some of your staff and to ask how the preparations are going for our journey.'

'We will double our efforts and I can assure you we will be ready. I am short on staff, but I understand that the army needs good people to defend Raniel. We must all make sacrifices during these troublesome times.'

'That is very noble of you. The Queen will be pleased to know of your efforts.' The steward stood a little taller now after the comment. He led Freya to the door and along the corridor to a group of staff folding sheets in a large room. They all stood when they saw who had entered their work area. Freya had a chat with them and asked their thoughts. They were all very positive and patriotic, as was to be expected, given who was asking the questions. Freya was not in the least interested in their feelings, but made out that this was the Queen's request. Moving into a large high-vaulted room, Freya noticed some balconies looking down onto the area. An immense oak table was placed in the centre, with wooden workbenches around the periphery of the room, where a large fire crackled and spat at the far end. At least twenty folk were busy chopping vegetables, butchering meat, stirring pots. One elderly lady was barking orders at a couple of younger helpers in her charge.

'My, this is where it all happens. Thank you for all your lovely meals,' Freya said over the din. The head cook gave her a nod and continued to harass the apprentices. 'Can I speak to some of them?' she asked the steward.

'Certainly, my lady.' He beckoned a few of his staff over and they sat down next to Freya. She asked them the same questions. This didn't take long, but as she was about to finish, she changed her questioning slightly.

'On a more delicate matter, I am aware that there are rumours going around about me.' The staff sat rigid and glanced at one and other. 'Don't worry. No one is in trouble.' They relaxed a little. 'It's just this nonsense is making its way to the Queen's ear and she is under a lot of stress at the moment. I am not a dark mage. I can't turn people to goo or walk through walls.' She gave a chuckle. 'I don't really care what is said, but the Queen is tiring of it and that might not go too well for the folk concerned.'

'My lady, we can assure you that the feeling down here is nothing of that nature. I suppose that we do comment on your beauty.'

Another member of staff interjected at this point. 'That will be Millie. She's always spouting something off. She believes that the shadows are alive and watching her.' The man in question got a nudge from the person sitting next to him, which didn't go unnoticed by Freya. 'She's only young, but needs to learn to keep her thoughts to herself, especially upstairs, if you don't mind me being so blunt, my lady.'

Freya took a look around, as if scanning the shadows. 'No, not at all, my man. Like I said, no one is in trouble. But if you could let this Millie know her error, that would be lovely.'

As their conversation was finishing, Millie was on the top balcony sweeping out one of the servant rooms. Unknowingly, a shadow pared itself away from the coving and glided across the chamber and slid up her back.

Like a silk cloth, it enveloped her face. She was still sweeping as she made her way to the balustrade. Dropping her broom, she climbed up onto the banister, leaned forward and plummeted onto a workbench below. A second before impact, the shade left her body and she realised that she was falling. Millie's scream was short, and the crash as her body hit the table reverberated throughout the staff area. Shocked, everyone was quick to their feet.

'All the gods!' The steward was first to break the silence. 'My lady, please, you should not see such things.' Freya was ushered out and back up the stairs into the palace, with the steward apologising all the way up, and ensuring that they would look into it. Freya gave him a worried look.

'Please, pass on my sympathies to the staff on such a distressing episode.' She turned and walked away, feeling rather smug at how that had gone. *Look all you want, fool, but you'll get nowhere*, she thought to herself, content with her achievements.

Chapter Twenty

Gazing out to sea, the cool salty breeze was fresh against his skin. Maleth ran his hands over the grass, feeling every blade. Taking a deep breath in, holding it, then letting it out for the same time was his mentor's way of relaxing and stilling the mind. His thoughts drifted back to Marin and the rest of his friends in the camp. He wondered how they were progressing. Was Marin's mouth still getting him in trouble? He came back to the present and contemplated his study. Maleth found the training hard: reading book after book, large dusty tomes; having to learn a new language just to be able to find the damn thing in the library.

Master Falvor was kind and patient. Maleth had heard that some of the other tutors were not interested in their students, thinking there was no point in training them because they would all be dead in a couple of months anyway. That had led to a little uprising. Master Falvor had de-escalated the situation with some words to the tutoring mages. After that, maximum effort was given by all involved.

He entered his mentor's study with a concerned look on his face. 'Everything alright, my boy? You seem distracted. Did you read *The Anatomy of the Species* again? I told you; you'll go blind.'

'No, master, there are so many books to read. I feel that I'm only scratching the surface of what I should know. In *Heckler's Bestiary*, it mentions some odd creatures of scale and wing. Are these fantasy writings? And Jo'kals, the Tialan herb master, states that plants can open up a world beyond our own consciousness and even control us. It all seems a little fanciful. All my time in the Brovan order I saw nothing of the like.'

'You have your mind made up. If you think it is far-fetched then to you it possibly is. However, to Jo'kals and Heckler the truth must be told. Why, with all the novel things you have seen since arriving here, would you choose to disbelieve that strange beasts roam the world, or that plants could actually be a higher-level life form? When we are hungry, we eat. We have cravings for fruit or herbs. We get thirsty and we also get sick. It could be our body telling us something, or it could be what we have *eaten* previously telling our body what they want.' He smiled at Maleth, knowing that he had lost him with that little analogy.

A little downtrodden, Maleth confided in his mentor. 'I have concerns about the friends I have made. I want to protect them, but I don't want to hurt anyone.'

'Yes, you told me the story of the little girl in the town square. Very unfortunate.' Master Falvor was sympathetic to Maleth's views, as he was a healer first and foremost. However, he was an accomplished battle mage all the same.

Maleth sat at the reading table. He focused a little and produced a small transparent ball of energy, then started rolling it back and forth between his hands, lost in the simplicity of the light shining through it, making shapes on the wooden surface. 'I want to know more; I want to know it all. There is well over a thousand years of history, teachings, maps, philosophy and apparently fictional beasts and talking plants. I need more time, or at least be strong enough to help my friends and to come back and finish my studies.'

Master Falvor felt immensely proud of his new charge. He had only been there a week and he was soaking it all in like a sponge. 'All I ask is that a student pays attention and opens themselves up to their potential. We have students here who have yet to master a single spell because their mind is elsewhere, chasing girls or boys in their towns back home. One unfortunate chap had a soft spot for animals and tried it on with an imp. Terrible affair, that! Little Gife was beside himself and outraged that one of our students would behave in such a way. Sorry, I'm going off topic,' Falvor said with a wry smile.

'A teacher hopes that their student will one day be better than them and carry their teachings on to another student. This is how knowledge spreads and grows. I see within you, my boy, a destiny – one which is not yet written, I might add. You have empathy and respect, a keenness to learn and you want to do it for the right reasons. You may need to change your thoughts on battle magic though.'

'Master, with all due respect, I do not wish to pursue any art of destruction.'

Getting up from his chair, Falvor made a few groans and his joints creaked. 'Still agile for an old bugger, eh?' he said. Standing at a shelf he ran his fingers over a few books. Pausing, he hovered over a red leather book. Gold writing indicated that it was the *Citadel's Inventory for Vegetables, 1293–1297*. Maleth watched him. He was contemplating whether or not to pick up the book. 'Bugger it! Don't let me regret this, Maleth.' He pulled the volume out. The shelf gave a crack and opened slightly. 'What you are about to see is my own collection of books which has taken a long time to source. Remember, not all books live in a nice library.' He searched in the dim light, stopping now and again to reminisce about where he'd found a book. One particular scroll was still sealed with wax. He picked it up and paused, mulling over what the contents could be. Deciding against opening it, he placed it back. 'Now is not the time for a spell such as this. No.'

A couple of moments later, the Grand Mage emerged from behind a dusty shelf, climbing over boxes and forgotten editions of obscure philosophy from a distant land. Looking seriously towards Maleth, he produced a scroll with beautifully carved wooden ends. 'What I give to you is probably the most important spell ever written.' The mage handed the scroll to Maleth. 'I am putting a lot of faith in you, young man. These are difficult times and it has not gone unnoticed here that darkness stirs in this land. This is an opportunity. Use it wisely.'

Unrolling the scroll slowly to its full length, Maleth found only a few symbols inscribed in an archaic rune system. It took him a short while to decipher them. Eventually he had the first set of runes. Concentrating hard, he read them out. 'Know–ledge.' He said it again, a little faster. 'Knowledge. Okay, what does that mean then?'

'Keep going.' Falvor urged.

'See – tooth the knowledge gi–ven'

'Wow, you sound like a Rogane farmer. Read it back, and its *truth*, not tooth.'

'See truth the knowledge given.'

'Well done. When you use this spell, it will take a lot of focus and energy, but you will be able to read and understand everything that you see. Therefore, you may just be able to get through the entire library if you choose your literature sensibly. But beware: there are books within these walls that are connected to the dark arts, whose words should never see a curious eye. However, intertwined through the lines of hate and twisted evil are threads of hope, should we ever need them. Try it with this book – it's on fishing the Great Lake near Leal, in Senal.'

Maleth read the scroll and focused hard. Nothing happened. 'This is not just reading a page, my boy. You must empty all other thoughts; see the words in your mind's eye. Be one with the symbols and repeat the noises like a chant.'

All Maleth remembered before passing out on the wooden floor was a horrendous pain in his temple. Sitting up later against a wall, with the Grand Mage holding smelling salts below his nose, he came around with a panic. 'Ah the pain! You said nothing about the pain.'

'That's because it wasn't supposed to be painful. What happened?'

'You tell me. Shit, that hurt!'

'Hmm, let me see the scroll.' As Maleth had fallen to the floor in a spasm, he had gripped the paper tightly. The Grand Mage had had to wait until he'd come round to prise it from him. 'Oh! I fear that the runes have disappeared. Try the book.'

Maleth took the book, his head still throbbing. He read the cover easily enough, first page, second, third and on and on. He just needed to glance at the page and he knew the words. On through the book he went and in the briefest time he was finished. 'Well, the best time to catch black fish is in the morning, in the pools just a scant distance from the mouth of the river.'

The Grand Mage smiled at Maleth. 'Do you know what this means?'

'I'll not go hungry if I'm near water?'

'Well, there is that, but you are able to become one with a scroll. By doing so, you need not focus in order to use it: the words will augment you. This is fascinating. Now, you have reading to catch up on and none of it is fiction.'

Maleth set to work. At first, he picked up random books and amazed at the new ability he had, he commented childishly that he now knew the heights and names of all the peaks in Raniel. A pile formed beside him. Changing from mentor to assistant, Master Falvor called for other students to fetch and replace books, scrolls and maps for Maleth.

'I can recall everything!' Maleth exclaimed.

The Grand Master sat in awe at the speed at which Maleth was digesting the information. *'Balfour's Healing, The Mages' Tomes of Minor Healing Magic* – all ten volumes! That's six months' tuition gone in ten minutes.' The work was taking its toll on Maleth, however. Headaches and painful spasms were crippling him. He used magic to treat himself, which wore him out even quicker.

After days of studious reading, Master Falvor had to stop him. 'You cannot go on like this. Everything has a price.' With a murmur of well-versed runes, Maleth fell unconscious and Falvor grabbed the book he was reading before it hit the table. 'Ah, *Wanders in the East*: *Gurthrop's Expedition to the Lands beyond Rogane*. Not sure why you're reading that, my boy. That's where all your fanciful beasts hide.' Falvor stared at Maleth. He had never met such an enthusiastic student. *'If only I had the time to teach him properly,'* he thought, *'this boy could become the strongest mage alive. Such a pity he's not going to survive this stupid war.'*

Chapter Twenty-One

The Queen sat at the head of a large oak table. Thick, simply cut legs held up a top that weighed at least the same as ten men. There was a sheen on the greater surface. However, in front of each seat, the beeswax had worn through to the bare dry wood. The shape of the table was such that the eight other seats were angled to face the top seat. This made it difficult for guests to eyeball each other and the regent could see everyone's face.

Leaning on her elbows, the Queen pondered the importance of her position while being swamped by the large chair that had been placed at the centre of the table. It was supposed to be intimidating. Her father had sat here before her, and his father before him. The line went back generations. She had never been allowed in here; it was strictly forbidden, However, being an inquisitive child, she had found a way to get past the guards. The palace was such an old building with an abundance of gaps and holes for a sprightly little girl to use to her advantage. Remembering the row she had got when caught made her smile, but at the same time, she recalled the feeling of disappointment in her father and recoiled at the sadness this invoked inside her. Now was not the time.

Her expression mirrored that of an apathetic teenager, weary with the tedium of existence. She had propped her feet on the table and her gaze fixed on the door at the other end of the room. The fire had gone out and the embers gave off their dying light, cloaked in wisps of thin smoke. The door opened and the embers gave a last fight for life as fresh air entered the room. One of her advisers, crossed the threshold and stopped in shock at the position she was in. Stumbling words on his lips.

'My apologies, my Queen. I did not think you would be here. The council is not due to start for another twenty minutes.' The middle-aged, well-groomed man was one of the last advisers on the council that had served her father. The late king would not have stood for feet on the table, but he kept his thoughts to himself, well aware that some of the other advisers were no longer on the council after speaking their mind. Their replacements were of an uneasy nature.

'This is my house, is it not, my lord?'

He swallowed to ease his dry throat, obviously uncomfortable. Looking around the room he seemed anxious of the dark. 'I meant no disrespect, my Queen.' He bowed his head.

'Relax, sir.' Guessing where his unease came from. 'Why do you fear Freya?' Swinging her legs round and taking a more formal position as she asked the question. He was not ready for such a direct assault.

'I have no quarrel with her ladyship. You are the best judge of who you keep counsel with. Some of her suggestions at these meetings are perhaps *questionable* and ...' He paused. '... there have been rumours.' He saw the Queen frown and was quick to add. 'I take things as I see them, your highness and don't give any time to such gossip.'

'I have heard the rumours and the tales and I can assure you that she is no demon.' Her adviser blushed as his thoughts ran away from the moment. 'We are sitting on an unstable ledge. I need strong and loyal people around me. I also see the fear that she instils in everyone. Do you fear me as much, my lord?'

He was not in a wonderful position – out on a limb searching for answers. His reply would either hang him or help him. 'My Queen, I knew your father well. Although I cannot attest to know the mind of a king, or a father, I am sure, however, that he would be proud of the strong young woman who now sits on a war council ready to engage the enemy abroad.' The Queen gave no hint of whether his words were changing her feelings one way or another. Grasping for a little more courage he continued. 'Some of your decisions of late have been *uncharacteristic*: quick to dismiss loyal advisers who would query your actions. There have been many changes within the palace: strangers now appear with no contest from the guards and, with all due respect, your highness, that business with Lord Hal was very unfortunate. My feelings are that there is something else at work.'

Looking in his direction the Queen gave no response.

'You see much, my lord,' Freya said, as she walked out of the shadows. Both had been unaware that she was there, nor knew how long she had been listening. The adviser's blood ran cold. He had answered the question; his response would get him killed. He gave a low bow as Freya made her way over to the Queen's side.

'Our conversation is over, my lord. You may take your seat and I welcome your honesty'

An uneasy silence fell on the room. Freya sat to the Queen's right, the place of Chief Adviser. The others filed in and sat after paying their compliments to the Queen.

The Queen stood and surveyed the occupants of the room. 'You are my trusted advisers. We are about to embark on a trial that will see the ruin of Kolgoth. Are we agreed on the reasoning for what we do?' Whether or not their responses were from the heart, they were unanimous in their agreement. 'They burn our villages and terrorise the townsfolk. My father went to the aid of the border towns and paid with his life. If accounts are true, Kolgoth will meet us on the field as soon as we cross the border near Enokas. General, is the army ready to move?'

'Yes, your highness,' replied the newly appointed general. 'A couple of weeks will see us able to march. We have just over 12,000 armed and ready. As we speak, officers are taking command of their units: 500 heavy horses; 400 archers; 500 light cavalry, namely, lancers. We also have a household guard of over 500. The rest, your highness, are the general ranks of spears and militia.'

'What of the Citadel? Are the battle mages ready?'

'They will join us at Enokas.' Seeming content with this The Queen glanced over at Freya, who gave her a reassuring smile.

She returned to her seat and let the conversation flow. Losing focus, an hour or two slipped by. Unlike her father, she was not interested in the details – all she wanted was revenge, or so it felt. Sitting with her own thoughts and reminiscing about her father, she became aware of the gathered council staring at her.

Breaking her daydream, she stood and called for an adjournment. They rose and bowed. Freya was the last to leave. Normally, the Queen would have called her back at this stage and they would have bitched about the advisers. However, they both felt that there had been a change in their friendship. Toying with De'sal's bracelet on her wrist, she recalled the meeting. Whenever Freya had spoken, all attention had been on her and everything had been agreeable. She had a special way with the advisers and got things done.

Remembering the frustration that her father had shown after such meetings and he was respected. A solitary tear fell. It landed on the table and soaked slowly into the bone-dry wood. A minute later there was no trace of the miniature dome of water. At the same time, the last embers of the fire gave up their light and died in the hearth.

The escape through the toilet window was a little undignified. Hal remarked on the aroma coming from the Emissary as he was balancing on his shoulders.

Letting him down, Hal took a step back for fresh air, or as fresh as he was going to get in a Weelan alley.

'I need your help, De'sal. You are well aware of the reality. You have witnessed first-hand what that bitch is capable of. Wouldn't you like to reclaim your bracelet or at least some revenge?'

'Well, indeed, but I'm done with your country's nonsense. You're power-hungry and consumed by vanity. The slightest wrong word to any of you and outcome the fangs. A Tialan sage once said that anger comes from a place of selfishness. I think that place is called Raniel.'

'Very good, but our past engagements have seen a lot of gold go Tiala's way. And I would also add that trade going south has also been of benefit to your people. If Freya is what I think she is, then Raniel will be crushed and a far darker presence will rule. Do you think whatever their plans are, they will stop at the border? No! Tiala will fall, then Senal, Rogane and I'm not even sure we are right about the part Kolgoth is playing anymore. Maybe those big bastards are being coerced into something. Who knows? But what I do know is that Freya is a threat to the Queen and to Raniel.'

Hal was very animated. De'sal could see the distress the former General was in over the current way of things.

Taking a couple of minutes to think, De'sal was reluctant to offer his services. He wanted to go home, but his ordeal over the last couple of months had put a strain on his ability to think. All he wanted was to sit in his house, beside his fire and hold his sons. Hal was correct in his assumption though: logic dictated that Tiala was only as powerful as her allies – they had no warriors or magic-users, although they were very smart and produced weapons, armour and clothing of the finest quality.

'Okay, I will help, or at least do what I can for the protection of Tiala and reunite with my family. If we get to catch that harpy, that will be a bonus.'

Hal stretched out his hand and offered it to De'sal. They shook on an oath that would see the demise of Freya. 'Thank you, friend. I will do my best to keep us alive until you see Tiala again,' Hal promised.

'You'd better, because my wife will kill you if I return with so much as a scratch.' They laughed, sharing a moment of a new friendship. 'I warn you now, sir, that I am no fighter – I am a diplomat; my words are my weapons.'

'Then how about using those words to get us a couple of horses?'

'Yes, but the only horses worth riding are in the ownership of the house guard. And if I could talk them into giving us horses, then surely, I'd be able to talk myself out of helping you.'

They crept along slim side streets, ducking behind boxes and crates, trying to stay out of sight of the very people that they were going to speak to. 'Really? This is madness. Let's just jump on a cart heading south,' De'sal suggested.

'No, my long-eared friend. We need horses. They will be quicker.'

'If we're back in jail or dead, then it won't matter.' De'sal despaired. 'Getting out of jail was an extremely positive step in my long-term goal of living. This is not!' he said brusquely.

'Shh! That's the barracks over there.' Looking between two slats in a fence, De'sal saw two guards brushing two large pure-black horses; huge muscular beasts that were clearly enjoying being groomed. The two guards were chatting idly to each other. 'Okay, here's the plan …'

A few moments later De'sal strolled up to the guards, introduced himself and started asking a few equine-related questions. 'Lovely day, gentlemen, and I must say that you are doing a wonderful job of looking after those.' He checked behind a guard and spied Hal edging closer. 'Ah, yes, stallions. Difficult to know them sometimes, wouldn't you say?'

'You're wasting our time, Tialan. Please be on your way.' The guards turned back to their grooming.

'Could I have them?' Perplexed and slightly agitated the guards' gazes at a fidgeting De'sal who was now perspiring. 'I mean, such wonderful animals and in tip-top condition ... I'd really like to have them.' As the first guard made to move towards De'sal, Hal was at the back of the second. Grabbing the unsuspecting lad by the shoulders, kicking the legs from out beneath him, Hal forced the guard onto the ground. He pinned his knee to the guard's chest and knocked the guard out with one swift but powerful punch.

At the commotion, the horses started to rear and whinny. The first guard grasped that his comrade was down, he turned on Hal, taking the couple of paces between them at a lightning speed. The guard made short work of getting his brawny hands around Hal's neck.

Where is De'sal? Thought Hal struggling for breath.

The Tialan was still cowering, waiting for the first blows of the guard to land on him. It was only now that he gathered that he was okay. Hal managed to break the choke. With roles now reversed, Hal lay into the guard with a ferocity that made De'sal uneasy. A man possessed. Blow after blow. The guard had stopped defending himself. Pulling Hal off the bloodied body, De'sal wide eyes conveyed the shock. Hal's teeth were showing and there was almost froth around his mouth, his eyes piercing and focused like a wild animal. Realising that he'd lost control, he stepped away from the guard. De'sal checked that the man was still alive.

'He'll live, but was that necessary? I think you had him with the first volley.'

Breathing loudly, his hands shaking, Hal stood, mute. Calming slightly, his reply was curt. 'He would have done the same to me. Remember, I trained most of these guys.' Brushing himself down and going through the guards' effects, he picked out a folded-up piece of paper. He opened it out.

Orders:
Divide the house guard, remain with the Queen. Freya will give the order to split before ambush. Rendezvous with my acolyte at the copse north of Enokas. Make sure the Queen survives.
Lord General

He folded the note and placed it back in the guard's pocket. He now knew that the Queen was in danger.

'De'sal, we need to hurry,' he said. 'The Queen will be kidnapped on her way west. Saddle up.'

With steely determination, the two companions raced through the streets and out into the countryside, driving the horses, staying low on their backs and encouraging them on.

The Clamour and uproar from their pursuers intensified, echoing between buildings

Chapter Twenty-Two

The clouds boiled with rage, straining to hold back the deluge within. Towering grey and black giants filled the sky, from the northern mountains to the southern plains. The wind blew fiercely in the faces of all the soldiers lined up in their ranks. The diffused light that penetrated the clouds added to the sombre mood. The soldiers faced three weeks of marching and then had to be ready for battle. Their packs were loaded with all they needed: bed roll, armour and camp gear – all had to be stowed neatly. Anything on the outside would surely be drenched in the ensuing storm.

Standing in close order on the parade ground, many concentrated on the approaching weather front. Some of the more rural conscripts called it a foul omen. An eye-blinding flash of electrical energy lit up the ground like the first daybreak. A short time later, the earth-shaking roar of thunder eclipsed any chatter within the ranks. Skittish horses pulled on their reins almost unmounting their riders. The officers did well to stay in the saddle.

Marin winced and adjusted his belt. The sword, standard Ranielian steel, hung uncomfortably down his left side. His pack was heavy and slightly unbalanced. Every soldier had the same pack, regardless of their physical size. Steeling himself, he heaved his pack and adjusted its position on his back. His spear offered him a little help with balance.

'Shit! We've not even started this march and I'm buggered.'

Mounting her charger, the captain strode up the lines of waiting soldiers, her finest regalia dull in the low light.

'I would have hoped for better weather on such a glorious day.' Speaking loudly, fighting over the wind, she addressed the battalion. 'We leave today as the last hope for Raniel. The savage beasts are making plans for the destruction of our fair land. Our task is to stop them before they cross from their guttural wastelands. Some would say *peace* and claim *warmongering*, but I would say *nay*! They killed our king and that is a true act of war. Long live the Queen!' There was a unanimous reply.

'The time for departure is on us.' The resonant echo of horns filled the air and the command reverberated through the ranks. Like a new foal starting to walk, the somewhat disjointed units fell into line behind one another. Upfront the captain settled in for the march to Weelan. The battalion was followed by a baggage train of ten or so carts filled with food and weapons. A short time later, the camp was empty. The Ranielian flag snapped in the wind, playing with each breath and gust, but no one admired its dance, bar crows and rats. Empty and still were the barracks, with no apparent thought of return. Tent flaps flailed, cold stoves their only occupants. One tent gave an account of its tenants. Carved on the large centre pole was an inscription: *Marin, heading to hell. See you soon*!

Late that night, the order to halt and make camp sounded. Collective relief swam through the ranks. Some were posted on sentry duty, others made up cook tents and officers' quarters. Everyone else put their own tents together: four people to a tent and each person carried an integral part of the shelter. Marin was first to drop his pack. He had been struggling with it for hours now. Flushed and gasping for air, he bore a crimson hue. Beads of sweat trickled down his furrowed brow, their relentless path blurring his vision and stinging now weary eyes. Every now and again a small salty droplet would make it past his unkempt beard and on to his lips. In a dishevelled mess, he dropped down and tried to catch his breath.

'C'mon, ya lazy bastard, help put the tent together so we can get a brew on. That storm has been following us, threatening to rain all day.'

The next morning after torrential rain, the ground was a quagmire of mud and stones. Anything on the ground had been soaked, boots were waterlogged, and any packs left outside were half-drowned in muddy water. Some tents had even collapsed under the weight of the deluge. That morning was a hard start. Packing everything away and trying to get the carts moving slowed the advance. They needed to be in Weelan in three days. The Queen was to lead the army west and the captain didn't want to be the one to hold up proceedings.

'What is it you have there, boy?' Master Falvor was an inquisitive soul, especially when something was happening in his library. Maleth had not moved from his spot between the bookshelves and loose scrolls strewn on the floor.

Looking rather sheepish, Maleth gave a curt reply. 'Nothing, master.'

'You are neither five years old, nor I a fool, boy! What is it that you read?' Maleth realised his error and apologised. He had been engrossed in his reading ever since gaining the ability to speed-read. He just needed to scan a page and turn it over on to the next one. He was now even fluent in languages he'd never heard of previously. And his learning of spells was just as quick: he knew the shapes and sounds instantly. Within the walls of the Citadel, a great magic spring gushed forth with unceasing vigour, allowing students to test their abilities without succumbing to weariness. Maleth slipped the book under his cloak and produced another small tome. He handed this to his mentor.

'Ah, *Krassic's Album of Gardening in the Southern Lands*. A first edition too. A pleasant read. But what of the other one?' Maleth shouldn't have been surprised at being caught. The old man seemed to see and know things.

Flushed with embarrassment, he transformed into a mere child caught red handed clutching a sweet bun. With a sheepish demeanour, he reluctantly surrendered the book he had been immersed in. Master Falvor took the black leather-bound book and placed it gently on the reading table.

'I am disappointed in your choice of literature, young Maleth. Necromantic tombs are of ill words. You wanted knowledge that would help your friends, but this, I feel, is the third such book you have taken to study. The pages within should be read in isolation. It is dangerous to have such a concise understanding of the dark arts.'

'I would not use such ways, master. And it is my understanding that their use ceased after the Great Disaster and all knowledge was lost.'

'Sadly no! These books were made as a reminder of the deviance of their followers. You will be aware of the origins of the human species and how the Great Disaster came to be.'

'I remember a little: The Brovan clerics regularly put out leaflets,' Maleth said.

Master Falvor filled in the blanks in Maleth's education. 'Over time, the fallout from the Disaster caused changes in the peoples of Kalnath. The mages from the northern tribes of Zinjal wielded too much magic and became obsessed with power. They found a way to summon demons and create monsters to terrorise the other tribes. Some, you will know, are still around today. However, very few remain.'

'I read that they also practised healing and regeneration,' Maleth said, trying to find a purpose in his actions.

'You are correct, but they also coveted eternal life, and in the grim cities of Zinjal they succeeded. One particular mage and his followers gave themselves never-ending life. For years they made artefacts of death and destruction. The Brovan Order vowed to eradicate this foul rot from the earth and, in doing so, the destruction of a necromantic artefact caused such devastation that the lands to the east were devoured into darkness. Hundreds of tribes and many thousands of animals were eradicated from the earth. After the accident, when the survivors rallied, dark mages were hunted down and killed, with no trial or second chances. Some – very few – survived, and if stories are true, the Dark Lord himself has returned. Talgameth was buried for all eternity in a tomb, so with the power of everlasting life, his return would be the thing of nightmares. Somehow, he walks again.'

'He's a myth.'

'If only that were true. The books you have read, along with your ability to recall and understand all you see, could prove useful to Talgameth. Be careful that the darkness does not take you, Maleth.'

'I don't wish to hurt anyone, Master.'

'That may not be your choice. If you feel any doubt in the light or a pull to hate your Ranielian friends, you must leave them. Having the knowledge contained within those books makes you a danger to them and all that is good in this world.'

Maleth's insides were now reeling and boiling at the thought of what he had done. He bowed his head and with heavy shoulders, and cursed the books.

'And of the Emerald Knight,' said Falvor gravely, 'I believe that it's been found. It must not reach the hands of Talgameth.'

Leaving Maleth to his thoughts, Master Falvor made to leave the library. Stopping, he turned to his apprentice. 'You are strong, gifted and pure of thought. You have the ability to fight this, if it comes. I believed in the man that alighted from the ship. And I believe in the mage that I see before me. The ship leaves in a few hours. Gain what you can in the time that remains and I will see you on the dockside.'

Master Falvor left Maleth and the library. The well-trodden wooden floor made slight groans of acceptance as he made his way along the corridor. Spitting flames on candles made his shadow dance and hop from left to right along the smooth stone walls. Arriving at a wooden door, the handle noticeably much lower than normal, he rapped a few times, stood and waited for an answer. Silent on its hinges, the door opened inward to reveal a well-kept room. A fresh airy breeze blew through from the open window at the far side. Standing at about knee height to Master Falvor was Tep. The little blue imp was sharpening a dagger, big enough for him to wield as a sword. Master Falvor strode in.

The door gently closed behind him. 'I have a task for your skills,' he said.

'Click, click ... crackle.'

'Yes, you will be getting on that boat again. Now, listen ...' Master Falvor crouched down to Tep's level. The imp still held the dagger. 'Would you mind putting that away?'

'Clack.'

'I have a concern about our new friend.'

'Click?'

'Maleth, the boy that I'm mentoring.'

'Crackle, click.'

'Yes, the person that you found on the boat. What do you mean they all look the same to you?'

'Click.'

'Good. Now, I may need you to kill him.'

'Click, click?' Master Falvor relayed his thoughts to Tep, ensuring that he understood the task and that it had to be kept a secret. The imp nodded and replied, 'Clack!'

'The boat leaves in a few hours and yes, you will need your battle armour. Remember – only if you feel it's necessary. I would quite like him to come back and finish his studies.'

The wind was up and the tops of the waves were breaking. All the new mages were on the dockside. The *Dying Siren* was unloading supplies and loading up horses and crates of bottles of all shapes, colours and sizes. Some crates were labelled 'Dangerous' and many of the sailors were not impressed by their new cargo.

Maleth and Master Falvor stood together solemnly.

'Those are fine horses, Master. What is the need to take them on board?'

'You will not find a better breed of stallion. They are powerful, fast and agile. They also have a little magic in their hooves.'

'Can they soar through the air?'

'Don't be silly! Horses can't fly.' Maleth felt a little stupid at this rebuke. 'You must take one on arriving ashore. The mages must get to the battle quickly for their task. I hope that you will return and continue studying. This war is an awful business. Here!' he said, handing Maleth a rolled-up set of robes. 'May these protect you and give you power. Where you go is weak with magic, but these should help.' They shared an embrace that was interrupted by Tep. The imp carried a large sack full of small steel armour pieces.

'Tep is going with you for protection. The imps are a special lot and he's quite handy in a fight, is old Tep.'

'Click!'

'Oh, yes,' Master Falvor handed Maleth a small green leather book, 'you may need this – *Falvor's Guide to Northern Imp Speak*.'

Chapter Twenty-Three

The Queen's steps echoed softly along the corridor, muffled by the carpet beneath her feet. Anticipation hung in the air, mingling with the distant hum that penetrated the palace. Having arrived the day prior, the first battalion made their presence known with a resounding drone. The captain of the battalion trotted along with her. He had a friendly manner about him: Very patriotic and could not contain his appreciation of meeting the Queen. For most of the day, she had met with the commanding officers one by one – a break from normal palace life. *But what was normal these days*? she wondered. She felt like a child, with everyone pandering to her. At least Lord Hal would have told her straight, if he'd felt the need.

Reflecting on her actions, the Queen felt a pang of remorse. She couldn't deny that she had been severe with him, however it was inconceivable to kill a guard without just cause. Her position demanded a measured response.

This was no time for sentimentality. It was what it was, she had to follow through with her task. However, there was anxiety where there once had been confidence. Maybe the bracelet was not helping her cause. Freya no longer made her feel better. Deep inside there was a feeling of hunger, emptiness.

Stopping at a balustrade, the captain bade his farewells. looking out onto the courtyard, she saw the bustling house staff and the royal carts and carriages. She remembered when her father had left: everyone had cheered and her father had been so proud and triumphant. He had met with the staff and soldiers of the guard. They'd loved him. All she felt was anger and resentment from them. *When had their attitude changed?* she thought.

When she was young, she'd played in these halls. The cooks and maids would drag her to her father when she'd stolen a cake or put muddy footprints on beds. Now they scurried past her and didn't look her in the eye. Freya reassured her that everything was fine and that there was still respect for her within the palace.

Backing out of a room which she had been cleaning, a maid didn't notice the Queen.

'You there!' As the words came out, she instantly thought they were intimidating. That's what the old house steward used to shout until she'd realised that it was the young princess. The old crone would then apologise and bow her head, giving her a very polite telling off. The maid was startled, eyes wide, heart thumping. There was a lot of talk downstairs about dreadful things happening to those who stepped out of line, and clear worry in her face. 'Sorry, I didn't mean to give you a fright,' said the Queen reassuringly. 'What is your name?'

Cautiously, the woman cleared her throat. 'Beth, your highness.' She gave a neat, well-drilled curtsey.

'You seem anxious, please, don't be afraid... How old are you, Beth?'

'Twenty-four in the summer, your highness.' Her heart was racing faster now, feeling that she might not make her next birthday. Confused by the questioning, she stood silent.

'What of your family? Do you have any brothers or sisters?'

'I have a brother. He went west with ...' There was a pause.

'It's okay. Please, speak freely.'

'He went west with the king. He has not returned, but my mother still sets a place for him, your highness.' The Queen could see now that she was not the only one to have suffered loss.

'Let's drop the *highness* bit for now. What of your mother? Do you have a father?'

'My father is ill. He used to work in the mines, but struggles with his breathing. My mother used to cook here in the palace, but she was asked to leave after the king ... after the king died.'

'Why was she asked to leave?'

Beth felt vulnerable. The Queen was asking personal questions and she didn't know where they might lead. 'By your order,' she whispered, her eyes fixed on the patterned carpet. 'You didn't know who to trust so most of the staff were changed out for new folk. My mother often talks about you fondly, even after–' She stopped, realising that she was letting her mouth run away from her.

'After what?' The Queen's mood was changing slightly.

'Please, your highness, I must excuse myself.'

'No, tell me what troubles you.'

Reluctantly Beth spoke again. 'There are rumours that you are in league with an evil mage. I am sorry. Please, forgive me. I'm only repeating what I have heard. Foul things haunt this palace now. I have seen nothing, but I have lost a couple of friends.' Moving to Beth's side she witnessed the girl flinch. A small tear formed in the corner of her eye.

A wave of empathy washed over the Queen, followed by the realisation that she had been looking outwardly for revenge. Hate had been driving her actions. 'It is I who should shed a tear. I have been blind to what is happening within my walls. Thank you, Beth. I can assure you that I do not practise dark arts. Those things are not real: scare stories, nothing more.' She gave the frightened Beth a smile and held her hand. 'When I return, your mother will be welcome back in the palace and I will send a healer to your home for your father.'

Beth, confused and a little relieved that the encounter was over, gave a tight smile. 'Bless you, ma'am.' She gave another curtsey before hurrying past the Queen.

Entering the main audience chamber, the Queen found the room empty apart from the four house guards on duty. Climbing the polished steps towards the throne, she called a guard.

'I want you to go to the prison and find out the condition of Lord Hal. Don't speak to anyone of this. Go!' The guard looked uneasy, then bowed his head and saluted. Backing away, he walked towards the door. 'Run!' The guard covered the rest of the distance in quick time. When the door closed behind him, the Queen settled into the throne. Enclosed within the chair she felt alone, the soft furnishings of velvet and silk not bringing any comfort.

Freya was in the courtyard looking over the provisions that were due to head west. Counting the furs used to line the royal carriage, she was interrupted by the guard.

'Mistress.'

Freya took a cautious look around. 'What is it?'

'The Queen has requested that I check on Lord Hal.' The guard stood straight, awaiting his orders.

'Ah! Return in a short while with the news that he is comfortable, fed and watered. But report that he shows no remorse for his actions and thinks that the Queen is acting like a spoilt child.' The guard gave her a distrustful look. 'I shall be there. There will be no rebuke.'

'Yes, mistress.'

The Queen's adviser gracefully glided into the audience chamber, moving silent grace. As she approached, the Queen shifted her attention towards her friend.

'I am disturbed by some of the things that have been happening lately, Freya. There are stories, rumours, and I've seen things myself which bring your loyalty to me into doubt.'

Shocked at this change in demeanour, Freya had two options: act now, or restrain the Queen. But this was not the plan and there were 12,000 soldiers camped outside the city with around 50 commanding officers within the palace itself. Her followers were outnumbered and escape would be difficult to say the least. No, what she needed to do was to play the naive girl, as that was what was expected of her.

'Your highness, please. I don't know what you're talking about. I've heard the rumours too, but they are peasant nonsense. I know not what else to say. We are good friends. I have stood by you through these difficult months. You are all I have.' Freya was crying, catching a breath in between sobs as she continued to plead her innocence. 'Please, don't cast me aside as well. I need you. You are the only friend I have.'

Softening and showing the beginnings of tears in her own eyes, the Queen took Freya's hand. 'I need you too. I need my friend: the one who doesn't skulk in corridors and speak to strange, cloaked figures; the one who is nice and pleasant to the staff; the one who makes me laugh. Freya, you have changed into someone I don't know.' She let that hang in the air.

The door opened, breaking the moment. The Queen's head snapped round. A guard ran to the foot of the throne steps. Saluting, he steadied his breath. 'Your highness, I have spoken to Lord Hal and he seems comfortable. He is well fed and watered. But ...' He trailed off.

'But what? Speak!'

'He said that you have been acting like a spoilt child and he shows no sign of remorse about what he has done.' His eyes darted towards Freya, though she offered him no comfort.

Both sadness and rage filled her heart. 'How dare he! Leave him then. I will deal with him when I get back. You are dismissed.' Bowing, the guard took up his position within the chamber.

'What am I to do, Freya? The people loved my father, showered him with respect and praise. All that's left for me is hate and fear, even though I'm trying to save the country from the Kolgothians. Maybe I should just let them take over the realm.'

'No! You cannot leave them to a fate of servitude or slaughter. They may fear you, but it is better to be feared than loved.'

'How so?' said the Queen, disapproving of Freya's statement.

'No matter what you do, not everyone will love you. But you *can* make everyone fear you. Be strong. We will finish it together, loved or not.'

Glistening in the spring sun, the gaps in the drapes shone through the window. Specks of dust reflected the light causing bursts of intensity. The Queen had been in her chamber for a few hours, sitting staring at her armour. As one sunbeam diminished, the beautifully crafted plate work lost some of its elegance. The suit hung on a manikin with an under cloth of the softest southern weave. A leather jacket and thigh protectors were laced with the thinnest and most supple leather straps. The plate itself was designed for comfort and maximum movement: thin, gold and silver-plated leaves of steel were interwoven and moved like snakeskin. A black cape was arranged over one shoulder, showing the fine trim inlaid with gold thread.

The sun had moved and a shard of brilliance now illuminated the armourer's work. She didn't want any confusion over who was leading her army. Feeling alone and scared, she needed her father, but he was gone.

The creak of the door awoke the Queen from her daydream. Freya approached. The same spears of light that had caressed the armour now fell on Freya. Her unblemished skin glowed and there was a fire in her eyes.

She sat down next to the Queen and touched her arm. This gave some comfort, but she still felt alone.

'Are you okay?' Freya's question was warm and tender with a genuine feeling of concern.

'I can't do it.'

'We are ready, and your people are relying on you to face down these beasts. But I understand your reluctance.' Freya focused on some healing magic and tried to sooth her friend's worries. 'Is that better?'

Feeling no change, 'It seems that you are losing your touch. I'm sorry, but I still feel overwhelmed by what I must do. I feel so alone.'

'Please, hear me when I say this: I am your friend and I'll be with you until the end. Even if Talgameth returns and unleashes his demons, I will be by your side.' She said this jokingly, but the Queen did not see the funny side.

'That is too close to some of the rumours to be funny. I don't have people I can trust around me anymore. What happened to Lord Hal shocked me. He was a close friend of my father's and he felt like family, even though I treated him poorly. I need to be able to trust you, Freya.'

'You can trust me. I won't leave and I'll be riding out with you. I don't know how to reassure you, but I will do whatever it takes to prove it.' She was losing the confidence of the Queen, his could be a problem for her master's plan. Anyway, it would all be over soon and this charade could come to an end.

'C'mon.' Freya urged, using both hands to lift her up. 'Let's see if it fits.' They approached the manikin together. First, the Queen donned the leather under armour, sliding her left arm through the supple sleeve. Her right arm was hindered by De'sal's bracelet on her wrist. Noticing the new piece of jewellery, Freya was intrigued. 'Oh, that's new. When did you get that?' Glancing nervously between the bracelet and Freya, the Queen had to think quickly.

'I've had this old thing for some time now. I rather like it.'

'I've never seen it before.' Freya was cautious. 'That's fine detailed work, and beautiful inlaid stones. Is it Tialan?'

'I've no idea. It belonged to my mother. I inherited a box full of jewellery from all over the realm and beyond.' She took the bracelet off long enough to get her arm through the jacket, then quickly replaced it on her wrist.

Making a mental note of the bracelet, Freya helped with the rest of her armour.

Stepping back after tying the last buckle on the chest guard, Freya admired the sight of the gold and steel plate armour radiating with the power of Raniel. Nibbling her lower lip, the Queen squirmed, 'It feels so heavy.'

'The weight of what it represents far overshadows the material it's made from. These are the lightest alloys that the smiths could forge.

The Queen took a breath, her chest heaved in the little space that was afforded in her armour.

'It is time.'

Chapter Twenty-Four

Through the verdant grasslands, the mages rode scattered in small groups. The breeze whipped at the manes of the majestic beasts brought to hasten their travels. Amidst the light-hearted banter, the stories of their rigorous and arduous training crept into their tales. Regardless of the memories the treacherous sea voyage, agreed by the mages, was the most wretched journey. Maleth trotted alongside another newly fledged wizard, their cloaks billowing.

'Not long now, Mal, eh? Just a few more days.' There was an excitement in his voice that unnerved Maleth, who was sticking fast to his stance of only using magic for healing. Any talk about killing Kolgothians didn't sit well in conversation.

'You are that eager to hurt?' Maleth asked him.

'Well, it's for the realm. We're only protecting our own people. If we kill them before they hurt us, that's all the better.'

'I've read a lot about the Kolgothians. It seems they're very spiritual beings with strong family ties and a connection to the earth and stars. Although I also read that there used to be dragons, dwarves and all manner of creatures before the Great Disaster.'

'You must have read too much and cooked your brain, locked up in the Citadel library. The rest of us were practising for the battle to come: real power that will save lives and keep Raniel free from those Kolgoth animals. Mal, we need you on the field. You have the ability to harness more power than the rest of us. Ain't sure how that came about, but glad you're on our side.' Maleth didn't say much after that. He wasn't on any side. He was a Brovan brother caught up in a neighbour's fight, all he wanted to do now was help his friends. Besides, some of his companion's kind enjoyed beating children to death for stealing. There was no high ground in this conversation, so he let it be – some fights were not worth fighting. They rode on in silence.

'Hal, I think someone's coming!' De'sal had good hearing, which came in handy now they were outlaws. There was chatter from further down the track. Hastily halting their steeds, they concealed themselves in a clearing off the road, making short time in disappearing. With plenty of lush vegetation and rocks to hide them, aware of the need to evade any form of attention from guards or anyone else tasked to look for them. De'sal's apprehension surged at every squeak and caw. Crouched low behind a thicket of brambles and long grass, the two surveyed the clearing.

'I'm stopping here. I think my companion needs a call of nature. I'll catch you up.' Pulling up on his reins near to the clearing, Maleth got out Master Falvor's book on Imp speak.

'Click!'

'Yes, *piss*. I understood that. On you go then. Mind and shake it.' He gave a chuckle, then a shiver came over him, horrified that he was thinking of an Imp's private parts, as he now had an image in his head that wouldn't go away. Maleth sat upon his horse, flicking through the translations of Impish.

'Oh, you have to sit down?'

Running behind a bush, Tep relieved himself quickly. A slow click left his mouth, clearly thankful of the stop and the cover afforded by the bush. Buttoning himself back up, Tep noticed a shiny boot just below the bough of a shrub.

'Click?' Not to anyone in particular, but he thought he'd ask the question anyway. Following his own advice, the little blue imp circled round, low and out of sight. There was no point in calling out for his big companion. He would investigate himself. Now behind the boot, he realised that there was a foot in it, which was attached to a leg ... and a Tialan.

Loud enough for the Grand Master back in the citadel to hear, the imp made his presence known. 'CLICK, CLICK CLACK!' The two watchers were caught unaware by the little figure. All they knew was that a man had stopped on the road. Startled, the two turned. Hal had already drawn his sword, ready to run someone through.

'What do you mean *two bastards*?' Confused, Maleth turned in his saddle.

Hal relaxed a little. He eyed the imp. 'Shit, I've never seen one in armour before. Hey little fella, you shouldn't creep up on folk.'

'Click, click!'

'Maybe you shouldn't be watching an imp take a piss.' Maleth had arrived to see the two facing down his pal. 'It seems we have a situation.'

Hal, calculating the odds of survival, took the decision to launch an attack at Maleth. Springing like a young buck, he barged past De'sal. Tep didn't make a move to stop him, he just looked confused and scratched his chin.

Hal was almost up to full speed, but in an instant, he found himself hanging free in the air, unable to move. A bewildered expression adorned his face as Maleth stood with an air of tranquillity, his arm outstretched gracefully. 'You attack me, but I am unarmed. What is your cause, sir?' He could see the anger and frustration on Lord Hal's face. De'sal watched, mildly entertained as he recognised the robes of the High Citadel.

'Let me out of this bond. I'm going to cut you in half. De'sal, help me!'

Folding his arms and relaxing, De'sal was glad that Hal had not killed the imp. 'Oh, I do apologise, I cannot. This is far too humorous to intervene.'

'Sir, you want me to let you go so you can cut me in half? That's not much of an incentive.' Maleth looked intently at Hal, bobbing in his force barrier. 'You look familiar.'

De'sal enlightened the mage. 'Yes, well, he would be the Former General, Lord Hal.' He was cut off quickly by Hal.

'Don't tell him anything, you pointy-eared fool.'

'Oh yes, from the cells. You came to see another poor bastard who was in with me. Why are you not heading out with the army?'

De'sal stepped in again. 'Sir, that would be a conversation best told with my friend out of his restraint.'

'Well, my lord, if you make one move on me or my companion, I will set you alight.' Dropping his hand, Maleth released the barrier, a faint opaque mist left his eyes. A little distrustful of Maleth, Hal sheathed his sword and composed himself.

'Click?' Tep sat on the ground and looked up.

'Ah, yes,' Maleth set a small fire in front of Tep. 'My friend is a bit peckish.' Picking up a stick and removing the bark, Tep held it over the flame until it charred. Then delving into his waistcoat under his chest armour, he produced a small dead rat. which he skewered to the stick and roasted slowly over the flame. De'sal and Hal looked on with mild disgust.

'His ways are a little unconventional, but you get used to them after a couple of days.'

Hal's stomach gave a jealous rumble. 'That's just making me hungry, but I am not eating rat.'

'You need not fear that, my lord. If you tried to take it off him, he would probably eat your arm.' Tep looked up from the cooking rodent and gave a hostile glower.

The same faint mist that had sheathed Maleth's eyes when he'd used the barrier now reappeared. Hal went for his sword hilt, but at the same time his hunger pangs receded and he felt full. 'A little warning, please, before you try any of that shit on me.'

'My apologies, but I have nothing else to offer you, and you did say that you were hungry.' Still cautious, Hal gave his thanks.

Sitting around the fire, with the smell of charring rat meat filling their nostrils, there was more of a relaxed atmosphere and an understanding that Maleth and Tep had not been sent to capture the two runaways.

'So, friend, what's your stake in all this? You're a magic-user who was in jail for roasting a couple of guards. You were sent to the High Citadel and now you and this little blue chap are heading north.'

'Well, it was lies about me killing innocent guards, but you have the most of it, my lord.' Maleth was cut off.

'I'm no lord now, son. But that is a story for another day. I'm just Hal and this is De'sal.'

'Well met, mage. It seems that we have all fallen foul of misunderstandings. I am an emissary from Freehold. My task was to extend trade with Raniel. However, the Queen has a vile consort with whom we have both crossed paths. This man saved my life and I owe him a debt, and to that I am tied until … well, see that morsel your friend is eating? That is what shall become of the Lady Freya, and in doing so, maybe save Raniel,' said De'sal.

'I want no part in this war, but I have friends who are fighting for their lives in a conflict they don't believe in. My name is Maleth and this fellow is Tep.'

'Clack. Click, click.' Tep was now licking the dripping skin like an ice lolly. Hal screwed up his nose in distaste.

'He says well met, and that you smell of good intestines.'

'CLICK!'

'Ah, no! You *have* good *intentions*. I'm still learning, Tep.'

'Clack.' Tep shook his head and returned to gnawing on his meal.

'Yes, that ability still works, but I'm conserving energy. The barrier took some focus.'

Hal, looked confused. 'You can understand Impish?'

'I'm learning. There are mistakes in my notes, but yes, I have the basics. I seem to have been given an extraordinary gift. While I was at the Citadel, I read some scrolls. One in particular ... well, the best way to describe it is that I absorbed the rune and now I can pretty much learn anything I read instantly.' Hal gave out a whistle of admiration.

'Handy trick in a card game.'

'Indeed. But all magic takes its toll on the user. I would probably fall asleep using it and then get robbed.'

They passed a little time with some more idle chatter while Tep finished. Licking clean the stick, the Imp gave out a burp of contentment. 'Click.'

Hal and De'sal looked at Maleth. 'Oh, he says that the rats out here are of a higher quality than the city vermin.'

The conversation turned serious. Maleth opened up. 'There are rumours that the Dark Lord, Talgameth, has risen and he descends on the world. This will be the time when Raniel and Kolgoth are at war. The lands will be easy pickings. I have also read books and parchments in the Great Library of the High Citadel that concern me. The black arts are not of this world. Talgameth has kept his presence hidden. Raniel's feud with Kolgoth seems petty if the dark one makes his move.'

Nodding in agreement, De'sal spoke first. 'We may have come to the same conclusion. It seems that the royal household may have been manipulated to advance Talgameth's plans. There is the possibility that–' Interjecting in a rage, Hal let fly his anger. 'As I was saying, there is a possibility that the Queen has been driven to war with Kolgoth. We are in possession of information that she will be kidnapped and our plan now is to stop this and save her.'

'I would help, but I must protect my friends,' Maleth said. 'There is also the worrisome fact that the Emerald Knight could still be found. It is not a secret that the followers of Talgameth have been digging in the old cities of Zinjal. Why would he make his move now? Unless it's been found.

'If there is the possibility that Talgameth has the knight, then they will need all the help they can get.'

'Maleth. We believe that Kolgoth has also been manipulated to go to war. If his enemies fight each other, he will be victorious. He means to wait until the battle is almost over and the blood of the people nearly spent, then unleash his host upon the weary.'

'Then we must warn the general. Our orders are to meet with him before the battle to get our deployment.'

'Reval is an idiot. Freya put him in charge because her magic works best on weak, wanton men. He only listens to himself and would counter any idea because it's not his own. He will drive the army over a cliff and drink wine while he does it.'

'Then what do you suggest?' Maleth asked.

Hal shrugged his shoulders. 'I have no idea. All I want to do is protect the Queen. I suppose we must trust in the common soldier to stay alive long enough to fight whatever Talgameth puts on the field.'

'It seems then that we are lost against such a tide,' De'sal added.

'Click. Click!'

'What's he saying?' Hal asked.

Laughing, Maleth caught his breath and translated: 'Looks like we are going to Weelan first, Tep here's going to ask for help from his kin.'

'Clack, crackle?'

'Seriously? You're less than two feet tall. Yes, you have a mean bite, but c'mon.'

'Click!'

'And you have as much to lose as any other being walking the earth. I know. Fine.'

'Click.'

De'sal gave Maleth an inquisitive look. 'He has a point – every blade and claw will come in handy. And he said that he would eat me and go anyway.'

'All that from a little scratchy noise?'

'It's a complex language, quite difficult to get your head round,' Maleth said.

Hal stood. 'We must get going, De'sal, if we are to make the ambush point.'

Maleth put out his hand and shook De'sal's, then Hal's. 'Well met, indeed. If only these were better times. May the gods protect you.'

Turning to Tep, Maleth smiled and was met with a snarl – Tep's attempt at a grin. All it showed was a few rows of sharp pointy teeth. 'I'll take you to Weelan then I'll head west.'

'Click.'

Waving them off, Maleth hopped on his horse. His thoughts turned to the torment that lay ahead.

Chapter Twenty-Five

Striding past the imposing bulwark, Guldr's mind fixated in a thought that lingered, refusing to dissipate: Helda. The memory of their walk on the night plain had rekindled the connection between them. This had made Guldr's departure more arduous. With a heavy sigh he pressed on, his heart burdened with longing. Helda's gentle face and wide smile filled his thoughts, as well as her long flowing curls, herb twigs and all. His mind filled with the scents of lavender, jasmine and rose. 'Tears will soon dry,' he'd told her. Thumbing a pendant that hung around his neck, unconsciously. Inscribed upon it was a rune to protect the wearer from evil thoughts. He wore it now to remind himself to live through the battles to come, so he could see her again.

'Uncle, how big is this place?' Sokal had never left Fethal before apart from tending the cattle in the lower fields. This was a journey of enlightenment and excitement for him. The young Kol had been taken aback to find out that he was the nephew of the Guardian and was fit to explode when asked to accompany Guldr back to Droth'Ka. The air was heavy and still, a big change from being out on the grasslands and camping under trees. It was afternoon and the sun was at its highest, the unfiltered spring sun gently warming the dusty track they were following.

Both Guldr and Sokal were wearing leather and cotton leggings with heavy woollen jackets. They were also wrapped in dust-covered cloaks, to keep the sun off their pallid skin and hide their identity. Guldr was interested in how the city had faired while he was gone.

'Shh, boy. Do not use that term here. Some may harm you, to incite me to a challenge. That time is not now. So, keep quiet.' They walked steadily through the street, not giving much attention to the surrounding city folk. There were cries of meat and vegetable vendors and the clash of hammer on anvil. Guldr disliked the noise, smells and the claustrophobic nature of so many huts and people crammed into a relatively small space. Fights were frequent, brought on more often than not by cheap ale. Boredom was also a factor: young males trying to find a purpose in life. Merchants brought back stories from the eastern borders of murders and cattle-reiving; the blame put solely at the feet of the Ranielians.

The two continued their journey through the tight streets, where mud- and-wood-built homes gave way to more sturdy dwellings of stone; large, round, solid buildings with heavy thatched roofs. A crowd had gathered at the junction of two streets, where two males were knocking lumps out of each other. The massed spectators were egging on their prospective champion. Both were bloodied and weary. Given the audience, they had probably been at it for some time.

Sokal took an interest in the boys, watching the moves and finding that he was captivated, he was drawn into the crowd. A lust for the fight was growing in him. 'Do not get involved. We have other business,' Guldr quickly pulled his cowl up and dipped his head, before he dragged Sokal away from the entertainment.

Only a short distance now and they would be at the central round – an immense stone circle containing a fire pit. The fires were constantly lit and tended, and the space was said to be the soul of every city, town and village in Kolgoth; the meeting place for elders and townsfolk alike; and a place to challenge and question their leaders. It was quiet today. Only a handful of young folk and some of the older population were sitting in the shade smoking a local herb. The Great Chief's lodgings were next to the central round, where tribal chiefs would meet and feast. Arriving cautiously, they entered the round and sat on a carved wooden bench.

'What are we doing, Guardian?' Sokal was aware that he had to speak in hushed tones to avoid being noticed, but could not contain his curious mind.

'We are watching who is speaking and who is listening. We must also be cautious of others who are looking.' They didn't have to wait long before an argument erupted between two farmers – nothing to do with land or livestock, but more to do with a family feud. There was no referee: all things in Kolgothian culture were settled with a display of aggressive behaviour. Again, a crowd began to form. Even though the pair exchanged heated words, there was still respect – there were rules and all accepted the outcome.

There was a tap on Guldr's shoulder. 'Stranger, I noticed you at the street fight. You look familiar.' A little annoyed that his plan had been ruined, Guldr stood and removed his cowl.

'You should.'

'Guardian, my apologies.' The thin-framed Kol took a step back and bowed his head. He was a regular at the centre round, or gossiping on street corners.

'I wanted to hear for myself what had been transpiring while I was away. I guess hearing it from you is just as good, if not better.'

'My honour, Guardian.' He relayed the most mundane of goings-on, from stallholders dropping food to the saltiness of the water in the wells, only stopping for breath when dramatic effect would allow. His ramblings went on. 'And then Chief Golth sat in the Guardian's chair, proclaiming to challenge him on his return.' He stopped in a panic, aware that he had said too much. He dropped to his knees with outstretched hands. 'I beg forgiveness for my disrespect. I forgot to whom I was speaking.'

'Calm yourself. It was not you who made the false challenge.' His head lowered the gossip kept his position. 'Get up. There's no need to be down there.' Still, he did not rise. The gossip-monger had noticed Golth within the centre round.

'Guldr!' Sokal edged away from his uncle when the challenger called his name. He saw Guldr's knuckles whiten and his chest heave. As he watched, the Guardian stretched and flexed his hands. It was evident that his uncle was an extremely powerful warrior.

'Do not disrespect me, Chief Golth. I am still Guardian.' Guldr was making every effort to contain his anger.

'There is the smell of war in the air,' Golth declared. 'I wanted to see what you human-lovers are doing. I hear of friendships with those weak bastards. Surely the great Guardian has not succumbed to such depravity,' said Golth, taunting.

'Be careful where your tongue leads you, Golth. Guldr noticed that a crowd had gathered.

'Guardian or not, I will tear the flesh from your back, you are nothing but a Minal tribe runt,' Golth spat. Some other Kolgothian chiefs from the north were doing their best to hold the challenger back. They knew this was not the way – it would be sorted at the council meet.

No more words were exchanged and the gathering dispersed, leaving Guldr and Sokal. 'Uncle, what would you have done if he had managed to hit you?'

'Have faith, it was not going to get that far. Know your enemy: learn, watch and respect them.'

The invited tribal chiefs were sitting round the central fire. Even some that weren't particularly welcome shared the heat. Thick smoke was building around the wooden rafters, enveloping the ancient timbers with a herb-and-spice-filled blanket. The incense was to calm the gathered chiefs so that tempers were dulled and conversation kept amicable.

The low hubbub of conversation stopped as Guldr entered the low-ceilinged building. He took his seat and gave respectful nods to all present. Some tribal chiefs from all across Kolgoth had travelled for weeks to be at this particular meet. Chief Golth sat smugly, eyeing the Guardian. Guldr had asked Sokal to join the meet and sit close to Golth. Should he make a move to attack, at least he would get some warning. This act would be highly disrespectful, but Guldr didn't think that would worry the young warrior much. A hush settles on the gathered chiefs.

'Great tribes of Kolgoth, thank you for bringing your counsel. We face an enemy who is under the control of the Dark Lord Talgameth.' There were mutterings and shaking of heads from those gathered. 'I have travelled to the night plains and spoken with the ancestors. Our threat is not from Raniel.' Guldr was drowned out by shouts of angry protest. Guldr knew this would be difficult, but he had to trust in the elders. 'Let me finish! The Great Father told of a darkness from the north. Talgameth has risen and corruption has spread throughout Kalnath. Raniel is weak and easily manipulated: they covet power and wealth. Dark mages have the ear of the rulers and the common folk have been subjected to lies and deceit.' There were more grumblings. The incense did not seem to be having the effect it should. A few older southern tribal leaders listened intently, some stroking old scars, others turning braid rings between their thumbs and fingers.

In a booming voice that made all conversation cease, an old chief called for calm. 'It is not by chance that you are Guardian, Chief Guldr. You have scars, both bodily and etched on your soul. If you have spoken to the Great Father and taken your journey on the night plains, I wish to hear what you have to say. Let the Guardian speak. We shall all have our say at this meet.'

Giving the old chief a respectful bow, Guldr cleared his throat. 'If we do not meet the challenge from the north, it will be the end of Kolgoth. Talgameth means to enslave all living beings that walk the earth, from the grasslands to the east, the high mountains of the spine of the world across Rogane, and even deep into the lands of the Great Disaster. He has awoken! He may have found the Emerald Knight,' many knew the stories and shook their heads in doubt, 'which he intends to use to unleash demons upon these lands. Raniel moves to war on false pretences.' Guldr paused, trying to summon the courage to ask these war-hungry tribal chiefs not to fight.

'Continue, Guardian,' the old chief said.

Sokal was aware that they sat on a precipice. This could mean the end of Guldr's rule and, if it was to believed, the end of Kolgoth.

Steeling himself, Guldr continued. 'I ask that we request aid from Raniel and do not meet them on the battlefield.' There was uproar. Most were on their feet, lambasting his foolishness. Chief Golth stood, pointing and shouting, calling for Guldr to be stripped of the guardianship. Only the old chief sat contently, staring at Guldr. There was a familiarity to his features. He gave a thin smile and a shallow nod.

Then, loud enough to be heard over the din of anger and calls for a challenge, the old chief spoke to Guldr. 'Well done, Guldr. Remember, we are always with you.' More tribal chiefs stood to be heard, walking between Guldr and the old chief and obscuring his view. Moments later there was no sign of the old Kol'. There was, however, the rage and anger of all the tribes manifest in the face of Golth, his eyes blood-filled and wide, set on Guldr.

'I challenge you! You are unfit to meet the needs of our great race.' Golth threw down his overcoat and stood for a second, his muscles tensed. He leapt for Guldr. Still lost in his vision of the Great Father, Guldr was caught unawares, still sitting when Golth landed hard on him. In a splintering of wood, the chair gave way and both Kolgothians landed on the compacted hard earth of the tribal meeting hut. Other chiefs were knocked out of the way.

His senses dulled by the calming vapour emanating from the brazier, Sokal was stunned by the events taking place. He made to intervene, but felt dizzy. His hands moved slowly before him and a light hum registered in his ear. Seeing his uncle pinned to the floor energised him to fight the dullness. Gradually his hearing and vision became sharper. The roars and shouts were now almost ear-splitting. Swimming through the gathered ranks was difficult. A rough looking brute held Sokal. A small blade appeared at his side.

'I do not know who you are, boy, but you chose an ill friend. Make another move and I'll gut you like a war boar.'

Blow after blow landed about Guldr's head with the ferocity of a possessed animal. Barely able to defend himself, his brain clouding over, Guldr slowed his breathing. His adversary was straddling him and throwing meaty fists of rage in an effort to not only subdue, but kill Guldr. Other tribal chiefs called for a halt. To their astonishment, Guldr replied with an order to let the battle play out.

His face bloodied and the taste of iron on his tongue, he felt a change in Golth's weight. Able now to swing his hips out to one side, he grabbed an arm and pulled in close. With unnatural speed for a body of his bulk, Guldr pushed his hips up and sent Golth slamming into the ground. With a look of disbelief on his face, the attacker was pinned. Guldr could scarcely see, so he was acting on feel alone. Still holding his arm, the strain on Golth's shoulder could be seen in the firelight, his muscles stretched to bursting point. Letting out a cry as he tried to release himself from Guldr's arm hold. Then it came: a pop and a crack. Golth's scream was blood-chilling. Those who witnessed the fight would recall the sound of a wet branch being split in two.

Knowing that he had just broken Golth's arm, Guldr released his hold and drove the heel of his foot into his opponent's gut, cracking a few ribs and adding to the agony. Rolling and getting up on all fours, blood poured from Guldr's mouth and an open wound below his left eye. Pushing away any help to get up. Guldr rose slowly to his full height. Knowing that tradition would see him kill the challenger.

'I accept your challenge.' He paused to spit out some of the blood accumulating in his mouth. 'You have shown this council much disrespect. You dishonour your tribe and your father's name. In times past, your life would end here. It is not an idle comment when I say that there is a far greater threat to our world. We will need every warrior to face what is to come.' He looked around the room. There was silence apart from the crackling of the fire and groans from Golth. Some of those present bowed their heads and stared at the floor, not wanting to make eye contact with anyone – especially those who had hedged their bets on the would-be successor.

'I name you *Berserker*, like those in ages past. You will be needed to face this darkness. Your fate shall not be determined today.' Golth eyed Guldr. He had been bested and had expected death. He said nothing but closed his eyes and tried to manage the pain without sounding like a crying child.

Turning back to the council, Guldr made a plea. 'Is there any who would challenge?' In the stillness, no one made to move or utter any word for fear of Guldr's wrath. 'No? Then know this: we are heading for war, but we will *not* engage with the Ranielians. We must look to the north. Prepare your tribes and speak with the spirit ancestors.' The mood around the fire was subdued. Not fighting in a battle was a challenge for any Kolgothian faced with a foe.

Guldr's gaze swept the surroundings in search of Sokal and among the chieftains he spotted his form hunched over. With an urgency he cleaved his way through the crowd. Guldr's attention was drawn down to the trembling hands of Sokal, a crimson stain seeping through fingers and shirt. Guldr's hand lay gently but firm on Sokal's shoulder, a comforting touch with an unspoken understanding. Looking around at the gathered chiefs they too now understood that darkness had reached the heart of Kolgoth.

Chapter Twenty-Six

The cold spring morning caused the dew to lie still, even on the Ranielian troops' armour. A damp chill penetrated leather and cloth to sap any heat out of the body. The whole army was lined up in marching order. Horses snickered and pawed at the hard-packed, stony ground. The odd shake of their heads broke the natural sound of the morning with a tinkle of bridle against thin plate armour.

The troops were getting restless, there was a rising sound of steel plates scraping together. Soldiers shifted in their ranks, trying to alleviate the discomfort from the packs and weapons they carried.

The general stood on a parapet of the city wall, the weak low sun endeavouring to glint off his well-polished armour – a set that had not seen action. Indeed, he himself was not a military man, but had been thrown into the role owing to his own ability to follow orders. He revelled in the role though; he didn't need to earn respect anymore; he felt that it was owed. Whether lacking confidence in his abilities or genuine nervousness at addressing such a gathered crowd, his was a poor attempt at a speech.

'We are on the cusp of battle and are ... fighting for the very land that you have toiled over. Many of you will not return, but that's perfectly fine. Those that do will receive a hero's welcome.' The rows of soldiers were losing interest, unable to focus on the speech's content. After a temporary pause, he began again. 'The battlefield is where respect is earned and honour given to the valiant! The Queen orders you to fight and take courage in the fact that we will be there with you.'

Ending his speech, he held out his hands as if to embrace every single one of the lined-up troops. He may also have been waiting for applause, but none came.

Walking back down to meet the Queen and the rest of the royal entourage, the General felt quite content with himself.

The ruler of Raniel sat upon her horse, resplendent in her fine crafted armour. 'How went your speech, General?'

Stopping and taking a bow. Reval replied. 'Very well, your highness. I got the feeling that I really inspired the troops to follow you with a little more vigour. And I must say that they look strong and ready.'

The Queen looked at him uncertainly. She felt he had just made a fool of himself. Oblivious to this, he continued. 'May I also say that you are looking radiant, your highness.' He waited for a response of congratulations or at least a smile. None came and the awkward moment played out until Freya interrupted as she passed between them on her own horse.

'Enough, you fool! Get on your horse.'

'Yes, my lady.' Reval mounted and fell into line behind the Queen and Freya, who was also wearing fine detailed armour, albeit with black shoulder plates and chest guard. Moving closer to the Queen, Freya placed a hand on her forearm. 'Are you okay?'

'I take our people into the west, to a battle I know not if we can win. Reval put more doubt in my mind.'

'You know him to be an idiot. Trust in the other officers. Trust in the soldiers themselves. They all fight for you and this cause. It is their land that they protect. They do not want to see these beasts farm their soil and fish their rivers, while they are enslaved to work for them. And that is if they survive the raiding parties.' Freya gave a smile. 'It will be over soon and Raniel can look forward to a peaceful rule without the threat from Kolgoth.'

'Yes, you're right. I must see this through.' Steeling herself, the Queen took a deep breath of chilly spring morning air and nodded to the guards on the gate. A horn sounded. With a slide of a heavy oak beam, the brace was released and the huge wood and steel gate opened with a moan – a last lament from the city to which many would not return.

Other horns now blew. Way off in the distance the forlorn tones could be heard carried on the breeze. The shouting of officers and the clinking of steel on steel was loud enough to shake the birds from their roosts and cause deer to run and flee. The Queen and her retinue passed through the gate and joined the head of the army. The gathered officers saluted sharply.

Turning to face the path, Freya gave a quick look around. The plan was in place and nothing could stop it now. She had done all that had been asked of. Those loyal to her were within the Queen's guard and her advisers were either fools or in the employment of the Dark Lord. Any seeking to oppose her had been dealt with: she gave a contemptible snort at the thought of Lord Hal and that creepy Tialan emissary starving and rotting in the palace jail. She was ready and her master would surely reward her.

Pausing once more, the Queen collected her thoughts, trying to block out the din and commotion of such an amassed amount of people. This war was to avenge her father's death. She had felt no empathy for the people until recently. Now she thought about all the families that would lose fathers and mothers, sisters, brothers, cousins, and the like. She could not turn around and head back to the comfort of her brushed-cotton bed linen, warm baths and freshly prepared food, leaving her army to meet the foe in a distant field. *No!* she thought. *I must be strong. These are my people and I am my father's daughter.*

At a nudge from her heels into its flanks, her charger walked on slowly and smoothly. One by one, like a spring being pulled, her retinue followed. Freya gave a smile and a contented sigh. Almost all of Weelan had emptied. There was no one left to wave them off, no crying, no flowers thrown onto the road in front of them, no music or fanfare, only the thump of boots on the packed ground.

The march would be long and hard and they would need their strength to fight at the end.

A fierce wind blew through the empty street. A lone figure wrapped up against the elements side-stepped a puddle. They arrived at a building on the corner of Hill Grove and the main thoroughfare that headed down to the merchants' quarter. A sign swung violently on a rusty chain: Croft's Alehouse. On reaching the door, the figure turned the latch and the door burst inward. The wind howled through the bar, causing the window drapes to come alive and dance on their rails. Paper and bowls were blown onto the floor and one unfortunate customer had the froth removed from the top of his mug.

'Shut that door if it's still on its hinges!' Croft shouted from across the bar.

'Sorry, Crofty. It's blowing a gale out there. Is your fire on?'

'Aye, come in, Elora.' She managed to shut the door, but it was clearly an effort. Hanging up her coat on the rack by the door, she noticed that it was quite empty. Squeezing down next to a couple of men at a low table in one booth, she smiled to the group.

'Malcolm.' She nodded to the other gentleman at the table. 'Terbut. Nice to see you back on your feet again after the accident.'

'It wasn't an accident, Elora, and you know it. Those scum bastards that are running the Watch did me over because I wouldn't pay up.'

'Keep your voices down.' Croft came over to the table with some stew. 'Especially you, Terbut. You don't know who's listening.' He gave a sly look around. His bar was empty except for a few folk next to the fire.

'Aye, well, you all know what's happening. And we do nothing about it,' said Terbut.

'Look, yes, thirty years ago when we all served, you know I'd have been the first to start a fight.' There were confirming nods from around the table at Croft's declaration.

'Even when the place was empty, old boy.' Malcolm's manner hadn't changed much over the years. When he was in his twenties, he'd sounded like an old man. Now he was an old man he'd kind of grown into himself.

Croft sat down and they huddled in a little closer, either for warmth or, as would normally be the case, to put the world to rights, but not wanting the world to know about it. 'My boy is gone: four months with not even a note. You remember, we wrote home at least every week.'

'Can your Jack write?' Said Elora.

'Well, no, but he'd have a damn good try at drawing a picture. My point is that nobody knows what's going on.'

Malcolm sat quietly, looking into his bowl of stew and using the spoon as sort of a paddle, moving the contents about. 'What's in the stew?' They looked round at him with puzzled expressions. They knew better than to ask. It might ruin your appetite.

Croft was straight on the defensive. 'What do you mean, what's in the stew? It's meat.'

'What kind of meat?

'It's the chopped-up bits of the last guy that asked is what's in the stew!' Malcolm looked him in the eye and without asking another question, he made Croft buckle and give in.

'Okay! It's white meat from Foth Lane.' Again, Malcolm didn't move a muscle. The other two turned slowly to face Croft. 'It's cat, alright!' With a unanimous vote of disgust, they all pushed their bowls into the middle of the table. 'What do you expect? All the proper meat has gone to the army and any decent cuts go to the palace for that daft bint to scoff. Her dogs are better fed than us down here. And anyway, I thought you liked a bit of pussy.' Malcolm shook his head and took a gulp of ale and try to get rid of the taste. Which, incidentally, had been quite alright prior to him asking for the recipe. He looked at the ale mug and then back at Croft.

'Now that's enough. That's proper ale that.'

They sat and chatted a while longer. However, their conversation got a little darker as the evening wore on.

'I'm telling you, she's mad. Did you see her eyes at her father's funeral? Honestly, she's not right.' Elora was a bit of a gossip, but she said things as she saw them. 'And as for shacking up with her maid! May the gods protect us.'

'I think the gods have more to worry about that whether that girl likes meat or veg.'

'I'm not talking about what she likes to eat, Terbut.' The confused men looked at each other and wondered if they'd heard that right.

'I heard that Kolgoth was going to invade and that some of the border towns have been sacked already. The guy I get flour from said that he spoke to a farmhand, who'd run away from Enokas. That's only a month's ride from here,' Croft said.

'I think not.' It was Terbut's turn to put in some wisdom. 'Why would Kolgoth invade? A thousand years have passed, so why now? What would make them break an age-old pact? They base their political system on besting the tribal chief, not on gaining land and riches. I spent many a year studying Kolgoth culture and they're fascinating. Still wouldn't trust them though.' He thought for a little longer while the others mumbled into their mugs.

Elora was about to say something, but Terbut interjected. 'The current climate is agreeable. No drought or plague has befallen our neighbours. No impact from the skies or godly intervention has laid waste to their lands. I can only think that they've been provoked.' There was a silence around the table and Croft looked slowly over his shoulder to check if they had company close by.

'Look, you senile old fool, you can't be going around saying shit like that. They will hang us. They do that for fun these days, so imagine what they would do for treason?' He shook his head and pulled in close. 'I've heard stories.'

'And made a few up,' said Elora.

'I've heard that evil times are upon us. The dark arts are being used again. Some say Talgameth is reborn.'

'Bullshit! That's kids' stories. Aye, there's magic around, but nothing like back in the days of the Great Disaster.'

'I'm telling you what I heard, and I believe it. Did you see the Queen's adviser?'

'Aye, she was a looker, eh?' said Malcolm.

'Well apparently she set a man to tears at court.'

'I'd probably start crying too if she spoke to me. At my age I'm pretty much useless for anything she might want.' He gave a cheeky smile and raised his eyebrows. Elora sat oblivious to the reference.

Croft had a stern look about him. 'The man apparently stood in her way and she used some sort of magic. He's gone completely white now and at the time, folk say he was crying and bleeding out of his eyes. He also pissed himself and screamed like nothing anyone had heard before. She then walked calmly by while he sobbed on the floor.'

The three other members around the table thought about this and recalled other stories about strange goings-on in the city. 'Do you think then that the Queen is a dark-magic user? Terbut was again a little too loud, and the others hushed him rather quickly this time.

'Maybe they all are. All her advisers have been changed out and posted to far-off places.'

'We're in the shit then!'

'Why has she sent the army away, eh? All the good men and women of the city have been called to fight. Those left protecting the city are nothing more than thugs and thieves. There is no one to stop the evil from getting into the city. Yeah, we're in the shit and all that is left is old farts like us thinking we have it all figured out. If the Dark Lord does come back at least we can say smugly that we knew this would happen.'

A muffled cough came from behind the group, causing them to startle. Given their advanced age, with fragile hearts and bladders, moments like these were unwelcome.

'I'm looking for the proprietor.' As one they pointed at Croft, who was trying to register how the stranger had got in without him noticing.

'How did you get in without opening the door?' The rest of Croft's friends, given the nature of the conversation that night, were wary and a little spooked at the stranger's arrival. Malcolm unconsciously picked up his spoon.

'Are you Mr Croft?' The tall stranger's fine complexion shone with every flicker of the firelight. He wore a well-groomed robe with a leather belt on which hung a scabbard. To Croft's relief his sword was still in it. He had piercing red eyes, which gave him a sinister look and were fixed on Croft. Malcolm rose.

'No need to get up, sir! I shall sit, and given your uneasiness, age and general appearance, I believe I have the right place.'

'Alright, shitbag! Have you come to kill us for getting a bit lippy about the Queen? What do you expect when the taxes go up, there's no food and scumbags like you are roughing up the old and frail? If I were ten years younger, you wouldn't have even been able to sit down.' Terbut was sitting closest to the door. He had one leg in the walkway outside the booth. 'If my Jack was here, he'd pull your arms off with just a look from me.' With this last tirade in full swing, Terbut made a run for it. The stranger didn't move, but watched him head for the door with surprising speed for a gentleman of his years. The others in the group watched him go too.

Elora was the first to break the silence. 'The bastard ran out on us!'

Softening slightly, seeing as the stranger hadn't attempted to stop Terbut, Croft cleared his throat. 'Okay, sweetheart. I'm Croft. What do you want?'

'May I ask that your friend put down his weapon?' Malcolm still had his spoon gripped tightly in front of him. As everyone stared at him, he placed it gently back on the table. 'My name is Maleth. I'm a member of the Brovan Order from the northern Senalian city of Shoul. I apologise if I gave you cause for concern. And if I were here to kill you, I would not waste my time engaging in conversation. Will the other member of your party be alright? He left in rather a hurry.'

'Aye, he just forgot that he had to be somewhere else and didn't want to be late. So, Maleth, why would a fine gentleman like yourself come all the way from Senal to find me?'

'Oh, my reasons for travel were not to find you, Mr Croft. No. I am heading west to join the army, and my friends. On that note, a good friend requested that if I were ever in Weelan I should track down a Mr Croft who owns Croft's Alehouse and say, *hello*.'

'Well, maybe you should have started with *hello* rather than creeping us out. Poor Elora there is a nervous wreck.'

'No, I'm fine thanks, Croft,' she said, dismissing her old friend's concern.

'Who's your friend then?' Croft was at a loss.

'Jack.'

'My boy? Replied Croft with a quivering lip. 'How is he? where is he?'

'He was fine the last time I saw him. We were at the training camps together. I was sent to the High Citadel as a magic user.' At this, the group recoiled. 'It's a long story but I'm heading west, my intention is to keep them safe.'

'Bless you lad. There didn't happen to be an unsightly little runt with him? Said Croft quizzically.

'Ahh, that would be Marin.'

'Be sure and keep him safe too, he owes me money. Maleth you can have a bed here for as long as you like. Just don't kill anyone in your room.' He tried a slight smile to lighten the mood.

'I thank you for your hospitality, but I will not be staying long. I have a little friend in town doing some errands and I must be ahead of the army before they deploy.'

'Oh, how so?'

'My order has been tasked for the last thousand years with protecting these lands from the perils of dark magic. At a time before the Great Disaster, many artefacts were infused with powers that were deemed too powerful to be given to any man or beast. An age of looting and adventuring by every race imaginable has seen these artefacts scattered across the six territories of Kalnath. Before I left, word had reached the High Citadel of a relic of such power that it could doom all that walk the earth. I was asked to ensure that it did not fall into the wrong hands.'

'Talgameth?'

'Yes.' For the first time in the night, they were silent.

'Would you like something to eat?' Croft said finally. Elora looked at Maleth and shook her head, hoping that Croft would not see.

'No, Mr Croft, thank you. I'm fine.'

'Okay, lad. And just call me Croft.'

Chapter Twenty-Seven

The weary company gathered for their evening meal, a water gruel of porridge and dried fruit. Clad in their tattered armour, the soldiers sought solace in the meagre warmth of the cook pots, the feeble flames flickering against the chill night. Long days marching had taken a toll on morale. The fireplace, once been a place to catch up at the end of the day, now it was quiet. The soldiers deep in their own thoughts trying to will the aches and pains away from their feet and legs.

Darkness had fallen and the small glow from the fire lit their faces and played with the shadows – the real ones. Some of the soldiers told stories of seeing places where the shadows were not quite right.

Marin dropped his spoon into the small wooden bowl he used for his meals. He gave a sigh, intending to break the silence and start a conversation. Continuing with their meals the rest paid him no attention. In a day or so they would be on the field, lined up and waiting for a Kolgothian charge. The general's motivational speeches had done nothing to inspire any of them. If anything, they made him look more foolish every time he took a notion to impart his knowledge. Marin's thoughts turned to deserting. In a company of 12,000 depressed, tired and hungry Ranielians, no one would see him leave or even know he was missing.

His struggle was, however, letting down his friends: he needed to protect them; stand beside them with his shield; and pick them up if they fell over. If he left, he'd be a coward. *Would it matter?* he wondered. *We will all probably be dead in the first charge with only the Highborn to pick through the spoils of war and proclaim victory. The mud will take the rest of us.*

Turning his bowl thoughtfully in his hands and watching the less than appetising liquid wash over chunks of oats and dates, he mulled over the reason for him ending up in this spot. He hadn't signed up for it, so why stay? *In the end all we are is what's in our heads and if someone has an issue that's their problem*, he decided. He steeled himself, certain of his next move. A burly girl with swept back, jet-black hair tapped Marin on the leg. Looking up Marin saw a small thin smile. She nodded and handed him a piece of sweet bread.

'Everyone's thinking the same thing,' she said knowingly.

'I wasn't ...' There was a brief pause as he thought of his next words. 'Thanks,' he said.

She went back to playing with her own food. The heat and the taste had left a while ago, but food rations were getting low and it wouldn't be smart to waste it, regardless of how it tasted. A distinct rattling of armour made huddling group look up. The sergeant was on his rounds checking in. They shuffled up instinctively to make space for their new guest.

'Thanks, but I'm here for guard duty. Marin, you're up. You're on west detail. Get some food in you. Be there in twenty or you'll be digging the shitters again.'

'Yes, sir!'

'Carry on.' The sergeant stalked off into the gloom. Marin took his last few mouthfuls and stood up. As he went to turn, he was stopped by the same girl.

'Don't do anything stupid, Marin. We'll need every shield and spear, and that includes yours.' Without responding, Marin left the fire, and as he did, the void he'd left was swallowed up by the others, as if he'd never been there.

A short time later, Marin arrived at the crudely erected guard post made up of hastily cut trees driven into an embankment which stretched all around the camp. A torch flickered and silhouetted the Sargant on the makeshift wall.

'Sir, I'm here for detail.'

'Ah, Marin. I'm in need of a little humour.' The rest of the troop is in poor spirits. It's obvious why, but we've got to get on with it, eh?'

'Yes, sir. I'm not much company these days though. I feel as rough as a troll's toenail.'

'There you go! Even that nonsense will lift the spirit.' The Sargent smiled and turned to look out into the surrounding fields. 'Any news or gossip?'

'None, sir.'

'Let's drop the *sir* until someone else comes. The old ranking doesn't sit well with me; probably why I didn't join the army in the first place,' said the guard

'What did you do back in Weelan?' Marin asked curiously.

'I'm not from Weelan, I'm from a small village to the west, called Jamesford. I was a thatcher, with a wife, two girls and a pony called Sprite. I was doing okay until all this bollocks. I thought the best thing to do was shut myself off and let the world happen. Then the guards came knocking and a few of us were taken to the training camps. What about you? You seem like the military type.'

'Nah, I didn't amount to anything. Didn't see what I had. Kept drinking to forget, then forgetting to stop.' They both gave a short laugh, then Marin continued. 'I had finally decided to sort myself out, get stuck into my chores on the farm and repay the Simpsons for all that they had done for me. I went to apologise to some friends about the way I had behaved, then the guards entered the bar.'

'Aye, life's a bitch,' The guard replied.

'Yup, then she starts a war,' Marin added. This again lightened the mood slightly. Marin had a knack for adding the odd witty comment, which unintentionally made people laugh and forget the situation, if only for a moment.

A few hours passed and the night was going well, with both of them reliving stories and talking about what they would do if they survived.

Marin went out on his sentry rounds. All the while the conflict within him was raging. He could leave now ... make a run for it. His chances were running out. *Survival*, he thought.

The girl's voice from the fire came into his head, followed by the thought of his sentry companion getting a beating for him running away. He couldn't leave; his fate was decided – stand with the rest and fall with his friends. At that moment of realisation and change of heart, a noise pricked his attention. Horses and men talking. Unsure as to who they were, he crept softly, thinking to himself that they may be guards, and if he were found, they would hang him for desertion, even though he'd made his mind up to return. He'd been away for a while now.

Snooping closer, he noticed that they were men, dressed strangely in oversized clothing. The horses were odd-looking too and covered in some sort of pelt.

'Mount up and remember no talking.' Marin assuming the leader of the group.

'Set fire to a few tents and harry the soldiers. Most of them will be in the tents playing with their dicks.'

'What of the guards?' One of the other riders spoke in a Weelan dialect that was familiar to Marin. A realisation of the impending attack froze Marin to the spot. He knew he should make his way back to the wall to warn the Sergeant. However, motionless he couldn't move.

'If they get in the way, run them through. That'll make fewer to get in the way later. Now move.' Twelve in all rode past where Marin had concealed himself. Noticing now that they were wearing headgear made to look beast-like. *Were they Kolgothians?* Marin wondered. Their blades were wide and jagged, not Ranielian. Breaking free of his paralysis, he ran as fast as he could and was soon out of the thicket and running headlong through the field. As he neared the embankment, he heard the shouts and saw a glow against the cloudy night sky. Shouting, Marin scrambled over the earthen ridge.

Not stopping to look where the Sergeant had gone, he picked up his spear and sprinted towards the shouts. The riders were charging through the camp causing utter confusion. Tents were alight, along with some of their occupants. Those running to help were cut down by a second wave of riders. Watching the first set of riders turn for another attack, Marin ran to position himself to stop the assault. With lungs rasping, shouting to get their attention, Marin steadied himself and rammed the back end of his spear into the ground. He heard screams and shouts of. 'Kols! They're Kols.' All he could focus on was driving his spear into the chest of one of their mounts. Sweat ran down his forehead, but he didn't have time to wipe it away.

The raiders charged. The lead rider swung his blade and gave out a loud raging battle cry. Holding his nerve, Marin stood firm. Only a few paces now. He could feel the thundering hooves thumping the ground. He closed his eyes, gritted his teeth and waited for the impact. The impact did come, but not from the front. Marin was charged from the side and thrown onto the ground just as the mounted attacker charged past. A large body pinned him to the earth. Marin was winded. Struggling for breath, he couldn't shout or cry out in pain.

'Get up, you fool!' Marin came to his senses and saw a familiar face with creased brows snarling at him.

'Jack?'

'Get up! Move!' Jack pulled Marin to his feet and dragged him away. Marin then noticed that some of the soldiers had rallied and formed a shield wall. At the same time the raiders realised that they would not get another charge in. Standing up on his mount's saddle, the lead rider uttered some bestial noises and levelled his blade at the rank of spears. A shout came from the back of the lined-up defenders.

'Archers!' At that, the raiders made their escape without a scratch, leaving behind screaming, burning bodies, tents ablaze and the wounded and dying sprawled wherever they'd been run down. A volley of arrows was loosed, but none hit their mark.

The captain, who had been in the middle of the shield wall, broke rank. 'What in the gods just happened? How did those bastards get across the bulwark? Shit! Tend to the wounded and put those fires out. Those not helping, get up on that embankment and make sure there are no more.'

Walking over to where Marin and Jack were standing, she had a stern look on her face. 'Stupid thing to do. We've lost enough tonight. You could have been trampled by that war boar and it probably wouldn't have felt your spear.'

'Ma'am, that was no war boar.' Marin was full of adrenalin and felt the challenge was justified. Jack, however, thought otherwise and tried to shut him up.

'What's your name?' The captain was in no mood for games.

'Marin, Ma'am.'

'Okay, Marin, brave as you may have been, they were Kolgothians, sent to attack and leave us in disarray before the battle – a raiding party of ten or so riding war boars. We saw it and you can still see the fear in the dead's' eyes.'

'I saw them before the raid.' Marin began reluctantly. 'I went for a piss and came across them mounting up.'

'Those were Kols,' she pressed.

'No! They were *men*. One even had a Weelan accent. Their horses were covered in fur skins. They wore some sort of headgear to cover their faces. I will swear on any god that's listening that they were men on horses. Their leader said, "Set fire to a few tents and harry the soldiers. If they get in the way, run them through. Less to get in the way later." Honest.'

The captain stood confused. 'Why didn't you shout the alarm?'

'I was near a thicket of trees, across that field.' Marin said nervously, not mentioning that he had been on guard duty.

'You went all that way for a piss?' Marin's head dropped. His superior understood without any words from Marin that he'd tried to leg it. 'Well, you made up for your ...' There was a pause, '...*excursion* by squaring up to the intruders and taking their mind off the tents and stores.'

'That was no Kol raider.'

'Get back up on the embankment and put this to bed. And Marin, if you take anymore extended late-night walks, I'll flog you myself.'

Marin knew what he'd seen and was now more confused. Turning to Jack to acknowledge that he'd saved him from being trampled or skewered by the archers. 'Thanks, Jack.' Jack gave no response and headed to the embankment to take up a space on lookout. It was going to be a long night.

Chapter Twenty-Eight

'We are but the space between all that we are not.' The slave that listened at Talgameth's feet was at the end of his life. His torment would soon be over and he knew it. Talgameth had been draining the Ranielian farmer of his life essence for the last day or two.

The incumbent man, once well fed and strong, had been brought up in the northern fields, driven by the constant cycle of ploughing, sowing and harvesting in all weather conditions, rearing, feeding and butchering livestock. In the last years, he had also found the need to be a protector for the local village. Raids were common: money, livestock and children all taken by bandits in heavy woollen cloaks the colour of darkness.

That last afternoon he'd heard the screams from a mile away, carried on the wind, along with the acrid smell of burning pitch. Above the hedgerow, smoke rose into the air. Dropping his tools and unhitching his horse from the plough, he galloped bareback to the village. Only faint shouts could be heard, the high-pitched shrieks silenced, given over to the crackle of flame and the collapsing of thatched roofs. Dismounting and running headlong to the village square, he was met by the scene of the village folk cowering on their knees – women, children and the menfolk, all with looks of despair.

Grabbed by two bandits as he took cautious steps towards his kith and kin. His huge muscular arms no match for whatever demon curse his assailants had over them.

Confused he was dragged by the two invaders in front of the kneeling villagers. Dropping to the ground from a kick driven hard into the back of his knee. His lowered head jerked back, responding to a pull on his hair. In front of him he remembered seeing a tall figure, larger than a normal man, draped in many layers of cloth and leather. He seemed to have tattoos all over his exposed skin. The farmer was made to look directly at the individual. He recalled his eyes, containing a blackness he'd never seen before, a contempt for life, and a malice that bore into his very soul. The robed figure gave a nod to those holding him and he was thrown into line with the others.

He knew not how long ago that had been. Days, weeks, months? There weren't many of them left now, the villagers taken screaming from the cells one at a time. He supposed their fate was like his own.

'Come, farmer.' Rising from an oak chair Talgameth walked to the window. Unable to walk, a shade released itself from a gap between some crumbling blocks and enveloped the farmer lifting him to the side of the dark mage. His eyes, grey and lifeless, looked without seeing. He was made to face the horizon.

'Look upon this day. I make my final roll in a game that has played out over a thousand years. These events are to my design. Division and hatred are easy seeds to sow, wouldn't you say?' The farmer had little energy to respond. Breathing was an effort. 'The field will be ripe for harvesting and it will see an end to the Kalnath kingdoms. The shadow will come. It is said that there are other dimensions, realms within realms; places of such evil that comprehension itself is torturous. Beasts of myth and legend, nightmares made whole, will manifest on this earth. Having this knowledge would see me more powerful than any Great Father, God or spirit. I have the power of the Emerald Knight and it will be unleashed upon Kalnath with ferocity and an abhorrence of life in all its forms.'

Turning to the near inanimate farmer, Talgameth placed his hand on the man's chest and drew the last life from his body. 'I thank you for your part in my success.' The farmer's body shrivelled and contorted until it began to break up and fall to the dusty flagstone floor and settle like ash from a fire. Rejuvenated, Talgameth walked back to the chair. The room was an old library – the very same in which he'd once studied for many long hours as a young acolyte. It was now cold and draughty. No light from sconces danced across detailed tapestries that had once hung on the walls. No student voices chattered in the hall nor did the vellum turn in the tomes he had studied. The millennium had not been kind either to the blocks of stone. The mortar, worn and crumbled, had loosened and collapsed. Talgameth knew that the great cities of Zinjal had hidden many magical items and tomes of knowledge. They would have to stay entombed for now. His prize was a greater bounty – to rule.

'Lord Talgameth, I have word from your agents abroad.' The acolyte was nervous in the presence of such a being. He kept his head bowed and waited for a reply. The same shade that had carried the farmer to his master floated close to the acolyte's head. There was a faint hiss, and an earthy damp odour. His hands trembled, knowing that some of the news would not be to his lord's liking. Having witnessed the pain that could be inflicted by a shade entering his body, his trembling was well placed.

'Speak!' Talgameth's tone was cold and sharp, almost as lifeless as the dry corpse of the farmer.

It was a gamble as to which news the messenger should tell first. His thinking was that maybe he would live longer by telling him the good news first. 'The Queen has left Raniel. Your servant Freya sent word that all is going to plan. They will be at the border in ten days, master.' There was a pause and the acolyte shifted uneasily.

'I sense there is more. Do not game with my time. You are lucky I had a soul from your filthy kind a moment ago.'

'Master, the plan to usurp the Kolgoth Guardian has failed. By all accounts he has knowledge of your intent.' The messenger was struggling to breathe now, as fear had taken hold.

'It matters little. Kolgoth is a war-hungry race. The slightest hint of prey and the beast will charge.' The Dark Lord sat in his chair watching his servant become increasingly uncomfortable. A cool breeze blew through the open window. Talgameth had long since lost any sense of physical pain. Cheating death had come with some side effects and this was far from the worst. A haze of white light gathered across his dark sunken eyes. The temperature dropped and the acolyte's breath could clearly be seen hanging in the air in front of him. Still staring at his servant, Talgameth watched him hold on to his life with all the will he could muster.

'Why do you cling to life? You must know that you are going to die. Give in to the pain and free yourself.' The follower of the Dark Lord was now shaking uncontrollably, teeth chattering and holding his arms in an attempt to retain what little body heat was left in him. Ice formed on his skin. The moisture that escaped from his mouth had already frozen on his lips. The pain of muscle spasms was clear in his face. He could barely stand and was now wishing for a swift end.

Talgameth stopped his icy blast. The acolyte started to warm up slowly. Still the dark mage studied this weak frame. 'You didn't give up! I could feel your life leave you and yet, you didn't give in to death.' A few moments later the acolyte was able to speak.

'I'm sorry that I disappointed you, master. Thank you for sparing my life.'

Talgameth gave a subtle snarl and raised a finger. In that instant the shade entered the acolyte and caroused through his insides, turning all to mush – bone, organs and muscle all mashed and contained within a thin skin sack. The shade burst out and the body popped like a balloon, splashing on to the stone floor in a wet slippery mess. Returning to a dark corner of the room, the shade settled back to watch and wait for its master's next command, content that it'd had a little fun.

'Oh, you didn't disappoint me. Your kind have a will to survive, but your bodies are weak.' Getting up and walking around the pool of cloth, flesh and moist innards, he gave a call, which was quickly answered.

'Ready the tribes.' The northern tribes were loyal to Talgameth. They were human – mostly – and had, at some point, been rejected by various villages across Raniel. Some had been adventurers, waylaid and picked up by his acolytes. There was a steady stream of men and women with no place in their societies. Talgameth was happy for them to stay. He needed fresh souls to rejuvenate him. To ensure that his plans would work, he offered incentives – the mere whisper of eternal life could make any fool do his bidding.

'Empty Zinjal. Kalnath's time is up!' The acolyte bowed and scurried off; no questions needed. This was the end of the play. Talgameth would unleash everything that he had amassed on the world. There was no match for his magic. He had seen to it that, within the realms of man, the practice of magic had been outlawed. Only fools with cheap tricks were left, and without battles to fight and feuds to settle, Kolgoth had become weak and hearth-happy.

'All by my design,' whispering to the city.

Guldr sat in the round, catching the sun's rays as they spilled through the old trees. He was content and unafraid of the future. The journey to the night plains had given him visions and a relaxed acceptance of whatever fate befell him. Refusing to succumb to thoughts of what might happen if Talgameth were to succeed in his efforts to bring darkness to the land. He knew that Helda would be safe, at least from the battle to come. She was strong, as were most of the women – he had seen childbirth and was more inclined to take a beating from ten Ogres than go through that.

He had control of the tribes ... well, most of them. Golth had not been seen since the challenge had been laid down. That little event had done a great deal for Guldr's place as Guardian. Letting Golth live had earned much respect from the older tribal leaders. The younger ones saw him as an even stronger and capable leader.

As he sat, watching and listening to the general sounds of market life, he was aware that this would all change. Today would be the last time many of his kinfolk walked these streets. If they were lucky enough to return, they would have witnessed such horrors that sleep would escape them and waking dreams would steal precious memories. It had fallen to him to lead, but it would be up to them how they survived.

'Uncle?' Sokal approached.

'Ah, you are up and about. The healers have worked their magic.' Guldr gave a smile and offered him a seat on the bench. 'How fares the scratch?'

'I am tender, Guardian. It was more than a scratch. That bastard cut me deep.'

Guldr was amused at Sokal's response. 'Yes, I know, nephew. I remember you holding your entrails out to show me. I'm playing with you. I know not where Golth has gone. Let us hope that his end will befit his heart. The Great Father will ask him to prove his worth before allowing him to sit in his hall.'

'What do you sit and watch?' Sokal winced as he sat. The wound was still weeping and the herb balm stung a little when it opened. Guldr was unlucky not to have been blessed with children, and since Sokal had arrived, he had felt a paternal love for the young Kol'.

'Some of these folk will not return. They are spending their last hours here with the people they love. There is pleasure and sadness mixed with honour and ritual. I cannot share in this, as Helda is as far from harm as she can be. I said my goodbyes when we left Fethal. I may not survive the coming battle and those memories are the most precious thing I have. These brave souls are making their own – something to fight for, survive for, come home to. We are on the edge of a void, young Sokal.'

'It's not fair that we go to war, even though we do not want it.'

'There are brave Kolgothians among us who crave destruction. Lacking purpose and direction, they are led easily down that path. Life is cruel and unfair, never forget that. And sometimes the rules change.'

'When do we leave?'

'As the sun rises, we will muster 10,000 war boars, twenty tribes fulfilling their oaths.'

'Will the tribes hold as you have asked?' Sokal saw in Guldr the fear of what might happen.

'I trust in the Great Father.'

'What of the Ranielians? I hear they have magic-users who can set fire to ice and make the ground swallow us up.'

'That is true, but I have had a few dealings with them. They are shorter, lacking in muscle and the earth spirit. However, they make up for this in sheer determination. Most are honourable folk: farmers, merchants and crafts people. Like every crop, there are bad grains. Hold your shield tight and your axe ready. It is not the Ranielians that we fight. Far worse will come from the north. We will need the Ranielian magic and they will need our strength.'

A mild wind whipped up the dust from within the round. Guldr smelled the air and took solace in the fresh scents of herbs and cooked meats. Children chased one another, oblivious to the impending encounter. 'We must protect life, it is precious. For our descendants, stories must be told. I am Guardian, I am protector and I fight for their future.' The two talked long into the evening. The sun had set, the stars unveiled and the brilliance of the cosmos clear to see. As teacher to student, Guldr told of the ancestors and the night plain; what the alignment of the stars meant to their place in time; and the omens for the future.

Before dawn, after only a few hours' sleep, Guldr was already awake. He knelt before an altar of a carved figure. Meditating, slowing his breathing down and clearing his mind of noise, he was able to focus, looking within himself to find the strength he needed. Dark were his thoughts. A shadow lurked, watching. He had the feeling that it had been with him for eternity. A hiss, then it was gone as soon as he looked to find it. Centring himself again, it reappeared and this time it spoke; a strained whisper of a voice, painful and hollow.

'You see me, Guardian. Long have I waited for you. Kolgoth will know no freedom henceforth. You will meet your fate on the slopes of stone and grass. Long will your bones bleach in the sun, with no pyre or grave for your kin.'

Guldr felt only pity, not fear or hatred for this apparition. Speaking from deep within his unconscious mind, his reply was level and calm. 'If my fate is so, then I have no fear of what is to come. I shall honour my ancestors and fight with courage. Long may I walk the night plains, but know this, before I leave this earth: I will come for you; I know who you are.'

A laugh echoed around his mind, pulsing in and out of hearing. 'Then you should know that I cannot die, fool.'

'I will find a way.' In a burst of blackness, the phantom evaporated, leaving behind only a feeling of hatred and spite. 'I will find a way,' Guldr repeated.

Awaking from his meditation, he donned his armour: heavy leather plates interlaced with steel mail. Preferring not to wear a helmet, his long hair was braided in a high topknot. On his belt hung two short axes, a bag full of herbs and potions and a ceremonial dagger. The dagger would be handed to the next Guardian if he should fall in battle. It was not a jewel-encrusted blade of gold and silver; instead, it had a wood and leather handle and a blade made of a material not seen for many an age. Some said it had come from the stars of the world past – a meteor of such destructive power that it had wiped out whole civilisations, leaving only a metal so hard and light that, once worked, it could make a blade so slim that it would cut the very fabric of reality. To be Guardian also meant being the wielder of Heaven's Blade.

Outside the air of the morning was fresh. The stars were still out and this gave Guldr comfort, knowing that the ancestors were watching. Entering the round, various tribal leaders greeted him, all in full battle gear. He gave each one a braid ring from his beard.

'I see that Golth has not shown face.' He had one more ring to give out. Nineteen in all had been given to the gathered chiefs. 'I have one last braid ring to honour an oath. I do not hold his tribe accountable, only Golth for his cowardice.' Turning to face each chief, he gave thanks. Beyond the round he saw Sokal and called him over, Sokal ran to the Guardian's side. 'I give the last braid ring to you, nephew, to honour your family for their support for me. You are strong and wiser than you seem.'

'I am not a tribal chief, Guardian. To bestow greatness on me is false. Surely there are warriors among those here that are more deserving of this tribute.'

'That reason alone is why you shall have it, Chief Sokal.' Smiling at his nephew, he continued. 'You must survive and build that tribe and grow a family: share our knowledge, tell of our mistakes and triumphs. We will meet on the night plains far into the future and drink with our forefathers.' Sokal felt as if he had grown ten feet in that moment. The other chiefs accepted him as a chief of his own tribe, even though he had no one to follow him.

Each chief, including Sokal, bowed and headed off to mount their war boars. They had about five days' ride to the border. The few souls that remained lowered their heads, thoughts weighing heavy in their hearts. A hushed stillness, the very air held its breath witnessing the departure of the last war host.

Chapter Twenty-Nine

Dawn broke and there was a low mood around the camp. The previous night's raid had removed any remaining notion that this would be a walk in the park. The Queen's guard were first to get in order. Checking saddles and tying down their bedrolls onto the backs of their horses made for a welcome distraction. They all feared the same thing as the common soldier: that this venture would end in disaster. None would say it though. If word got around, they would be stripped of their duties and put back with the mob. There was a subtle safety in being part of the Queen's guard; at least they would be last to take to the field.

Perched in her saddle, Freya impatiently awaited the General's attempt to rein in his horse. A weary sigh escaped her lips, accompanied by a disapproving shake of her head. With a quick gesture of her hands and a playful white mist around her eyes. The General's steed bucked violently, hurling the general to the ground. There were muffled sniggers from some of the guards. He scrambled to his feet; his dignity bruised.

'Sort yourself out, Reval.' Came the blunt reprimand from the Queen. She was in no mood for his stupidity. In a day they would be at the border and the threat of raids was now an increasing danger. Turning to Freya, she asked, 'How did he end up being general of my army?'

'Because the last one was a murderous drunk.' Freya gave a wry smile towards one of the guards. 'Are you ready, my Queen? Shall we make progress?'

'No reason to wait. Reval, are you done?' said the Queen.

'Yes, your highness, I do apologise.' After fumbling for the reins, Reval climbed onto his horse. He gave a nod to the guards at the front to move off. There were almost a thousand armoured soldiers and Reval felt quite happy to be in the middle of the column. He was hoping not to see any action in the coming days, but maybe help to mop up or dispatch a wounded Kol or two.

It would be a few hours until the last of the camp would be able to move off. The column was travelling in close order and there was little chat among any of the soldiers. Upfront a scout galloped up to Freya. Out of breath and her horse sweating, she waited to be given leave to speak.

'Calm yourself. What is your news?' The scout pretended that she needed to speak to the general. 'It's fine, tell me your news,' Freya said. 'The general is occupied further along the column.'

'Yes, my lady.' Catching her breath, the scout continued. 'There is a large raiding party heading this way. They were keeping to the road three abreast. I estimate there are about ten to fifteen Kol warriors.'

'Thank you. Return to your duties. You have served well.' Looking at Freya the Queen thought it was an odd thing to say – *'You have served well.'* Freya turned to the Queen to find her inquisitive gaze. 'I think it in your best interests to split the guard and get you off the road safely until the skirmish is over.'

'You served well? What did you mean?'

'She was helping to protect the column and her Queen, so she served well. Sorry. I'm very nervous and it just came out like that. Have I offended you?'

'No, it just seemed an odd thing to say.'

Freya called out for the captain. 'There's a raiding party some way down the road.' Noticing that the captain was one of her own, she offered him an opportunity to give a solution. 'What would you have us do?'

'I suggest that the guard splits and sets up an ambush. The Queen must be protected.' Pausing for effect, he added, 'The first section should take the royal retinue off the road. Keep heading west to the border.' Quickly the soldiers organised themselves, with the first section of around a hundred soldiers leading the Queen and Freya into the fields next to the road.

'The rest of you keep sharp.' The captain led the rest of the army along the road with no intention of setting an ambush. Any questions about a raiding party were quickly stifled and the long march continued.

Rounding a bend, the Queen's guard were met by a cloaked figure sitting on a tree stump at the side of the track. On seeing the troop of mounted guards, the figure arose and held up its hand to bar the way. The order to halt echoed along the tree-lined track. Some guards looked nervous, surveying the wood to either side. Their horses, sensing an unknown menace, snickered and danced beneath the soldiers who were trying valiantly control the beasts.

'Friend, please be on your way.' The lead guard's request was polite, but the figure did not move or respond. 'I say again, be on your way.' Taking a few steps forward, the guard's horse began to roll its eyes. Curling its lips up and baring its teeth, the steed's moist gums frothed like a rabid dog. With ears flat back against its head and more of the white than pupil showing in its eyes, the horse lurched forward. Other guards were now taking notice and becoming a little fearful.

With a second lurch and the rider was thrown to the ground. The horse writhed in agony, giving nightmarish screams, then dropped to its knees, convulsing. The rider sitting up and backing away witnessed his steed, that he had cared for from a foal take a last sorrowful look at him and fall silent. A heartbeat later the horse's body exploded and out came two shades that rushed past the rider and into the trees. The guards at the front who saw the horrific scene quickly went for their weapons and moved to protect the Queen – or at least, most of them.

The figure stepped forward towards the shocked rider, removing its cloak hood to reveal the face of an old man, gaunt and drawn. Liver spots covered his skin and the dark rings around his eyes gave notice of a troubled life. Kneeling next to the guard, he removed a glove from his right hand. 'You were brave to step out of line. I'm sure that your horse would have rather you'd stayed at the back.' Petrified and unable piece a sentence together, only faint squeaks and whimpers passed his lips. 'Lord Talgameth thanks you for your service.'

Moving to help his comrade, a guard broke rank only to be stopped by another, a small dagger held at the would-be rescuer's side, poised to plunge into his ribcage. Confusion and concern ran through the Queen's guards. The Queen herself now looked around for an answer.

'Guards, kill this old wretch.' Again, some of the guards made to follow her order, but were held back by their companions. A commotion ensued, with bumping horses and shouts of traitor and bastards.

'What is the meaning of this?' The Queen was quick to anger. A slight panic in her voice gave her thoughts away. 'Freya, do something.'

'Shut up, you snivelling bitch!' Freya let out a sigh of relief. 'I'm so glad that this moment has finally come. For too long have I been holding back my true feelings.'

'What?' The Queen's face now bore an even more perplexed expression.

'I found purpose in the night, away from the drudgery life. My master found me and taught me to use my powers.'

'But—?'

'Be quiet and wait. Watch.' Freya pointed at the old man.

Holding the guard's head as if in the caress of a father, the old man tried to calm the young man down. 'Shh, child.' A lustful grin came over the old man and with lightning speed he plunged his hand into the guard's chest. The very life was now drawn out of the guard, with a black haze enveloping them both, with a groan of pleasure ensuing from the miasma. Quickly the body of the guard began to contort and became emaciated. Freya watched on with delight. Others were repulsed and sickness spread among the guards. The limp body was thrown aside like a worn cloth. The cloaked figure now resembled a man of vitality and strength.

Horrified, the Queen's heart raced. She wanted to run, but there was nowhere to go, surrounded by her guards but none able to help her.

'My lord, another fine display of your power.' Freya dismounted and walked over to her master. 'My duty is done. Please, may I present the spoilt brat that is Queen of Raniel, vessel of the king's blood. May our lord give blessings upon us for her delivery.'

Trying hard to understand what was going on, the Queen let out a soft sob. 'Freya, what have you done? Why do you say such things?' Looking around at her guards, she saw that most had their weapons unsheathed. She shouted to the nearest guard. 'Do something. Protect your Queen,' she pleaded.

'No Queen of mine. You'll have to wipe your own arse now.' A guard spat a glob of phlegm from deep within his throat at her. Another guard made to protest at her treatment and won a mailed fist to his jaw as a prize for being foolhardy.

'I don't understand. What is happening?' The Queen gave a delicate last shout for help. 'Please, help me. One of you must be courageous enough to protect your–' She was cut off by the nearest guard.

'Why?'

'What? I am your Queen.' Her eyes glazing over. The strong-willed young woman that had left Weelan was now retreating from the harshness of the world. She no longer had sway over her subjects.

'What is my name?'

Barely audible, the Queen replied. 'I don't know.'

'Do you know any of the guards' names that you demand help you?' She was silent, looking down at the reins held firmly with her fine, soft leather gloves.

'Thought not. You bastards are all the same. I'd cut your throat, but Lord Talgameth has need of you.'

Leaving the husk of the guard abandoned at the side of the track, The dark acolyte and Freya made their way towards the ruler of Raniel. 'Ah, Queen, the fruit of Thomas and only heir to the throne of Raniel.'

'Who are you? Why have you done this? Freya, please help me,' she pleaded once more with friend.

'I am done with your childish acts and the demands of a spoilt whelp. I follow a different path, whose reward far outweighs coin and title.'

Searching deep within Freya's eyes to find the person she knew, 'You are my only friend, like a sister,' said the Queen.

'Enough! Too much time has been wasted.' The acolyte's shout startled even Freya. He was eager to fulfil his own task and deliver the Queen to his master. 'To those not in the service of Lady Freya, I offer this one chance: renounce Raniel and pledge your service to Talgameth.' None of the Queen's guard uttered a word. 'Ah, stoic to the last, but foolish. Kill them!'

Some had no chance as blades were driven into their side by the very companions who they had trained and eaten with. The luckier ones managed to draw their swords and defend themselves. A clash of steel rang through the trees and the cries of dying soldiers was only stifled by the screaming of panicking horses.

In the chaos an assassin seized their opportunity to strike. Clad in the same armour as the Queen's guard he was now perched atop his horse.

With a flourishing of his blade, he made a lunge for the Queen. Knocking her to the ground, the assassin's blade poised an inch from her exposed neck.

'The Emerald Knight shall forever lay dormant; I will end the king's line,' vowed the assassin with unwavering determination.

The dark mage, noticing a glint in the air turned his deathly gaze on the assassin. With time-honed skill, the attacker pulled from his belt and released a vial of blue liquid. It exploded at the dark mage's feet into a swirling miasma of dust and ash, then imploded into a vacuum. Shielding himself the mage let out a cry of pain. As the dust cleared Talgameth's acolyte was on his knees. Looking up, he gave what looked like either a grimace or a grin. Through gritted teeth he threw shadowy enchantments, seemingly without care for the Queen. Stalking closer to the assassin, each dark set of words broke a bone in the assassin's body. The Queen broke free and tried to run, but her escape ended in the arms of Freya. The pain brought on agonising screams

'Who are you, assassin?' No words, only screams, as the dark mage continued to manipulate the bones to break within. Seeing now the features of his foe. 'A Brovan assassin!'

With a twist of his hand, another few ribs broke within. This brought on his crying out in more pain, his face contorting. 'Your antiquated sect of righteous fools will not stop my master this time. You thought to kill the Queen before we could use the artefact. You have failed and I know that cuts you deep. What now? Should I let you crawl out of here for the world to see your demise? I think not.' With a last clench of his fist, the mage spoke his final set of enchantments, The assassin fell silent and limp against the tree, his body hunched like an old ragdoll.

Turning, he noted that Freya's men had taken care of those loyal to the Crown and that his prize was still alive. 'Secure her and get moving. Our master awaits.'

Chapter Thirty

'Sir, a rider approaches.'

'What?' The general had been a little distracted. The weeks in the saddle had given his arse a lot to complain about and the food was not up to the standard he was used to. He had thought his ascension to general would give him ultimate status. Even now there was a thought deep within that this battle would not happen and they would turn around and go home. General Reval was not the brightest candle on the alehouse table. He was intent on making sure that his armour had more of a shine than that of those around him. And all the while he lost the respect, if he'd had any at all, of the soldiers. Desertion was also high. He was not a leader; he was a pleaser. It weighed heavily on his shoulders, this task which lay ahead of him. Command the entire Ranielian Army? They were supposed to meet the Queen again after the ambush. *Ha!* he thought. *The road was empty. That fool of a captain had left the Queen exposed.*

A rider pulled up alongside the General. She saluted and waited for a response. Reval gave her a brusque wave of his hand. Still, she waited.

'Well? Go on, what is your message?' Without much interest, Reval listened.

'Sir, we have almost reached the Valley of the Wellspring River. Our scouts suggest that the enemy is on the far bank.' Reval took notice. The reality now set true. With a dry throat and struggling to contain his emotions, beads of sweat began to burst forth all over his body making him even more uncomfortable.

'How many are there?'

'An estimate of around 10,000, sir.' The messenger's horse snickered and paced sideways.

'Hold that animal still there or I'll have you in the front rank.' The rider tightened the reins and nodded apologetically. 'We have more troops and numbers are key. Kolgothians are foolish to think they can match us. Captain, any word from the Queen's party?'

The captain gave a solemn response. 'None yet, sir. However, it will be another few hours before *we* reach the valley ridge.' This bit at Reval, who insisted that he be placed in the middle of the column, so the rank and file saw their leader rather than being up front with the knights. 'There is still time for her to arrive.'

'Yes, quite. Well, at least there will be someone there to welcome her after her detour.' Their discussion was interrupted by another rider, who spoke directly to the captain.

'Sir, the mages have arrived.'

'Ah, by the gods, we may yet survive until the morning. Please go and tell the other captains. There should be a mage per section and any leftover are to protect the command tents.' The captain's smile was evident.

'How, sir, is it that you feel we may not last the night? We have superior numbers. I think your lack of faith is alarming.' Reval's confidence was buoyant now that the mages had arrived.

'With all due respect, sir, have you experience of Kolgothian tactics?'

'Well, em, no, Captain. Be careful what you say next.' Reval did not like being made fun of. From a young age he'd used his family's influence to barter for friendship, feeling that power was far more effective than earning admiration.

'I was with the King's Light Horse when they charged at us. The ground thundered and shook with an elemental rage. We had lost before a single sword stroke was made. Those in the centre had no chance, penned in by those behind and to either side. As the war boars crashed through, their riders left them. Fearless and lusting after blood, they were unstoppable. The only thing that brought them down was a hail of arrows. Unfortunately, some of our own were caught in the volley. We may outnumber them and, by the grace of all the gods, we have mages, but they are strong and ferocious. It took ten arrows to drop one of those boars.'

'Well, captain, the lesson is not to end up in the centre, eh?'

The column continued its slow march west. All were weary of the travelling and very few of them were ready for a battle. The mages would be tasked to give them a little vigour and strength. What they needed, however, was a hot meal, a warm bed and a decent sleep. The threat of raids and the shortening of supplies had taken its toll on every person. The horses were better fed than the soldiers, and the less said about the commander and some of his retinue, the better. They surely wouldn't starve.

Maleth arrived at his assigned section and rode up to keep pace with the column captain.

'Sir, I am Maleth. I have been assigned as your mage.'

'Well, spell-caster, I can see that by your robes. Where have you been? Our soldiers needed a little help with the march. Give them some of that which sustains them. And be quick about it: we are but a few hours from the border.' The captain's demeanour was foul. To be more accurate, he was an arsehole.

'Sir, may I ask what training camp this section is in?'

'I have no time for your kind or your questions. Be on your way. You have your orders.'

Acknowledging the captain's response, he went to take his leave. Then a thought popped into his head as to what Marin would have done, although Marin would probably have had his teeth knocked out and been dragged off to be lashed, so Maleth would have to be a little more courteous and subtle. Swinging his horse back round to engage a little further with the captain, he saw the rage simmer around his cheeks and the creases deepen on his forehead. 'Sir, could you elaborate on *your kind*?'

The captain's anger was boiling. 'How dare you address me after you have your orders. I'll have you hog-tied.'

'Ah, would that be after I turn you into a toad?'

'You are threatening me now, you whelp?' Pointing to two of the mounted soldiers in front of him, the captain issued another order. 'Put this abomination in chains.' Nervously, the two pulled up on their reins and stopped to look at the altercation being played out.

'Men with power are quick to anger. Gentlemen, please, there will be no need for chains. I have had my fill of incarceration and the Queen's justice.' Rubbing his face, he could still feel the scars from the beatings he'd received despite all the magic he had applied to himself. He was not a vain person, but every time he looked at his reflection, he was reminded of the little girl. As the two soldiers moved closer to Maleth, he projected an unseen barrier. All this was taking place as the column ground its way past, taking no notice. The soldiers were like those in the old stories of beings who had died and been resurrected to fight once more. Ghost stories – wonders of ink, quill and parchment.

'By the gods when this is done, you'll hang.' The captain was now frothing slightly from his mouth.

'You seem confident that we will survive the battle and that I will allow you to catch me, in order to hang me. This is madness. Look, we're on the same side and I have just met you, yet you treat me like scum. I have news for you, sir – Kolgoth is not our enemy. We face a foe far more sinister from the north. Have you seen the Queen lately? No? That's because she's been kidnapped. We are heading into a trap and the reason is unclear. What I do think though is that both sides have been manipulated to this end. All I want to know is what section came from the eastern camps.'

'I am a commanding officer and this is an outrage. Talk like that will demoralise the soldiers. It seems that you are a Kol sympathiser.'

'Take a look around: no one cares. These soldiers will not be fighting *for* you; they will be fighting to survive and helping their friends to do the same. And you, sir, shouting your orders and threats of punishment will be trodden into the earth with no one to help you up. I am looking for a friend who was in the eastern camps, so that I may help him, along with as many people as I can, to get home. This is not my war. None of us signed up for this shit.'

Seeing the futility of the argument and the fact that he could be turned into a toad, or worse, the captain backed down slightly. 'Mark my words, this changes nothing between us. Your kind, magic-users, defiled the earth and tore it asunder. Your kind broke the earth and allowed the Kolgothians through from another dimension. Along with them, you are the cause of illnesses and blight.' He spat on the ground.

'Ah, a man of the gods. I see that your religious texts have not left too deep a scar on your mind. That is your version of events and I must, most respectfully, disagree with you, you bumbling idiot.' This did nothing to calm the situation. 'Tell me where is the section that I seek, and I will be on my way.'

'Mage, if you are not downed in the first hail of arrows, I will find you on the field and run you through for your blasphemy.'

Let's hope the first arrow is between your eyeballs, Maleth thought.

'That section is behind us.' The captain turned away and gave no more time to Maleth. He stood down the two riders, who were amused and a little relieved at not having to restrain an annoyed mage.

'Thank you, sir!' He bowed to the captain's back. 'And may I wish you ill health and hope that your next shit is a hedgehog.'

'Piss off, mage.'

Content, Maleth headed back down the line, saddened as he looked into the eyes of the weary soldiers. Most did not even look up at his passing, their gaze forward, staring at the person in front. This was dangerous: if there was an obstacle or stoppage, the concertina effect would mean injuries and an even longer delay. He stopped at the worst looking and pulled them aside. After his time in the Citadel, he had grown stronger and these healing spells came with ease; little or no focus was required. A thin veil of green mist appeared around his eyes and reaching out, he touched each soldier. Like a rebirth, the soldiers gradually took on a new vitality, standing straighter and colour returning to their skin. Their eyes were brighter and, as if breathing clean air for the first time, their chests now heaved. Many thanks and blessings of the gods were given. This also brought an enormous sense of well-being to Maleth, even though religion meant nothing to him.

A light mist hung low to the ground. Every blade of grass carried hundreds of sparkling globes of moisture. Not a breath of wind challenged the precarious nature of the droplets that clung to the small shrub branches. The Wellspring River flowed slowly, meandering through the grass-covered lands. A heron stood motionless, its feet in the water, poised in its hunt for breakfast, almost invisible with its grey and white plumage against the drab ashen sky. A faint sound and a change in the air broke the concentration of the wading fowl. Snapping its head up and round to the west, the tall elegant bird calculated the nature of the threat. Stock-still again, no longer fixed on the riverbed, the creature waited. The quiet symphony did not grow past a distant drone. The heron's survival instincts gave way to its hunger. Returning the gaze of its yellow and black eyes to the river, composed once more, it continued its hunt.

Sloping up from the river on both sides, the knee-high grass revealed that spring had returned. Small green shoots emerged from the brown husks of winter. In the distance, from of the shallow valley where the mist had been burnt away by the morning sun, the horizon moved.

A beast gave a snort. A billowing cloud of warm breath hung in the air. The animal, a large boar, surveyed the vista, its thin black fur covering a muscular body, shoulders the height of a man, as broad as an old oak. The creature was bred for one thing – war! Atop this huge steed sat Guldr. His task was to hold the tribes back from entering the battle. His own tribe was under control. However, the eastern border tribes that had been battling the raiders for years saw this as a chance to once again meet the enemy head on and take revenge for the countless villages that had been burnt and the sacred sites desecrated.

'Call the chiefs!' At his order a horn blew, low and deep and reverberated along the valley. As he waited, the mist began to disappear as the sun rose. The river was not visible, but he could see the immense grass-covered ground that needed to be covered. Squinting towards the other side of the valley, he could hardly see the opposite ridge. A chief of the same age arrived.

'My Guardian.' He gave a shallow bow. His mount edged away from Guldr's and dropped its head in a submissive gesture.

'What do you see, my friend?'

'I see a victorious battlefield.' Guldr shook his head at this response. This chief was a proud Kolgothian who had seen many years and many battles, he was eager to show his patriotism and loyalty.

'Get your tongue out of my arse and tell me what you see.' Guldr was in no mood for bullshit.

Caught out, he composed himself. 'My apologies, Guardian. I see nothing but mist on the valley floor.' With a little confusion as to what he was being asked, he queried, 'What should I see?'

'I would expect you to see the Ranielian Army. Either it is small in number and hiding within the mist or we are early. Our scouts suggested that we had made good time. The Mother Shaman also made mention of this place.' Looking up, they noticed the flight of a heron laden with a plump fish.

'A good omen, my Guardian.' The eager chief tried to lighten the clearly solemn affair.

'Then let us hope that this day is as successful as that bird's fishing. But we must trust in our strength and resolve rather than omens.'

The other chiefs arrived on the ridge, all giving varying degrees of recognition. Some showed more respect to Guldr now that they had actually arrived and were ready for battle. Kolgothians by nature were hunters and warriors. The thirst for conflict ran deep in their blood. Among the twenty or so tribal chiefs, there were those whose bloodlust betrayed their true intentions and loyalty to Guldr.

'I see a few tribes not represented here. This saddens me. There is a bigger game afoot. The Great Father has foreseen an enemy greater than the Ranielian.' He let that sink in to the gathered chiefs. 'Do *not* engage with Raniel.' Murmurs rippled among the tribal leaders.

'You cannot ask us to take a charge from their heavy horse. We must initiate and take out their archers. We will not survive the arrow storm then the impact of–' The chief was cut off by Guldr raising his hand.

'What I ask is against all reason. I understand your concern. But our threat is from the north.'

'None of the scouts you sent north have seen any other force.' The chief's voice was cautious, so as not to offend Guldr. 'And with respect, Guardian, there is no enemy to the east that we can see.'

'You are correct. I ask only for faith and loyalty.'

A familiar voice came from the gathered chiefs. 'I will stand with you, Guardian.' An old northern chief rode up to Guldr. 'You are strong, wise beyond the length of your braids and you have a connection to the spirits. You say you have spoken to the Great Father and walked the night plain – that is all the faith I need. I have seen the changes in the north: there is darkness abroad and it comes this way.'

Guldr, finding a little more resolve as a result of the old chief's declaration, sat up straighter in his saddle. 'It is my honour for you to be at my side, Great Chief.' Rounding on the other leaders, Guldr made clear his intent. 'Hold the line. Do not engage with Raniel. They will not ford the river or attack up hill. Nor will their magic or arrows reach us here. Wait until my call and look to the north.' Fixing his gaze on those who he knew did not fully follow him, he repeated, 'I say again – do not charge.'

The chiefs left one by one, heading back to their tribal warriors. Guldr was now alone with his thoughts. Doubt crept in. *What if I'm wrong? We have the downhill advantage. We could hit them hard, making their arrows useless. Is there a threat from the north?*

A voice broke his waking dream. 'Guardian, steady your thoughts. We are with you. Do not falter in this.' As Guldr tried to find the voice in his mind's eye, it was silenced.

'What of Helda? She is my strength. If I fail, she will be left to ruin.'

Again, the voice responded. 'You have the strength, Guardian. Lead your people to victory. Join with the Ranielian, bridge the divide. Your task is to protect more than Kolgothian lands. The fate of Kalnath lies with you. You will leave this field when it is time and another will be Guardian.'

'Great Father, protect the boy Sokal and lead Helda to a safe life.' There was no reply.

The mist on the valley floor was just a wisp of memory, the clear water sparkling in the spring sunshine. In the distance a single black pennant flew, so small and difficult to see, but he knew that Raniel had arrived.

Chapter Thirty-One

It was easy to follow where any army had been. The footprints of thousands of soldiers left clear marks, and on either side of the track was the detritus of an army on the march. Getting off their horses for clues of a fight or a split, the pair scoured the roadside.

'Remember not to pick up a fallen leaf, De'sal. You might get a surprise.'

'How so?'

'Well, there isn't any soft parchment to wipe delicate arses out here. Just a heads-up,' said Hal grinning.

'Much appreciated.' De'sal was rather naive to the workings of an army and had never really thought of the bodily functions of such a large amount of people. 'Now, I can't get that picture out of my head.'

'There's nothing here. We should move on. We're getting close to the border.' Climbing back into the saddle, they continued in silence, each checking the side of the road for any sign. A short while later they came across a depression at the side of the track. It was difficult to tell if it was new or old. The column had stopped here, which was evident by the stench of shit and piss.

'Well, my pointy-eared friend, I have a feeling that some soldiers left at this point.'

'We've seen this before. There have been desertions all along the route. What makes this any different?' De'sal was weary of all the stops. Sometimes thinking it would have been better to rot in his cell. He also wondered where Hal got his drive from – the man was relentless.

'The branches have been cut at horse height and a deserter wouldn't have a horse. It would be too easy to notice. The track is deep with mud, which suggests that many mounted soldiers followed the same course. Most noticeably, I have a feeling that I'm right.'

'Ha!' De'sal gave a laugh and shook his head. 'Well, if you're right, my lord, I'll follow,' he said sarcastically.

'I am no longer a lord and you are free to leave.' The task was getting to Hal. He needed to find the Queen. He had been having lucid dreams of the peril that she might be in, even nocturnal visits from her father, King Thomas. Many nights he awoke in a panic, drenched in sweat, and always present in these dreams was a hooded figure, which he took to be a sign of the dark powers.

'No, I made a promise to help and I apologise. I don't mean to make fun. Please, lead the way and let us be done with this nightmare.'

The companions left the road to follow the well-worn track. Their mounts' hooves squelched in the deep mud, which was not ideal for a stealthy approach. However, the trees on either side were nigh on impossible to navigate. On they pressed.

A couple of hours later with mud still sucking at the hooves of their horses. Hal raised his hand, 'Stop!' he whispered. De'sal dutifully obliged and placed his hand on the hilt of the sword he carried. With eyes unblinking, both looked straight ahead. The faint sound of carrion birds squabbling and cawing was carried on the breeze. Edging forward and round a bend in the track, they saw the first suggestion of a fight and noticed one of the Queen's guard face-down in the middle of the track. An arrow had got him in his back just below the neck. 'That's a well-placed shot.'

Stalking forwards, the pair arrived in the middle of what had been a blood bath, scattering the birds from their feast. Feathers and fleshy scraps exploded from the ground. A clamour of resentment broadcast by the fleeing ravens. The smell made De'sal's eyes water and quickly he covered his nose. A scene of horror unfolded, as bodies lay bloodied and defiled. Hal had seen battle many times, when he'd served in the northern territories.

'Shit!' he raged.

'What would you have done, Hal? You would have been among the corpses. We don't know the size of the force that attacked them or if there was magic used.' De'sal glanced at the bodies. 'There's no sign of any gold armour, which would suggest that the Queen still lives.'

'These were good soldiers. I trained the house guard.' Most still had their weapons sheathed. 'Poor bastards didn't even get a swing. They were stabbed in the side by those they'd shared ale with the day before. This attack came from within; from scum in the pocket of that evil bitch!' Walking between the corpses, a sense of needless death rose in Hal. 'Why the game, De'sal? Why waste the lives of all these soldiers?'

'We are all pawns in the Dark Lord's plan. These souls are nothing to him and his minions.' A cough was heard. They spun round with swords unsheathed, both in a low fighting stance, gripping their hilts tightly. Another cough and a rasping sound of shallow breathing.

'There, by the trees.' De'sal pointed to a limp body lying next to a birch trunk.

'Kill the Queen.' Struggling to speak and in immense pain, the soldier kept repeating, 'Kill the Queen.'

Hal let out a roar of anger. 'I'll kill you, you bastard.' But before his sword fell on the wounded soldier, De'sal pushed him out of the way and his sword imbedded itself in the turf.

'What are you doing, De'sal? You fool!'

'He's already dead, you oaf. It's just that he's not drawn his last breath yet.' Kneeling closer to the soldier, De'sal pulled a small bottle of a dark liquid from his belt pouch. He popped the cork with his thumb and immediately a dark blue smoke rose from the slim neck. Shrouding the man's face, the smoke found its way into his nostrils. In a spontaneous burst of life, the soldier's eyes sprang open and he inhaled a huge breath of air. Strength returned to his features.

'By the gods, why are you bringing this murderous son of a bitch back to life!' Hal was ready this time to cleave him in half.

'It's just his soul that I've awoken. His body is a vessel and has seen some punishment. I want to ask him a few questions.'

'Then I'll cut his bastard head off.'

'Yes, if you must.'

'Who are you?' De'sal was compassionate in his request. Hal, however, gave a grunt of derision.

'Kill the Queen.' The voice was but a whisper, his clouded eyes searching through the countless memories.

'Yes, we know that much. What is your name?' De'sal wafted more of the incense under his nose. Another deep inhale of breath brought the solider to the present.

'I am a brother of the Brovan Order. The Dark Lord Talgameth has found the artefact and plans to use its powers. I must stop him.'

'And you intended to kill the Queen, to get to Talgameth?' Hal did not have a good bedside manner nor patience.

'Yes and no. The brotherhood found out about Talgameth's awakening over a hundred years ago. Many assassins were sent to end his foul and unnatural life. There are few of us left now.'

'One less after today.' De'sal gave Hal a look of disgust at his comment.

'Go on,' said De'sal

'Word came recently that he had found the artefact.'

'What artefact?' De'sal intervened.

'The Emerald Knight. He will use it to bring forth such horror on Kalnath.

'Shit! That sack of dust is going to turn up after the battle and use it on the survivors. But what's it got to do with the Queen?' Hal was a little more interested now.

'*By king's blood, the doors shall open. The souls of the dead will be the vessels of darkness,*' the assassin intoned. 'The Queen is the last heir to any Kalnath throne. She is the last in the royal bloodline. If she is killed, Talgameth cannot use the Emerald Knight. Her death was a last resort.'

Hal sat on the back of a dead soldier, his head low, a feeling of complete weariness flooding into his body. He had driven himself forward in the hope of saving the Queen. De'sal looked over at him.

'What should we do now, my friend?'

Shaking his head, Hal responded. 'I am at a loss to know which road to take, De'sal. Do we save the realm from darkness or save my friend's daughter? She's just a young girl with no family left. The only person close to her is a flea-ridden witch. Freya has been planted in the Royal Court. It was all part of the plan. I have to save her. If Talgameth can't get the royal blood, then his plan is worthless. We could keep her in hiding, change her name, clothes and hair. We must move. Time is running out.'

'And what of Freya?' asked De'sal.

'The evil within that one does not deserve words. But mark me, she will be dealt with.'

The last tendrils of blue smoke faded from around the assassin. De'sal watched as the light left his eyes. There was nothing more they could do for him. 'You want to lop off his head now, Hal?'

'No, let him be. Let's see what we can get from these unfortunate bastards. They might have food, weapons, maybe some potions that might come in handy.' They set to work scavenging the bodies, turning them over and checking pockets and satchels. They found healing potions a plenty and the odd dagger, but no food.

'All the rations must be in the baggage train. They didn't expect to be separated from the main column.'

A noise stopped their foraging: a rhythmic beat of tin ... and it was getting closer. They checked the Brovan assassin, but he was past the point of making any noise. 'What do you hear, De'sal?'

'Just because I have bigger ears does not mean I know everything I hear. I think, though that we should hide.' The trees were not thick enough to conceal such a burly frame as that of Hal, but De'sal, if he turned sideways, was almost invisible. 'If you lie down next to the corpses you will look like one of the fallen. I'll keep an eye out from the trees and let you know if it's safe.'

Reluctantly, Hal placed himself face-down in the mud. Keeping his head up just enough to see the track, he listened intently. The noise was getting closer. A few moments passed and the noise stopped. There was still nothing to see. Hal, for all his strength and courage, felt his heart pounding. He was exposed, lying on the ground, waiting for a foe he could not see. *Damn you, De'sal! It should be you lying here*, he thought.

With bated breath, De'sal strained his hearing to catch the distant murmurs. His keen eyes catching a glimpse of movement on the track. Knowing that curiosity killed many a fellow, with caution he edged forward. But not cautiously enough, inadvertently he stumbled upon a soggy furrow and lost his footing. An old and rotting branch snapped as he stretched out to brace his fall. Dropping to his knees, he cursed his clumsiness. Before he knew what had happened, he had a fork at his throat. *A fork?* he thought. *Maybe a blade of sharper persuasion, but a common kitchen utensil?* The owner stared intently at the Tialan. There was no doubt in those eyes that it would use the fork to deadly effect.

Putting up his hands and backing away slightly, De'sal realised that what was standing before him was an imp – the common alleyway type, with very sharp, pointy teeth. In an extremely threating manner, the imp gave a series of low ticks and crackles, just loud enough for De'sal to hear. It then backed away and gave a loud click. There was a commotion and more clicks and scraping. Through the trees came more imps, all in different arrays of armour, from pan lids to well-fitted chest plates. Their weapons were a mixed bag also. Along with the aforementioned cutlery, some even had what looked like enchanted daggers. De'sal could recognise Tialan work from a distance. 'Fine work,' he muttered to himself.

The stand-off was broken by a bluish-skinned imp with full battle armour. 'Click?' There was no response from De'sal. 'Click?' The imp pressed home the question.

'I'm sorry. I don't speak Impish.' De'sal recalled seeing this particular little chap before. 'You were with the mage?

'Click, click.'

'Well, you haven't stuck a fork in me yet, so I would say that we are on good terms, yes?'

'Click.' Tep gave a wave of his hand, which suggested that the boundaries had not been set.

Relaxing slightly, De'sal took a breath. At the same time, the fork-wielding imp licked his lips. 'Very disconcerting, that fellow.' Giving a nod in the direction of the hungry imp, Tep gave a click and the imp was off. 'I have a companion. If you remember ... the heavy-set gentleman.'

'Click.'

'Well, I'll give him a call before he starts hacking your little friends to even tinier pieces.' Giving a shout for Hal to get up, De'sal turned to the clearing where all the bodies were lying.

As if rising from the dead, the imps watched what they thought was a corpse get up and stretch his shoulders with a crack. With its fork stuck in one of the bodies, the hungry imp stopped, looked sideways at the rest of them and thought better of trying to eat the dead guard, just in case it got up as well.

'Well, you little buggers do turn up in the strangest places.' Hal looked around. There was a large number of teeth and claws ready for a bust-up. He looked over to De'sal and Tep. 'Nice to see you again. The mage was right: you did go and get some help.'

'Click.'

'What did he say?'

De'sal shrugged his shoulders and pulled himself out of the bog he had found himself in. 'Neither of us speak Impish, so tread carefully with what you say.'

Tep, once again, gave a chorus of clicks and the imps gathered round. He produced a piece of parchment and charcoal and drew a picture of two stick figures and then behind them a lot of smaller figures. 'Clack!'

'This is fun,' said De'sal, showing his excitement a little too much. 'You will follow us?' Looking to his left, De'sal's initial assailant gave a big grin, with a gaping maw of razor-sharp choppers. This reduced his enthusiasm a little. 'We are intending to protect the Queen from the Dark Lord, so your help will be much needed.'

'As well as a little luck on our side, De'sal.' Hal gave the Tialan a wry smile. 'Right, we follow the track. Tep, get your pals to take anything they need, but do *not* eat any of them.'

The two companions left the clearing, leaving the fallen guards to the forest. There was no time to bury or burn them; Nature would reclaim what was hers.

Far in the distance a horn sounded.

Chapter Thirty-Two

Across the valley the formidable presence of Kolgoth was getting restless. Shamans, draped in their bearskins and adorned with intricately carved wooden masks, chanted incantations that hung like mystical tendrils in the air. Wisps of incense wafted over the warriors, to the annoyance of their mighty steeds, who grunted with discontent. In this ceremonial spectacle the Shamans beseeched the blessings of the Great Father to find a swift journey to the night plains should they fall in battle.

Guldr chewed on a leaf, thought to give courage and dull pain. Grinding down the fibrous material with his powerful jaws brought a little clarity to his mind. The repetitive motion was almost meditative. He flexed his aching back and shoulders. He knew the rest of his tribe and those of the other tribes amassed would be feeling the same.

'Guardian, are you sure that we hold? We could attack now while they are still organising themselves.' Guldr knew deep down that this was the time to charge, downhill, before the enemy was ready. He fought back the urge.

'Guardian, we are losing the advantage.' This first warrior was a little distraught. Kolgoth's best weapon was the massed charge, and what presented itself here was a gift for victory.

'Hold, as I said. There is a bigger game being played here. Check your armour, axes and harness again.'

Far off to his left, Guldr saw the standard of Golth's tribe: red-dyed deerskin with three white discs representing the body, earth and the night plain. Golth was stoic and deeply connected to the ancestral ways. His adversary paced back and forth along the line of his warriors, taunting Raniel with roars and hoots – an old tradition to instil fear in the enemy. He hoped the brute would hold.

'Sokal.' Guldr called for his nephew. The newly enthroned chieftain was quick to be at his uncle's side. 'I ask a favour.' There was willingness in the young Chief's eyes. 'Go to Golth and stop him from attacking. Do not look for revenge today – that time will come. Prove that you are of chieftain material.'

'Should he fall and break his neck?' Guldr gave a roar of laughter and a wide grin. 'Just make sure he does not charge the Ranielian front lines.' Sokal mounted his boar and headed to where Golth was parading his might.

The order came for the archers to advance. Nearly 500 stepped out of rank, each with a bundle of arrows in their hands. Taking some paces in front of the spears they drove their ammunition into the ground, ready to pick up and loose. Nothing was in range; it was more a show of force and standard Ranielian tactics.

The river was shallow and slow-moving. Tributaries from the Yavel Mountains, filled with meltwater, poured into the Wellspring River. This made the water crystal-clear. Many kings of old had come here to bathe in the transparent waters. There used to be magic here too, but the mage spring had disappeared – the northern lands had taken care of that. Only four mage springs remained in Kalnath; the Citadel, Senal, Zinjal and a small but potent well in Tiala. Overuse and the contamination of dark magic had seen many mage springs evaporate.

Gifted mages could harness magic from the earth, but this took a lot of focus and energy. The site of this battle was not by chance – Talgameth had laid the foundations long before the king's death.

Guldr snapped his head round to the left at the same instant that Golth started his charge 'No! The fool!' Guldr raged. 'He's going to get himself killed.' With nostrils flaring and gritting his teeth, he sat and watched the chieftain thunder down the slope towards the right side of the Ranielian line. There was fear too as he saw Sokal ride the tide of death along with the rest of Golth's warriors.

'Guardian, should we follow?'

Rounding on the questioning Kolgothian, Guldr said, 'I say again – we hold!' This made it difficult. He knew he should follow. Many good warriors were going to die out there. He also noticed the other chieftains getting their blood up.

'HOLD!' he shouted. 'Or by the ancestors, I'll cut you down myself.'

Raniel held its breath, the valiant soldiers who were positioned on the right flank sensed an ominous tremor coursing through the ground. Fear coiled around their hearts and sweat beaded on their brows. Tightening their grips with white knuckles around their weapons. Archers had their fingers poised upon tightly drawn bowstrings ready for the call to unleash on their foe.

The Kolgothian charge was almost at the river. At this pace they would run right through the line. Baring his teeth, Golth roared along with the rest of his warriors. A noise as if the very ground would crack asunder pounded in rhythm with his heart. Sokal was within the charge. He had failed in his task to stop the charge, but overwhelmed by bloodlust he had been compelled to set his war boar downhill.

Taking one of his axes out from his belt, Golth swung frantically, rising and standing on his saddle and keeping a tight hold of the reins. He was ready for the killing that would ensue.

A horn blew and before the note had stopped, nearly 500 arrows were launched at the oncoming mass. The sky darkened above the charging Kolgothians. Many riders were knocked off their mounts, but the boars kept charging. In the water now, splashing up a frothy haze, their speed was relentless. The archers managed to get off another two volleys before retreating to the back of the lines, running for their lives between the spears and dropping their weapons.

The front two lines of infantry dug their spears into the ground and held them braced against their feet. The first row was aimed at the boars and the second at the riders. Other rows were there to impale the attackers as they flung themselves from their mounts.

Witnessing the first contact, Maleth felt his stomach turn. Giving himself a little spell of Yamen's healing, he kept the nausea at bay. Even at this distance, he could hear the clash and roar, screams and cries of both

Ranielian and Kolgothian. Looking back up to the ridge, he noticed that the other Kolgothians were not moving. *Why wait?* he thought. *This first group will be slaughtered, outnumbered, and the attack will not gain any advantage.*

From the back of his detachment, Maleth scanned the lines for anything that he could recognise of Marin's group. Surely, he would be able to spot Jack. A soldier broke rank and made a bolt for freedom … and life. As she went past Maleth, he grabbed her to force her back in line. With her tunic gripped fast by the mage, she struggled and writhed to break free. Their eyes met. Primal fear was etched on her face. He held her for the most fleeting moment, then let her go. *Who am I to seal her fate?* he thought. Given the circumstances, he would have run himself if it were not for the memory of his friends and the need to protect them.

He bathed the running soldier in an incantation of swift speed. 'May you lead your best life away from the suffering of battle,' he whispered.

Looking back at the ongoing clash, he noticed that the mages had set off a few war spells. Soldiers bathed in a blue haze now had extra strength to protect them against the heavy blows of the Kol warriors. He also witnessed some boars ablaze, which was causing havoc within the offensive. But those were big spells – the mages were soon drained and had nothing to protect themselves.

Chaos engulfed the army. Sergeants screamed at soldiers to hold the lines. The ensuing stampede split units and made it difficult for the captains to keep order.

Back up on the ridge, the other tribes could only look on as Golth's charge was swamped by the sheer numbers of Ranielian soldiers.

'Guardian, we must attack! There is no sign of this fabled army from the north. Your kin are falling and you do nothing about it. Lead the charge like you are supposed to do. You are Guardian, are you not? Call the charge!'

'NO!' Using all his restraint not to silence the tribal leader for good, Guldr looked him straight in the eye. 'I follow the Great Father. Golth charged against my orders. It is he who is allowing his warriors to die.' With a snarl of rage, the tribal leader rode off to his place in the line.

Those next to Guldr could sense his anger and tension. His sheer size and the wrath building within him made the Guardian a formidable sight. Moments later the Kolgothian line broke and the remaining warriors charged down the long slope. It was too much to ask of them to watch the butchery inflicted on their own kind.

On seeing the mutiny, Guldr's roar was deafening. He had lost control. Only a handful of loyal warriors waited with him.

'Guardian, we are with you.' The voice was near but sounded distant. The remaining warriors heard it too. They looked about to see who the speaker was, but there were only whispers of wind and dust.

The rest of the Ranielian Army saw the second charge. More soldiers decided to choose life over honour and ran for home. Marin was still within his lines. Seeing and feeling the imminent attack, he steeled himself: 'This is it! C'mon.'

A wave of fear washed over those who could see what was coming. Jeers and shouts were heard to boost their own courage. Their captain had left them and some of their comrades had also legged it. Few officers were left to organise the line. Horns blew, but no one took any notice. All eyes were to the front, on the wall of boar tusks stampeding towards them. It was too late to run away.

Bracing themselves for the impact, those around Marin clenched their spears and prayed for protection. The crash was thunderous. Spears broke like twigs and the cries of men were silenced. Kol warriors landed among the soldiers and began to hack and slash wildly through the lines. Some wielded two quick and deadly hand axes. Catching on shields, the warriors used one to pull shields down, while the other sank into the exposed necks of the soldiers. Other Kols had large double-handed war axes. Great sweeping arcs of ferocious power did not discriminate between shield, armour or cloth. Like a scythe reaping crops, soldiers were cut down in quick succession.

Marin survived the initial impact, jostled out of the way by the sheer number of soldiers. He found himself with free space. Two boars lay in front of him with snapped spears puncturing their necks. The one closest blinked and Marin gave a jump. Pointing his spear towards the boar, he made damned sure that it wasn't going to get back up. About to drive the tip through its tough fur-covered skin, a huge Kol warrior rose. Stained in dirt and blood covering his face, the brute made Marin his quarry. Marin swallowed hard. The Kolgothian picked up the haft of his axe. Marin thought of the old guard's description: *This bastard ain't green, but he is big and angry-looking.* The battle raged all around them, all Marin could see was the huge beast bearing down on him.

Backing away and holding his spear out in front, Marin used all his focus and courage to not run away. 'C'mon then, ya big–' He was cut off as the big Kol launched himself at Marin. Landing a couple of feet away. Marin could see that his spear was no match for this seven-foot-tall, trained warrior. The enraged Kolgothian ran at him.

Marin closed his eyes and thrust forward with his spear. There was a squelch, then some resistance. Waiting for the killing blow, he thought to himself, *I'm not dead.* Opening one eye, he saw the warrior standing looking at his leg. Marin had managed to skewer the big fella's leg. Both were in shock as they both thought of different outcomes. Looking up, Marin saw his opponent's fury intensify. With an ear-splitting roar directed at the Ranielian still holding the shaft of the spear, the Kol smashed the spear shaft away with a hefty swing of his axe, leaving the tip and a portion of wood imbedded in his leg.

Cowering, Marin waited again for death – there was nothing he could do. All his training was worthless. He had no weapons left, bar a small dagger on his belt. If he tried to gut his attacker with that it would probably piss him off even more. Two strides and the huge warrior would be on top of him and tear his head off. His final moments would be spent hunched up in a ball, covered in shit and blood.

Grabbing his axe in both hands, the brute brought his weapon high above his head in a triumphant show of power, before using all the strength in his upper body to bring it down on Marin's chest. Once again, death knocked on Marin's door. Paralysed with fear, he was unable to close his eyes. And just as well, for he witnessed the axe head stop inches from his chest plate.

'You may want to get up. I can't hold him for ever.' The voice was calm and recognisable. Marin, looking round, still in a state of fear and confusion, saw his friend.

'Maleth!'

'Get up and run!' implored Maleth.

'Maleth.' Tears now started to well up.

'Yes. Now – run!'

'Maleth, you're here.'

'Holy shit, Marin! MOVE!' Coming to his senses. Marin could see that Maleth was holding back his attacker. Scrabbling up out of the mud, he ran to where Maleth was standing. Hands outstretched; an azure haze surrounded his eyes. Words passed the mage's lips that Marin had never heard before. The Kolgothian fell where it was standing as if all of his bones had been removed.

Looking back over his shoulder, Marin still in shock, saw the collapse of the huge warrior. 'I'm glad you got over your phobia of killing, Mal. I was a goner for sure.'

'Oh, I haven't killed him; just put him to sleep using Jessica Feldman's *Goodnight, Incantation*. He should wake up tomorrow feeling refreshed, albeit with a sore leg.'

'What? I'm going over to kill the big bastard.' Marin looked around for a weapon.

'No! He's not the enemy. And it's not very heroic to kill a sleeping adversary.'

'Bugger heroic! He tried to kill me.' There was more to the scene that Marin couldn't understand. 'Wait a minute! Why aren't the rest of them attacking us? Not that I'm complaining.'

'They can't see us,' Maleth said casually. 'Look, we don't have time. We need to get out of here.'

The bodies of both Kolgoth and Raniel impeded the slow progress of the Wellspring River, with no distinction made of friend or foe. The glacier-clear water was sullied with gore and churned-up silt. Lips were pulled back over bloodstained teeth and eyes gazed up into the evening sky. The fallen warriors on both sides lay tranquil. The shroud of dusk enveloped what was left of the sun's rays. Illuminating the early night sky, the stars were beginning to parade their beauty; small constellations shining and unfaltering.

Wisps of mist formed slowly above the river and showed the night's intention. A coolness descended. For those that had seen their last day, it mattered not. For the unfortunate souls who had endured the horror of battle only to be wounded and left on the field, the night would bring a chill. Scared, alone and in pain, the shivering would start. Crying out for parents and loved ones would not warm their bones. Kolgothians offering blessings to the Great Father were intermingled with the Ranielians' quest for divine help. In amongst the rites and sanctifications were questions and shouts of a less than holy nature.

Unabated the battle squeezed and stretched, turned and fell in on itself; a fluid form of steel, leather and flesh. Those in the centre had no room to swing a weapon, but punched, kicked and pushed their opponents. Every now and again, a soldier or warrior would fall in the blood-soaked mud. The space created was quickly swallowed up by the loser being trodden into the ground, then the macabre dance continued. All regimental cohesion had been lost. The melee was now a living soul with a will of its own. The fiercest fighting was around the edges, where space to swing and air to breathe was in abundance. Roars and screams alike could be heard for miles around.

In the dying light of the evening Golth was ferocious in his fever for battle, hacking and kicking, using his weapons with murderous results. Panting heavily, his chest expanded to show off his huge frame. Blood haemorrhaged from a deep wound on his arm and shone like silk in the little light that was left. He carried two war axes, now chipped and bloodied, but still razor-sharp. Banging the two hafts together, taunting the nearest foe. 'Your kind do not deserve life.'

A Ranielian soldier was knocked into Golth's path. Without hesitation he grabbed the soldier's head, snapped it back and drew an axe across his neck. There was pleasure in the chief's eyes; a lust for the kill driven from within and almost out of control.

Golth's barbarism gave one courageous soldier no reason to question her actions. Squatting and keeping her adversary in sight, she picked up the wood and steel protection of a shield, fed her hand through the leather thong and gripped the handle. Raising it to below eye height, she braced herself for a charge. On cue, Golth ran at her and in long powerful strides, he was on her, bashing with full force into her newly acquired shield. She tumbled onto the ground, falling hard, almost taking the wind out of her lungs. Taking a huge swing with one of his axes, Golth brought the weapon down onto her shield. Pain coursed through her arm and shoulder. The blow nearly split the shield in two. The Ranielian soldier let out a scream. Drawing back for another strike, Golth raised himself up to his full height. Seeing the weakness in his prey, he dropped his axes and pulled the shield away. She heard a dull thud then a crack, as her arm fractured, sending more excruciating pain through her body. Flinging the shield to one side, the big warrior gave a sneer.

'C'mon then, you murderous bastard!' she called out defiantly against the inevitable. Golth picked her up by her chest guard with a meaty hand and pulled her close. Feeling his hot breath and smelling the foul bloody stench almost made her retch, fear overpowering her ability to defend herself. She cried out and Golth laughed.

His merriment was short-lived as he was charged from the side. The soldier was flung a short distance to land on the bodies of some dead Kolgothians. Clearing the glassy beads of tears from her face she witnessed another warrior standing over Golth.

'Get up, you traitorous sack of shit!' Anger was clear in the newcomer's voice. There was a groan from the prostrate tribal chief. 'We have a score to settle.'

'Ah, the guardian's newest little pup. I thought you would be too much of a coward to join the fight.' Golth gave a cough and spat some blood. Getting to his feet, he was clearly the more powerful of the two. 'They should have cut you deeper, whelp.'

'That was their mistake. Yours was charging. You were told to hold the line,' said Sokal

'Hold the line or not, this day will end in darkness. Talgameth will bless me with life ever living. Until then we may as well have our fill of battle. We are here now, little cub. Are you going to take me back to that human-lover of a guardian?'

Sokal growled and bared his teeth in rage. 'You follow that foul master? Then you are not leaving this field.'

'Oh! A kin-killer. There will be no place among the forefathers for the likes of you. This will be your last lesson and this time you'll get gutted properly.' Golth hurled himself at Sokal, the two meeting in a flurry of blows; two colossal warriors trading punches. Golth soon got the better of Sokal with an elbow to the jaw. Knocked out and lying on the muddy ground with the victor standing over him. Dropping and kneeling on Sokal's chest, pushing his weight down, almost cracking ribs, the tribal chief delivered his lesson.

'Who do you think you are to challenge me? You see *your* mistake, boar-fodder? I am too strong for you and your pathetic uncle. I will lead the great tribes against the Ranielians. I, Golth, will become Guardian and your bloodline will be no more.'

Grabbing Sokal's hair in one hand, he pulled his head up out of the mud. With his other hand, fist clenched, he delivered a punch that cracked the unconscious Sokal's cheek, then another, and another. Witnessing the fight, the Ranielian soldier could see his pleasure, his triumph in beating an opponent.

Dropping the limp body back into the mud,

Turning to his first prey with a grin, 'Well, Ranielian runt, your turn!' Golth moved to where she was lying, breathing hard and quivering in the mud. This made Golth grin all the more, as he placed his big hands on either side of her head and stared at her face, which looked small in comparison. 'You are right to be fearful – not for yourself, but for those who will survive this night. Talgameth comes!'

A look of surprise came over Golth's face, as he remained motionless, paralysed, with his maw open and eyes wide. Blood trickled from his stained teeth. He fell onto his side. The Ranielian then saw the axe imbedded in the back of his neck. Before her, with a bloodied face, Sokal stood panting.

'Are you hurt?' She was completely surprised by the question, so sure that she was going to die. A raft of emotions swirled round her head like a hurricane. Overwhelmed by pain, she blacked out.

Waking only moments later, she saw the pale blueish skin of, for want of a better word, her *saviour*. 'Just kill me. I have no fight left.'

'If there was a need for that, I would have let that sack of shit to do it.' Sokal gave a nod to the body of his adversary.

'I don't understand,' she said.

'Nor did he, until I put an axe in his neck.' He gave a sigh. 'Can you move?'

'What? Why? I ... I think I can.' Her apparent puzzlement was not lost on Sokal.

'The battle still rages. You must get out of it if you want to survive. We are not enemies. But there is no time to explain and we are both targets if we stay here.' Picking her up onto her feet, he gave a smile through his broken jaw and swollen lips. 'Let's get to the other side of the river.'

Soldiers and warriors, though dwindling in number, were still fighting for survival: the stoic Ranielians calling out to the honour of the Queen; Kolgothians fighting for the protection of their homeland; both values driving each race to push back their enemy's advances.

Boars were causing havoc, goring anything that stood in their way. All around, the wounded cried out. A sickly smell rose from open wounds. Soon the flies would move in to banquet on the spoils of war. Thousands lay dead on both sides, and darkness shrouded the land. The ford over the Wellspring River would be a place of sorrow for evermore.

The night would be long and the coming of the light would show the true brutality of what had come to pass.

Chapter Thirty-Three

Dawn broke, the fledgling light bringing a golden hue to the grass. No lamenting birdsong in the eerie silence, not even the wind challenged the mood that hung over the plateau. Malice permeated the very fabric of life. The army stood motionless and quiet as if playing pieces on a game board, the dice ready to be rolled: rows of unkempt figures with various weapons, the most prominent a curved rusty blade with added copper shards, designed to tear at flesh and armour.

Dark were their coverings: black armour and furs. Some wore skullcaps, others helms adorned with spikes. The lost and the damned of Kalnath civilisation, banished from their homelands, now found and given purpose by Talgameth.

Revenge and destruction were all that these forgotten people knew. Incantations kept them under control and ready. Ten thousand souls called to the slaughter without a hint of remorse. The Dark Lord's plan was all but complete, the final act something that he had been planning for over a thousand years when entombed by the self-titled protectors of Kalnath. He cared not for the living; they were cattle, tools, playthings. He was ever-living and he would have dominion over these lands and wipe the great tribes and empires from memory.

The Emerald Knight would be the catalyst to their end. He would then turn east and Senal, Rogane and Tiala would fall.

Wearing a cloak of cloth so fine it moved like smoke on a still night, Talgameth surveyed the battlefield. From a ridge to the north, he witnessed the dying encounters between Kolgoth and Raniel. Small clashes of combat continued, although many from both forces lay on the riverbanks, still and lifeless.

'Good.' His voice deep and powerful, Talgameth summoned one of his acolytes.

Trembling, the robed female figure dropped to one knee. 'Master?'

'Send forth the army.' Within a few minutes, the first ranks began to lurch forward. Once close to their target, spells would be broken and they would be let loose on the battle-weary soldiers and warriors.

He gave his only order: 'Take what you want for your own needs and leave none alive. With their fighters gone, the cities will be easy pickings.'

Like dogs released from captivity, Talgameth's overseers mounted up and headed into the fray.

Some way off, The Queen lay on the cold ground. Hungry, scared and alone, she despaired at what was happening. Allowing herself to wallow in self-pity did not bring any comfort.

'Ah, it seems that slumber has released you,' Freya loomed over her charge and grasped the Queen's arm revealing De'sal's bracelet. 'You won't be needing this little trinket.' Nimbly Freya removed the talisman that was protecting the Queen from any magical influence and tossed it aside like common trash.

'I don't understand.'

'All will be clear soon,' Freya replied.

'What did I do, Freya? Did I cross you without knowing, or insult you?'

'You think this is about *you*?' Shaking her head and smiling in an almost patronising way, Freya continued. 'You are but a pawn; something that is necessary for my master's plan. I only did my duty, to fulfil his wishes.'

Searching her memories for signs, the Queen asked, 'How long have you been like this?'

'You say it like I'm ill, but I have never felt so free. For too long have I been at the heel of so-called betters, daring to display my powers.' Focusing on her hand, an aura of amber mist enveloped her eyes. Slowly a ball of flame began to swirl in Freya's palm. Turning it and manipulating the shape, it danced to her will. 'This is but a trick, requiring no more effort than putting on a pair of stockings.'

Kneeling in close. 'See how it's made of pure heat? No fuel. This little thing could melt your armour so that it would be as if it had never existed.

That said, there would be nothing left of you either now that you no longer carry that Tialan charm.' The Queen shied away. 'Ah, you show fear. Is that of this little ball of flame or of me, the one who holds it? Strong is the arm that wields the weapon.' She brought the flame closer to the Queen's face, singeing her hair.

'Please stop. I'll give you what you want.' Closing her eyes to blank out the heat given off by Freya's fiery ball.

'My master has a weapon of such power, but only he has the strength to use it. However, you are the key. *You* will bring about the end of Raniel and that savage beast of a race. I will then walk amongst my master's spoils, feared and powerful.' Freya's hand was now a mere inch from the Queen's face. Her cheek began to scorch and she let out a chilling scream. Smoke appeared, as the smell of burnt flesh filled both of their nostrils. Freya inhaled with pleasure as if smelling a rose freshly in bloom.

'Enough!' Another acolyte intervened and Freya pulled away. Dousing her flame, she turned: 'My apologies.'

'We have been summoned. Pick her up.' There was no light or feeling in the acolyte's tone. All hope faded from the Queen. Tied and bound, she was dragged to meet the Great Lord of Zinjal; a character from a tale she had been told as a child; a fable now made real.

'Don't cry,' Freya said. 'This is what you were born for. The pain of watching all the people you know die, because of you, will be far worse than that little burn on your cheek.'

Despite putting up some resistance, being dragged, stumbling and falling had taken its toll on the Queen. By the time she was brought into the chilling presence of Talgameth her spirit was broken. In the presence of the Dark Lord, her heart rate increased and she found herself holding her breath. In front of her was a tall, imposing figure, slim with smooth, tanned skin, his hair tied in braids with jewel-encrusted clasps. No armour or weapons were visible. His open cloak revealed a muscular body covered in small tattooed writing. She felt the energy emanating from him. More afraid than before, a feeling of claustrophobia took hold of her. She sensed it growing, her chest becoming tighter.

'I can't breathe.' Gasping, she clawed at her armour. Panic overwhelmed her. Talgameth raised his hand and it was as if she was breathing for the first time.

'I need you well enough for what is to come.' His voice was both in her head and surrounding her. 'The king's bloodline stops here with a scared little girl.' Still shaking with fear, she did not respond. 'You will bear witness to my ascension. I will be lord over these lands and have my revenge on Kalnath.' With unnatural speed, the Supreme Dark Mage was suddenly in front of the Queen, staring directly at her.

'You have something I have needed your whole life.' Grabbing her jaw and forcing her mouth open he snarled at her with utter contempt and pushed her to the ground.

'Bring me the artefact!'

A wooden box with iron braces was placed at his feet. Freya and Imrod looked on in awe: the size of the box seemed at odds with how the acolytes carried it. As it thumped onto the ground, those around witnessed that the grass began to wither and turn black. Like finding a light in the darkness, Talgameth caressed the box.

'Look out there. Witness your pitiful war.' She was dragged once again, this time to stand beside Talgameth. What she saw caused more tears to flow from her crimson, fearful eyes.

'What have I done?' she asked softly, with the sudden realisation that her own need for revenge had brought the army west.

'Child, it was not you! It was *I* who orchestrated this: *I* manipulated your father and the tribes of Kolgoth to fight; it was *I* who divided Kalnath and brought you here. However, it is *you,* who will destroy all that you see.'

Opening the box, he removed an item wrapped in animal skin. The wrappings had writing and symbols similar to those emblazoned on Talgameth's skin. He handled the artefact as if it were his most prized item, then the Dark Lord held aloft the Emerald Knight, turning it over and letting the soft light infuse the precious stone.

'Now is the time for Zinjal to rule Kalnath. There is no one who can stop me.' Freya gazed, awestruck, along with the other acolytes, at the majesty of their master. Truly he had returned and would now reign over the lands.

'Daughter of kings,' he turned to the Queen, 'now comes your part. With the blood of kings do gates open wide.' Recoiling, the frightened young Queen backed into Freya's arms. Held fast by her once friend, she could not move.

Producing an ornate blade with several snake-like curves, Talgameth recited an ancient text from the depths of antiquity. Grabbing her arm, he stretched it out to reveal the soft unblemished brown forearm. Trying with all her might to pull away, her fate was sealed.

As he ran the blade along the length of her lower arm, the Queen cried out in agony. The viscous dark-crimson fluid bubbled out of the deep wound. Holding the artefact underneath, Talgameth let the Queen's blood pour around the coarsely carved jewel, all the while mumbling invocations. Freya watched wide-eyed with anticipation. Some acolytes shied away, nervous of the unknown.

'Behold! Unto the world, I bring darkness. To the realms of death and decay, I set a task. Obey my command and come forth.' A violent wind picked up on the outcrop. Many could not stand. Freya did her best, but succumbed and dropped down grabbing on to what she could to save herself.

Talgameth was surrounded by a vortex of dust and small pieces of vegetation. A glow emanated from the Emerald Knight, softly at first, then grew in intensity. Freya, now shielding her eyes from the wind and debris, saw her master bathed in the ethereal light that came from the artefact. A dozen shades joined the turmoil, protecting their master. Screams and shrill screeches filled the air, along with the roar of the wind. The light, so bright now that none could look, swallowed the form of Talgameth. The Queen, bleeding and in immense pain, took the opportunity to crawl a short distance away while the lord of Zinjal was preoccupied. Not knowing where she was or who could help; what she did know was that it wasn't going to get any better staying where she was. Grasping with her good arm at roots and stones, wincing at every movement, she edged behind a boulder for the scant safety it brought.

A change in the wind was felt. All over the battlefield the breeze picked up, initially drawing broken shrubs and ripped cloth northwards. Moments later, a gale forced survivors to hold on to the dead for purchase. Guldr saw the flags snap and strain under the pressure. Standard poles bent. Horses tried to run but went nowhere. Boars dug in with their hooves, bracing themselves against the intense wind.

'Guardian!' One of his loyal tribal chiefs ran to his side. 'To the north!' He pointed to rows and rows of dark-clad warriors. A sickness came over the Great Chief.

'It is as I said, but none would listen. So many warriors have died and now the enemy appears.' Adrift for a moment, Guldr looked bewildered, caught among past, present and future, like a lost child, unable to cry out.

'Guardian!' with a ferocious roar, the chief woke Guldr from his paralysed state.

Getting into his saddle, Guldr addressed those who had stayed – almost 500. 'You see now the threat. Your loyalty will be renowned in the halls of your forebears. It was my honour to have been Guardian.' Lowering his great axe, he pointed at the northern army. 'We shall meet again in the company of the Great Father. Charge!'

Outnumbered tenfold, the last of the Kolgoth war host thundered towards the river.

Maleth wrestled with his cloak as the strong wind caused it to envelope his face and held on to the branch of a low shrub. Marin was tucked behind a boulder. It gave little shelter, but it kept him from being swept away in the wind. The bodies of the dead also started to move in the strong gale, which pushed everything towards the northern outcrop.

'It's hard to breathe in this wind.' Marin had to shout over the howling wind. 'What's going on? Did one of your pals get a little exited and set off some unholy storm?'

Struggling not only with the wind but also his free spirit of a cloak, Maleth returned to Marin. 'No! There is no one here with that much power. This is not our doing.'

'So?' Marin looked fearful and confused. 'Someone else has the power then!'

'There is unimaginable magic out there. The Citadel and the Brovan Order have spent that last thousand years collecting everything they could, to keep such spells and tomes out of the hands of common folk. There is much yet still to find. I have only been privy to a small part of the library.'

'Can you not stop this wind and make those big Kolgothian bastards drop dead?'

'I will not use magic to kill. And no, I don't have anything to stop this wind.'

'Shit! Well, what *do* you have to get us out of this?'

'I have Asher's protective bubble.' Maleth had studied many spells at the Citadel, mostly for protection and healing.

'Is that it?'

'It's better than a kick in the dick and it saved your arse from being smashed by that Kol warrior. I only had a short time to study it. Under other circumstances, I would have stayed in the Citadel and read for the rest of my days.'

'Our days might be coming to an end if you don't give some fiery nastiness towards those beasts charging down the hill.' He pointed in the direction of the remaining Kolgothian war band.

Maleth saw the mob thundering towards the river. 'We need not worry about them.'

'You've been at the herbs, Mal. That lot will run right through us and your fairy bubble ain't going to stop 'em.'

'No, look.' Maleth pointed northwards. In the distance they saw a large force of black-clad soldiers, their spears, shields and swords glinting in the morning sun. 'Hal was right.' Maleth's voice betrayed his worry, which caused Marin to brace himself against the thought of another army joining the fray. They watched as the Kol war charge turned and faced the approaching force from the north.

'Bugger this! Let's get out of here.' Marin's survival technique kicked in and made running and hiding the best option.

'We need to help them,' said Maleth.

'What? You are kidding! They've been raiding and burning villages all up and down the border. They killed King Thomas and I'm pretty sure they killed more than a few soldiers last night in the battle.'

'Don't you see? That was a ruse. Dark mages have been pulling strings in the Royal Court and, most likely, in the lands of Kolgoth. I don't know why that last lot of Kolgothians didn't charge with the rest, but they're heading for the newcomers and not for the remnants of the Ranielian Army. C'mon. We need to rally the survivors and attack that new menace.'

'Wait, Mal. We've just fought a major battle with those ugly child-killers. What makes you think our soldiers – who, I might add, have just seen their friends gored open by boars or hacked to bits by axes – will fight alongside them?'

'You do know that's all crap about baby-snatching and raiding villages? They love, laugh, dream and are civilised in their own fashion. The stories have been made up to make you hate them – and to bring almost 12,000

Ranielians here, I'd have to say they damn well worked. If we don't help, then we are all lost because, if I'm not mistaken, that's Talgameth's army.'

'Piss off!' Marin gave a snort of derision. 'He doesn't exist.'

'I'm afraid so. He is very real and he's come back. He was one of the most powerful mages before the Great Disaster, but he was buried, undead, for nearly a thousand years. I've read a few accounts of sightings and the Citadel has known about his cult for many centuries. We have to help if we want to survive.'

'That may have been the lot that raided the camps then. Shit, shit, shit! And double shit!' Marin, clearly frustrated, looked at Maleth. 'You're an arsehole!'

He put out his hand, inviting Maleth to do the same. There was a tacit understanding in the clasp. Readying themselves to face the howling wind and taking one last easy breath, they plunged into the violent gale, their task to gather as many soldiers to stand and fight... again.

Guldr stopped the charge and lined up on the edge of the battlefield facing the oncoming northern army. The intense wind still blew, but it did not seem to slow the forces advancing towards the ford. Slotting into position, the riders followed their Guardian's command. Behind them, small bands of warriors grouped together, heads bowed and ashamed at defying his order. Guldr was large, even for a Kolgothian. What was more intimidating was that he held 500 warriors by a single word, all staring down the black ragtag warriors that Talgameth had fashioned to end the realms of Kalnath. A war drum thumped a slow rhythm. A blood-soaked and beaten Kolgothian knelt in the mud. Guldr turned, as the warrior spoke.

'As the ancestors' witness, I was foolish to follow my lust for battle. Forgive me, Guardian,' the warrior shouted over the wind.

Guldr saw that more survivors were making their way towards him. Many were wounded, but still carried weapons, eager to swing their axes once more. One by one they all knelt. The drum still thudded deep and low.

'You see the enemy in front? This is what I foresaw. This is the doom of our time. Do not ask for forgiveness, for I cannot give it. Forgiveness should be asked of the souls who would survive this day and the families of those lost. Stand again and redeem what you threw away.'

Stopping, he noticed other figures beginning to stand and make their way to the gathered crowd of Kolgothians – Ranielians, in just as poor order as his own warriors. Some warriors turned to see what he was looking at and became agitated, snarling at the arrivals, unsure of their motives. The Ranielians, too, slowed on nearing the assembled Kols.

A lone mage stepped in front, approached and bowed his head to Guldr. With slight unease, Guldr reciprocated the gesture.

'I know little of your culture, but what I see is a warrior of high regard. I also see someone who saw through this delusion of this war between our peoples.' Maleth was taking a gamble – it could all be for naught if the battle started over again. 'In fairness, both sides have lost family and friends, but what we truly face is an ancient evil with the malice and will to destroy us all.'

Taking a pace forward on his boar, Guldr was a spear's length from the mage. 'There is distrust on both sides, yet I was given an insight of what lies before us.'

'Then may we have a truce to fight what will shortly be upon us?' Maleth asked.

A Kolgothian broke from the gathered group, eyes wide and snarling, two hand axes gripped tightly in both hands. 'I call horse shit!'

The figure wore no armour and was covered in blood. Taunting the closest Ranielian soldiers, he licked his lips – the Berserker. Many had witnessed him cause havoc within their ranks. Gripping their own weapons and shields tighter, they feared an onslaught once more.

'Hold your tongue and lower your axes. These are not our enemy. Can you not, see?'

'You are weak, Guardian.' The Kol warrior was provoking Guldr to a challenge. 'This is folly. Kalnath is finished.' He paused and spread his arms wide, showing his huge muscular chest. 'My master Talgameth will see to that.' With these last words, he sprang with unnatural power towards Guldr. Realising what the Berserker had just said, Guldr took up his axe to protect himself against the incoming blow. Those around him did not have time to react. All they could do was to watch the attack.

The warrior's axe was a hair's breadth from Guldr's skull when the assault stopped abruptly and the Berserker's body was slammed into the mud. Maleth moved forward slowly, hand outstretched, a haze of white mist surrounding his eyes.

'Your master will fall today,' he said to the prostrate Berserker.

Suddenly aware of what had just happened, Guldr dismounted and pulled the warrior up by the hair, and driving his axe in enemy's neck before dropping the limp body into the mud. 'I see now what tainted your heart. May you never reach the night plain.'

He moved to where Maleth stood and towered over him. Putting out his hand, he offered it to the mage. 'You saved my life.' With his other hand he removed a braid ring. 'With this braid ring, I offer a debt.'

Shaking Guldr's huge hand, Maleth replied, 'You may have saved us all. There is no debt to honour.'

'Well met, mage. I am Guldr, Guardian of Kolgoth.'

'I am Maleth ... just Maleth.' They smiled. However short-lived, a connection had been made.

Getting back up onto his mount and falling back in line, Guldr ordered the drum to beat faster and the line advanced, as Kolgoth and Raniel rallied together to face Talgameth's army.

Chapter Thirty-Four

The tempestuous wind encircled Talgameth, drawing shattered branches and dust in a vortex around him. Suddenly as if a cosmic breath had been withheld, the gale abruptly ceased, leaving behind an eerie stillness that muted the senses. Silence enveloped the battle field, fighters deaf but for their own thunderous heartbeats.

Talgameth was still shrouded in intense light. Shades, swirling and cavorting, gave glimpses of evil intent. Arcs of energy could be seen building from the ground to the tips of the grass, super-heating the air with a hissing crackle, lustrous and emerald in colour. Freya felt them on her skin in waves. Greater now, the noise became louder and the arcs more numerous, before they sizzled out of existence. An acolyte stood defiant against the powerful show. Feeling the power, the acolyte grinned. 'I have the energy inside me. This will be the gift that our master bestows upon me.'

The same flashes of energy started jumping between the metal clasps and pins on his cloak. 'Yes!' he shouted. More energy was directed at him. Freya wanted to turn and run, but something held her. Almost paralysed and struggling to take an in-breath, she noticed the same sparks of energy form on her armour.

An explosion erupted skyward from Talgameth. A beam of intense emerald-green light illuminated the clouds. So bright was the column that it contested the very sun for ownership of the day. A hum, deep and vibrating, grew. Pulsing energy flowed into the heavens. The uppermost portion began to boil over and infect the clouds with its ethereal green glow.

The shaft of light could be seen for miles around. Those on the field of battle stopped their advance to witness this new phenomenon. Talgameth's army took this as the sign to charge. As one, the mass of followers screamed out their battle cries and the overseers cracked their whips. The remaining warriors of Kolgoth and soldiers of Raniel met their cries with their own cacophony. The meeting of the two armies came in a bloody crash: one side fighting for survival; the other to eradicate them from Kalnath.

Further away, towns and cities saw the pillar of ominous light and protected themselves with religious rituals, many believing in the gods that they had never given fealty to before, asking for protection and forgiveness against the evil that might come. But what they didn't know was that the evil had already arrived. From within the shadows, shades, murderers and acolytes of the dark arts saw their signal and let their perversions loose on the common folk. Only strength and steel could help them now. Prayers were for the dead.

The unfortunate acolyte was all but consumed by the discharging energy. Smoke rose from him. Screams of pain could be heard, harrowing and blood-curdling. With his skin glowing, the figure began to break up and fragment towards Talgameth. 'Master, I have served!' he screamed. In confusion, the acolyte looked at Freya who was cloaked by the same green energy. Many other acolytes were also bathed in green fire, as sparks of arcing emerald energy flowed into Talgameth.

As suddenly as the outburst had reached for the sky, the column imploded. Drawing down power from an unnamed source, all those who were in range of the cataclysmic event were instantly immolated. Freya saw the fear and wonder in the acolytes face the moment he became one with the Emerald Knight. Freya herself did not escape the violence; the parts of her body she could not protect seared and blistered in the ferocious power, which emanated from Talgameth. Her face was scalded. Beauty no longer resided with her. With her hair singed and skin charred, she did her best to fight back the pain. Screaming, she recoiled and noticed the Queen's disappearance. Turning back, all that was left was Talgameth holding the Emerald Knight and a ring of scorched earth where some acolytes had once stood.

Using her own magic to dull the pain, she walked towards her master. 'My Lord Talgameth, I serve you.'

'Good.' He was still bathed in an ethereal green hue that was brighter around his eyes. No pupils could be seen, only an intense light with shades of green mist. As he moved, he left a faint residue which dissipated from view. He held the Emerald Knight in an outstretched hand, revealing that the same glow and residue radiated from the gem.

'The power to command is in my grasp. Long have I waited to wield the power of Zinjal. Kalnath will be devoured by demon kind.' Pausing and staring deeply into the carved eyes of the artefact, Talgameth relished the energy that flowed through him and the Emerald Knight. 'I am master of demons and the ever-living.'

Lifting the artefact high, he slammed it hard into the ground, smashing the gemstone into magic-infused shards. A wave travelled down from the outcrop and covered the battlefield, passing through the battling masses and on to the edge of the river. Freya stared, thinking the surge of energy would kill all those in its path.

Moments later, small dots of light became apparent – the same emerald glow as that of Talgameth.

The Dark Lord gave a grin. 'The door is open.'

Approaching the crest of the western ridge was another force. One that had not intended to be there. Noticing the pillar of light and the subsequent wave of energy washing down over the battlefield, their leader halted the advance.

'It is not for us to wait for the outcome of this day to slowly reach us in our homes. We are warriors too; warrior maidens that will not see our tribes fall to the northern threat. Be strong and fierce as the Mother Shaman would have you be. Give no quarter to the evil that would seek to destroy all life. Do not slow nor waver from your course. There is change coming and you too, sisters, will have places in the great halls of our forefathers.'

Helda stood up in her saddle and smashed her axe against her shield. As one, the gathered female Kolgothian warriors did the same, releasing a noise like thunder and a will to unleash the rage behind it.

Preparing to charge, Helda was stopped by the warrior next to her.

'Something stirs on the field. Look!' In the direction shown, Helda witnessed green orbs rising, then the ground itself move, as unnatural evil began to manifest itself in the bodies of the slain. All manner of grotesque-limbed creatures seemed to tear open the fallen warriors and soldiers. Inky black shapes with glowing green eyes sprang forth cavorting and whooping. Some were almost natural in shape with legs and arms in the right place. Others defied natural laws with appendages and bulbous sacks at odds with gravity. Each had one goal: destroy the fighting warriors and soldiers.

'Guldr will be crushed between the northern threat and this new horror,' Helda thought aloud. With a cry she rallied the shield maidens of Kolgoth. 'Charge now for your sons and brothers. Charge now for your husbands and fathers.' She crashed her shield once more and a thousand warrior Queens roared into the valley.

Spurring on the charge, Helda led like a spear tip. Reaching the river, they smashed against a wall of demon kind.

Some of Helda's force wavered and let their hearts control them, unable to comprehend what faced them. They were soon dragged from their boars and killed. Shouting above the din, Helda yelled, 'Do not fear! Let *them* fear your axe!'

Cutting a wedge through the ranks of hideous shapes and forms, the Maidens of Kolgoth turned and set up another charge. The remaining warriors still mounted fell into line, waiting for Helda's order.

'Charge!'

This time they sprang from their boars on impact and began hacking at the demons. Each warrior was as powerful and as skilled as their male counterparts. As each stroke fell on other-worldly tissue a spray of black viscous fluid drenched the warriors and stung their eyes. Wounding did not seem to slow the onslaught, only hacking and bludgeoning their foes stopped the emerald lights in their eyes.

Helda, now dismounted, was delivering blow after blow in expert fashion. One strike high, shield, then one low. Pushing through with her sisters behind they all earned their place in the great halls. 'Shield wall!' she cried, which gave the front line of fighters' space to breathe. This was happening up and down the line: pockets of warriors working together for the safety of each other. The enemy attacked the shields, but the strength of the warriors held them back. This also gave the warrior maidens time to regroup.

She was about to call for the wall to disperse and fight again when she saw a lone warrior. 'Open up to the left. There's a survivor.' She pushed forward with more effort, hacking at flailing limbs. Behind her, others took care of the demons and dispatched them. She recognised a Kolgothian by the tattoo on his face and by the braid ring that hung from his short beard – a young warrior chief carrying Guldr's braid ring.

'Sokal!' she shouted. 'Sokal!' Louder now above the clamour of fighting. The young chief saw his aunt and fell to his knees.

'Helda, why are you here? You should be safe in Fethal.' Sokal was delirious from the wounds he'd sustained. Covered in blood, his leather armour torn, mud had caked his eyes. 'Is this the night plain?' he asked.

'You've taken a few blows to the head,' she said.

'Helda, why have you come here? There is nothing but death.' Looking around all Sokal saw were women clad in bloodstained armour. He gave a smile 'This must truly be the night plain, but why does it hurt so much?'

'Be still. You have suffered much.' She checked his body. 'You're a strong son of a bitch, Sokal. Your Guardian will be proud.'

'I saved a Ranielian. We fought side by side as the Guardian commanded.' His words faded with a groan. Helda looked around but only saw the mutilated bodies of the fallen.

'Sokal! Stay with us.' Helda called for him to be pulled from the field and attended to.

Wiping the tears from her cheek she turned her thoughts to Guldr. Doubting that she would make it to him in time, all she could do was make sure as little of this evil made it in to the main fight.

'Click,' Tep called out telling the rest of the imps to halt and stay low, which was *really* low as they were only a foot tall. The lead imp made slow progress through the tussock-covered ground. With ditches and furrows, the woods were incredibly difficult to navigate for a creature of his stature. Nearing the edge of the tree line, De'sal was to the right of the imps and Hal was further away to the left, almost at the outcrop edge.

They had witnessed the intense light and knew it was too late to stop whatever weapon the Brovan assassin had described. Hal was intent on finding the Queen, praying that she had survived. His goal was to get her back on the throne of Raniel free from the darkness that had shadowed her. Killing Freya would be next on his task list.

Hal dropped his pack and removed some vials he had taken from the assassin. Gripping his shield and going over the plan one more time in his head, he readied himself. In all honesty, he wasn't really sure what the plan was, because he couldn't understand the imps, and they were doing all the talking.

'Just wait for a signal,' De'sal had said. He couldn't see the Queen or Freya. He counted about thirty hooded figures without armour, but all carrying blades. And then there was the star of the show: a thousand-year-old crazy bastard with glowing green eyes.

Checking his bracers and gloves, Hal missed the signal.

'Shit!' he said to himself.

The imps, en masse, emerged at speed from the trees and attacked the acolytes. A ragged bunch of fur, scales and hide carpeted the area, launching into battle with all sorts of weaponry, the most ferocious of which were their teeth. Shreds of cloth flew through the air, some still with flesh entwined.

Talgameth turned towards the distraction with little concern. The Emerald Knight had been used and the forces of Kalnath were almost spent. He knew not where this infiltration had come from, but his acolytes would take care of it.

Hal scrambled to his feet and charged onto the outcrop, running headlong at the nearest opponent. He was not expecting the blow to be so forceful. The two blades met. The wielder was a thin, gangly fellow, weak-looking with sunken eyes. How could such strength come from such a feeble frame? Hal took a split second to adjust his tactics. *This may not be a walk in the park*, he thought.

Removing his cloak, the acolyte showed his emaciated body, skin stretched over bone, with no muscle to talk of. Script tattoos covered his body. Hal could not make out any of the sigils. At any other time, he might have taken an interest. However, all he wanted to do was cut off his opponent's head and move on to the next bastard standing in his way. Side-stepping the acolyte, Hal thrust his sword towards the dark follower's ribs only to be blocked effortlessly. The reply was swift. A huge swing from the acolyte's sword ended with Hal on his knees under his shield.

The blow would have split any old wood and iron, but this was a quality Ranielian shield. Springing up, ready for the next bout of blows, the former general of the Ranielian was eager for more.

'Is that it, toast rack?' There was no emotion from the acolyte, just another vicious blow. Learning an opponent's moves in a short space of time was crucial to any fight, giving him something and luring him in. Hal dropped his sword and the acolyte took the opportunity to attack. This time the swing came from shoulder height and again in a big wide arc. Before the sweep was finished, Hal had managed to close the gap and smashed his shield into the unsuspecting acolyte's face.

Recoiling in dismay the Dark Lord's attendant was clearly in pain. Rolling and grabbing his sword again, Hal then drew his blade across the inside of the acolyte's leg, dropping him to one knee. The next cut was through his neck.

'Right, who's next?'

Talgameth stood engrossed by the view before him. His army, both living and demon kind, swarmed over the battlefield. No one had any hope of surviving such an onslaught. Reciting chants to imbue his followers with strength and speed, the Dark Lord continued to ignore what was playing out behind him. Shades hung ominously around him for protection, waiting and watching.

Guldr could see no end to the mass of black-clad fighters. As soon as he slew an attacker, two more would take their place. They didn't seem to weaken, had no fear in their eyes. He was faltering. All too often now he was taking cuts to his exposed flesh. The stinging bites from steel woke him up slightly to the next threat. Around him he saw his warriors pressing hard against the wall of Talgameth's followers. Some had fallen, but there was no time to mourn. Due honour would be given when the battle was over – *if* the battle ended.

All too visible was Guldr's inability to raise his axes above his head, his arms, heavy and slippery with blood. Underfoot was a mix of mud, stones, bodies and discarded weapons creating treacherous fighting conditions. He had to push on to the outcrop and Talgameth.

At the request of Maleth, Marin had made it to the edge of the fighting again. His task was to make it onto the outcrop and help Hal. Dodging fists, feet and swords, he used his spear to dispatch any of Talgameth's followers who came too close. To fight each one meant a slower ascent and increased odds of getting killed. The ground was getting steeper. The road that Talgameth's army had taken was a fairer route, although filled with murderous acolytes hurling magic. Scrambling on his hands and knees towards the outcrop, the scree slope was giving way and rocks were beginning to roll back down and smash against a couple of forsaken disciples. Unintentionally more rocks and stones fell. This riled the two black-clad followers of Talgameth to give chase. The closer they scurried in their attempt to annihilate those who stood in their way, the more panic set in to Marin's own climb. This gave way to mistakes in placing his feet. Even steeper now, his shield and spear were becoming a hindrance.

'Nowhere to run, Ranielian!' The shout was clear as was the menace behind it. Marin had never before been in such fear of his life. His heart thumped, his skin tingled and a cold sweat made it difficult to grip the dry rock of the slope. Glancing down, they were only a few feet away. In a moment of clarification, Marin took his spear shaft and rammed it behind a loose-looking boulder. With a mighty effort, he dislodged the boulder, which careered down the slope. Unaware of the impending contact, one of Marin's pursuers looked up just as the boulder connected with his face and ejected him off the hillside. Not far from the top, Marin gave an extra burst of energy hoping to make it over the ridge wall before he was caught by the remaining pursuer.

De'sal was no warrior. His role was to wait – well, that's what he'd understood from Tep's plan, his little hand gestures delivered animatedly. Hidden in the cover afforded by the shrubs and grasses on the edge of the tree line, De'sal kept watch. The imps were making short work of the dark followers and the sight made him a little nauseous. Even though he was not involved in the fight, he still held two daggers. The Tialan could just make out Hal ducking and parrying. Then he noticed a movement out of the corner of his eye – just the most fleeting of motions. He fixed his gaze on some boulders, holding his breath, as if breathing would make any difference to something forty feet away. The normally calm and composed diplomat feared what might be stalking him. Blades were all well and good, but if he panicked, any weapon would be near useless in his hands. He swallowed so loudly that in his head he was sure all of Freehold heard him. *There again. A movement,* he thought. Craning for a better view only made him more visible. He had to move.

Staying under cover of the trees, De'sal edged a little further north until he saw what had made him so jumpy. Stepping out from his hiding place and looking to see if all the acolytes were occupied, he ran for the boulder he had been so cautious of. Leaping and throwing himself behind the cover of the boulder, he found himself next to a frightened young woman.

She let out a scream and De'sal had to cover her mouth until she composed herself and quietened down.

'The Queen of Raniel, yes?' De'sal was a little smug.

'Get away from me.' She gave a kick and made to run into the woods. Holding her back, De'sal once again tried to calm her down.

'Shh!' He held a finger to his lips.

'Who are you?'

'Oh, my dear, do you not remember? I am a Tialan emissary. Many months ago, you threw me in jail.'

The Queen was slow to recognise him. 'You attacked Freya. Are you here now to take revenge on me?' Stunned by all that was wrong with her comment, he shook his head.

'Why would I come all the way out here in a war to *take my revenge*? Even now you believe that bitch of a mage, after all that has happened? She played everyone, your highness. You may just have been the last to realise it.' Looking around, he was confident that no one had seen him. 'No, we are here to rescue you, at great personal risk, I might add.'

'*We*?' She looked around.

'My other companions are a little busy.'

'He cut my arm. He needed blood.' Gingerly, she showed De'sal the wound that Talgameth had made. Her arm was covered in blood, some of which had hardened into a maroon scab. Weakened, she'd been trying to stanch the flow but had already lost a lot of blood.

'Ah, yes, you are in a bit of a mess. I am no healer. However, ...' He pulled a vial of dark orange liquid from his pack, popped the stopper and poured it over the wound. It gave a hiss and the Queen let out a scream of pain. 'Shh!' He had not anticipated the potion might cause discomfort. Within a few moments the gash in her arm began to close up and knit together. They were both surprised by the properties of the tiny jar.

'Is he one of your companions?' Looking past De'sal, the Queen saw a robed figure loom at them with a fanatical grin. Turning quickly, De'sal was met with a push to the body that hurled him back into the boulder.

'No!' De'sal managed, despite being winded. The acolyte raised his sword and, in that instant, a colourful volley of green, blue and red pounced on the unsuspecting attacker, as three imps leapt over the rock and buried their claws, teeth and kitchen implements into the chest of the acolyte.

They both sat in horror watching the imps consume their prey.

'Please tell me they're *your* companions,' The Queen hoped.

'Yes, and that is not their most endearing trait.' Gathering his thoughts, De'sal turned to the Queen. 'Right, we have to get you out of here. Hal will deal with Talgameth.'

'Hal? Where is he?'

De'sal peered around the boulder. 'He's currently indisposed, hacking the leg off one of these evil buggers.' He dragged the Queen up and they made for the shelter of the trees.

Chapter Thirty-Five

Guldr had reached the outcrop. The ferocity of his warriors and the tenacity of the Ranielian soldiers had led him to lay eyes on the Dark Lord of Zinjal for the first time. The huge being, shrouded in glowing green mist and dark shapes was truly the stuff of nightmares.

Sensing the Guardian of Kolgoth's arrival, Talgameth turned with soulless eyes and bared his rotten teeth.

The blow to the head came with searing pain, accompanied by a piercing high pitched ringing reverberating around his skull. Time slowed as he loosened the grip on his axe, the weapon slipping from his grasp. Sinking to his knees his gaze met with those of the lifeless and wounded. He saw nothing in colour; all was black and white. Along with the constant high tone were the muffled cries and shouts of the other combatants. He couldn't shake the fuzziness. Other thoughts came into his head: fields of summer grass, waist-high, blowing gently in a warm breeze; blue skies and lavender clouds; birds feeding on the wing in the early evening sun.

Talgameth gave an impassive grunt at the fall of the great Kolgothian by one of his lesser followers, before returning to observing the battle taking place below.

A mailed hand grabbed the back of Guldr's armour and dragged him away from the line of warriors who still had the strength to engage the enemy. The rescuer didn't get very far, only managing to pull him onto his back. 'Somebody, help!' the call went out. With no response. Gritting his teeth, the Ranielian soldier tried again. 'Help!'

All around, both warriors and soldiers were knee-deep in the dead and wounded fighting for their own lives. All Jack could do was defend Guldr as he lay, eyes open, staring up at the sky. What he looked at was not what he saw. Guldr was still in the grasslands, mumbling childhood conversations with his father. Jack himself was bloodied and scarred. He had lost his weapon and some of his armour. He had been using what his father had given him to survive. With his fists and feet, any follower of Talgameth would meet a brutal end. It seemed his strength was unending.

'Maleth!' he shouted through the clamour. 'Maleth! Where are you?'

Maleth had been attending to the wounded and giving much-needed energy boosts to those still in combat. He heard Jack's cries for help.

'Are you hurt?' he asked when he finally found him.

'Don't think so. What are you doing, Mal?' Jack's pleading tone was lost on Maleth.

'What do you mean? I've been helping the wounded.'

'Yeah! Can you not see that we need your help?'

'I am helping. There are hundreds back there in need of attention.' Said Maleth.

'Look, if you burnt half of the bastards that are fighting then you wouldn't have so many injured soldiers! Get it?'

'I'm not going to use battle magic and you know that well enough.'

'Okay then, help with this big fella. I managed to pull him back after getting a smack on the head.'

'That's Guldr, the Guardian.' The two dragged the big chieftain further back. Maleth closed his eyes and chanted a few words. Mist appeared, although this time in a few different colours.

'What's happening?'

'Shh! I need to concentrate.' A miasma of shimmering light enveloped Guldr. 'He is far gone but he should ...' Before Maleth could finish his sentence, Jack was hit by a fireball that catapulted him sideways thirty feet. He lay unmoving. More arcs of flame hit other soldiers and warriors. The line was in disarray. Burning bodies were screaming, running left and right. Maleth froze, as a flashback of the little street girl passed in front of his eyes. In his mind's eye she stopped and spoke to him: *'Help me!'*

'No!' he screamed. Drawing a protective field over the targets of the flames, he gave himself a moment to see where the attack was coming from. He saw a robed figure with red and orange mist surrounding his eyes, one of Talgameth's mages.

'Jack!' His friend lay in the mud with scorched armour still aflame. Torn between helping his friends or facing down the dark mage, Maleth's heart pounded. His rage increased. Anyone could help the injured, but who would face the mage?

Uttering a cry filled with anguish, Maleth rose to his feet. With arms outstretched to the skies, a blue azure haze enveloped his face. A whispered word and the heavens opened transforming into a thunderous rainstorm that pounded down upon the weary burning soldiers.

The mage rounded on him and immediately started firing missiles of ice, fire and magical essence. Maleth conjured a protective shield. The magical projectiles faded as soon as they hit the cloudy wall. A voice resonated within Maleth's mind.

'You are one of Falvor's runts. I trust he is in ill health these days.'

Maleth did not respond, and kept focus on his protective barrier. The dark mage came closer stalking around Maleth, sneering with a malicious grin. No one around could help, all consumed in their own struggle.

The mage threw another bolt of fire at Maleth. 'You are strong, but it will not last. You know that magic is weak in Ranielians and this place has very little natural magic. Indeed, that is why my master chose it.'

Maleth followed the dark mage as he stalked him like a hungry predator. 'I, however.' Another shot. This time a lightning bolt split the sky and earthed itself over Maleth's head. 'You will soon tire. That cute little protection field will start to fade. You will be weak and unable to defend yourself. I could burn you as you grovel, or my master might use your abilities. He could show you the dark ways.'

Maleth glanced at the wounded and noticed Jack getting up. *No*, he thought. *Stay down.*

Talgameth's mage perceived the change of focus. 'Ah, a companion. I see we have met before.' Jack's armour was burnt, the leather still smouldering. Jack's large frame rose to its full height and he gave a wince of pain. His skin was charcoal-black with red and yellow blisters. Some of his fingers were fused together, yet he tried to make a fist. Staggering slowly towards the mage, Jack was intent on brawling.

'No, Jack don't.' He took no notice of Maleth's pleas.

'Strong of will, but simple of mind – a common Ranielian trait.' The mage waited until Jack got a little closer. Holding up his hand, he ordered Jack to stop. Jack could not speak; he only uttered muffled syllables. He was stuck, unable to move. Clearly in pain, his will drove him to fight against the invisible chains that held him.

'Stop!' Maleth shouted. 'Leave him. He's had enough.' The dark mage looked at Maleth and smiled.

'You mean to barter? You intend to give me something in order not to hurt your friend? You misunderstand my role here. I am here to kill you all.' Jack's body began to shudder and move violently, contorting forward then back. His bones were breaking, snapping loudly. There was increased pain in Jack's face, so much so that he threw his head back. Lips that had melted together split apart and a roar of agony burst forth. His body fell to the ground and continued to convulse until stillness overcame him.

An uncontrollable rage washed over Maleth. Letting go of the protective spell, he unleashed a flurry of attacks on the murderous mage, which were easily brushed aside. 'I see that I have touched a nerve,' he said mockingly.

'You will pay.'

'Revenge is a strong emotion. Let's see what you have!' The dark mage's retaliation was to conjure figures out of rock and have them attack Maleth. One managed to knock him to the ground. However, a pulse of ice magic shattered the constructs, making Talgameth's puppet shield his face with his arm, which gave Maleth time to get up and compose himself.

Master Falvor had told him to stay calm under pressure. Setting off too-powerful a spell drained much-needed energy. Holding one hand out towards the dark mage, he focused on heat to burn him. As he did so, he apologised to the little girl from the plaza.

'Is this all you have, boy? Falvor said you were special and I know who you are.' Stopping, Maleth struggled to understand what he had just heard. *He's tricking me*, he thought.

'That got you thinking, boy?'

'What? You're trying to fool me.' Maleth's concentration was wavering.

'Oh, I know about the reading spell,' he grinned. 'And I know that you've read dark manuscripts. Falvor should check that light reaches all the dark areas in the Citadel.'

'No!' Maleth pushed harder with the heat spell, all the while readying another. Quickly a flash of green shot across his eyes and the roots of thorns grew out of the ground to ensnare his opponent, the barbs tearing at his robe and legs. Caught by surprise and unable to fend off the searing heat and the earth magic, the thorns encroached around the dark mage's body. Soon he would have to drop the protection against the fire magic and deal with the barbed stalks nearing his upper body.

Maleth walked slowly towards the struggling mage. The twisting and turning of his hand made the roots tighten around his legs and body. Maleth, with no remorse, waited until the dark mage let his barrier down then consumed him with heat, melting him from the inside.

Maleth stopped. The mage's cries of agony became a whimper. 'You underestimate your opponent. You may be old and of an ancient powerful race. However, you are easy to read and I like reading,' Maleth informed him. Without any showmanship, Maleth used his last magical effort to crush the mage with the briar roots.

Collapsing to the ground he lay, utterly spent. He'd broken his vow to never use magic to hurt anyone again.

Throwing his weapon and shield over the ridge onto the mossy ground, Marin gave thanks to whoever was listening that he'd actually made it. He heaved his body up and lay on the soft, comforting, natural carpet. Gulping a lungful of air that was less than fresh, made him cough. In that short time, he'd forgotten that he was being followed. Realisation hit him like a brick. Scrabbling for his shield and spear, he waited for the acolyte to emerge. He hadn't noticed much of what was happening all over the outcrop, as he'd been focusing intently on the spot where he'd climbed up.

'Clack?' A faint rusty noise came from behind and Marin spun with spear poised to strike any foe ... unless that foe was four feet smaller than him.

'An imp?' His confusion was clear given the lines on his brow. What bemused him more were the pot lids used as armour. He looked up to see a battle raging with hundreds of imps of different shapes, sizes and colours. However, all had the same ferocity. Among them he saw Talgameth and his acolytes. *He has returned*, he thought to himself, paralysed for a second and unable to take his eyes of the harrowing scene.

'Well soldier, don't stand there. Get stuck in!' Unsure where the shout had come from, Marin looked down at the imp with an inquisitive expression. The imp made a bolt past him. Just as his pursuer lurched up onto the outcrop the imp buried its teeth into the acolyte's throat. A short scream and the fight was over. The imp, however, continued to devour its catch with some pleasure.

'Hey! Are you going to help?' Looking round, still in a state of shock, Marin saw an armoured Ranielian being pinned down by what looked like a well-fed skeleton.

'Run him through, man!' The strain and effort were at odds to the bag of bones that lay on top of the man. Marin ran to his aid and thrust his spear into the acolyte's side. Turning its attention to Marin now the emaciated face gave a shrill scream. This gave Hal enough time to puncture its side with a dagger. Reeling, the acolyte sat up.

Marin rushed the figure and smashed his shield against it with all he could muster. Rolling to the side he observed more blood-curdling death given out by the imps as they set about the acolyte he had just knocked over.

'Thanks, friend. The name's Hal.'

'Yeah, it's a pleasure.' Marin was still stunned by what he'd witnessed. 'Sorry, I'm Marin.' They were interrupted by Tep.

'Click!'

'I still don't know what you are saying.' Hal was becoming increasingly frustrated that Tep kept trying to speak to him.

'Clack!' The imp was very animated with his hands and pointing back towards the trees.

'Bugger off if you want. I have to find the Queen.'

'Click, click.'

'Do you think I'm going to understand any better with your mouth full?' Tep spat out a chunk of flesh and shook his head. Jumping up onto Hal's shoulder, the imp pointed once again to the tree line. Noticing now what his little companion was trying to tell him, he saw De'sal run into the trees with a golden-armoured figure. A wave of relief flooded Hal's body. He could not relax though: there was still Talgameth to deal with. And where was Freya?

'Marin, can you go and help my friend?' Hal pointed to the tree line. 'Just make sure nothing happens to them. Keep them out of sight.' Marin nodded, happy to be away from anything to do with the imps.

Guldr rose stiffly and beheld the carnage. Unsure as to what the flashes of multicoloured spirits were, he did know that the darker figures were the acolytes of Talgameth. Blood poured from a wound in his head but his strength had returned. All around him he saw burnt and charred bodies as he stood in the middle of a scorched ring. The mage he had met earlier appeared to be dead. His own warriors were few in number. The Ranielians were also dwindling. Talgameth still stood. Guldr let out a booming roar.

'Face me!' Guldr levelled his axe head at Talgameth. The violent and powerful call woke Maleth. With a groan the mage clambered to Guldr's side.

'Don't fight him alone. He is too powerful. His magic is beyond what we understand.'

'Ahh, you live. Then you do it, mage.' The eagerness for the fight showed within Guldr.

There was no time to discuss the matter further as a couple of acolytes descended on them along, with a shade. The two dark minions leered with intent.

'You deal with that floating shadow, Mage. I'll take these two abominations.' Maleth found deep wells of energy within himself to imbue Guldr with extra strength and stamina. He left a little for himself. He needed to recall a spell that would work on shades. A memory of a forbidden book within the citadel brought an answer along with a raw, primeval pain. Wincing and crying out in agony Maleth stopped and cradled his head.

Guldr set forth and attacked the two acolytes. The big Kolgothian was powerful, but he was struggling to match the strength with which the followers of Talgameth responded. Blocking each swing of his axe it seemed as though they were playing for time. He saw an opening and drove the shaft of his axe into the face of an adversary. Flesh was ripped and bone was broken, but the acolyte shrugged it off and rounded on Guldr with immense force. The block rang and vibrated up his arms and shoulders. With gritted teeth, the Guardian of Kolgoth continued to defend and attack. Every now and then he felt another sting as his guard was dropped. However, for every one he received he gave back tenfold. Slicing through cloth, skin and bone made oozing ribbons of gore on exposed areas, yet they kept coming for more.

Maleth rallied. He mouthed some dark archaic words like venomous whispers. His fingers crackled with a power buried deep inside. Extending both hands and gripping the boundary between two realms, pain lashed at him once again. Struggling against the strain Maleth's power surged as he widened the gap enough to glimpse behind the veil to the unimaginable beyond. With each heart beat his body trembled more, his furrowed brows manifesting the agony, trying to harness the energy. Eyes now tightly closed; a black oily fluid pooled in their corners. The shade dropped low and aimed with intent at Maleth. Unseeing, Maleth knew that the shade was close by its cruel, malicious screams. With intense concentration he pulled his hands apart and tore asunder the opening to engulf the shade. As quick as it opened, it shut. Maleth had no strength to keep it open. His face stained with the black tears and muscles aching with the effort, he focused on Guldr, healing him and protecting the warrior as he battled with the two acolytes.

Putting his morals to one side again, Maleth created a blast of energy that hit one of the acolytes, knocking him off balance just enough for Guldr to make a killing blow.

'About time you showed up, mage,' said Guldr not realising that Maleth had been keeping him alive all this time.

'You're welcome!'

Now they fought together, with Maleth helping when he could and Guldr swinging his huge axe in great arcs at any black-clad follower that came near.

The Dark Lord of Zinjal turned to face the intrusion behind him. He did not expect what he saw; most of his followers were dead or being eaten.

'ENOUGH!' he roared and cast a wave of magical essence across the outcrop, knocking all to the ground. Waiting for the impact, Hal winced, but nothing happened. Darting a confused glance at Tep, then back at Talgameth. He gave a nervous laugh.

'Click.' It was clear that Tep thought something should have happened.

Talgameth drew his sword; an ancient blade imbued with runes. With a gentle movement of his hands the Dark Mage let loose the shades that cavorted around him. With lightning speed, the demon spirits closed the gap on Hal and the imps. The closest imp tried to catch the shade out of the air and was disintegrated for its trouble.

Searching his tunic Hal found a small glass container which he had taken from the assassin. It had 'void' written crookedly upon it. Throwing it towards the spirits with nothing to lose, the small glass vial smashed against the ground, opening up a dark vortex of swirling wind and lightning.

'I hope nothing comes out of that.' Hal gazed transfixed on the hole that had opened up. As the shades passed, three of the four were dragged in shrieking. In quick succession Hal threw the rest of the vials, the remaining shade managed to navigate past them all.

Picking out imps as it passed, the shade drew closer to Hal. Soon, it was on him, whirling round and round, trying to claw at him with spectral talons, burning his skin. The demon was relentless. Hal couldn't cut it or grab it; he was helpless. The shade tore the armour from his body. His skin would be next. Stumbling, trying to defend himself, he edged closer to one of the voids. He didn't know if he would be pulled in, but nothing was going to stop the dark spirit.

Talgameth had closed the gap to Hal. He was now bearing down on the struggling old soldier.

'Click, click!' Like a swarm of bees to a hive under attack, the surviving imps rallied and took on the Dark Mage. Magic had not worked on the imps. However, Talgameth had infused his own body with healing and strength spells. As the first wave of imps made it to him, he cut them like soft butter. For his size, he was agile and deft with the blade. He wanted Hal. The imps were a minor obstacle.

There were a couple of acolytes left. Freya saw the imps were getting the upper hand. Still hiding and reeling from the scalding she had received from the Emerald Knight; she was not about to step out and end up the same way. She had never really taken the time to notice them and was now amazed that magic had no effect on the rodent-like creatures. She also saw Hal in distress. Killing him would be a fine end to her day, shrugging her shoulders as she saw Talgameth grab Hal by the back of the neck and lift him off the ground. She watched the shade separate and find more prey. Witnessing the colour drain and fear take its place across Hal's features. Blowing him a kiss, she turned and ran.

The punch in the back took all the breath away from Hal. He landed, gasping on the scorched earth, his mouth moving like a fish out of water. 'Pathetic race! You are weak, with no power. Only a handful can use magic, and poorly to that end.' Talgameth straightened his robes and rubbed both hands over his head. 'My armies continue to destroy the forces of Raniel and Kolgoth. Your feral little friends are no match for me. I have surpassed life and, thanks to your poor excuse for royalty, I am now one with demon kind.' Hal groaned and coughed up some blood.

'Have a look! All your companions are dead. I have many followers. In every land and in every city, I rule.' Hal rolled over, wheezing at the effort. He mumbled a few words ... and laughed.

'Humour? At the end of all things? Curious. You should be begging for mercy. I can destroy you in so many ways or have you live forever, in pain and servitude.' Hal laughed uncontrollably, only stopping to grab a painful breath and cough up some more blood. This was starting to annoy the Dark Mage. 'Enough of this foolishness!' Hal once again mumbled a sentence.

'What is it you say? These will be your last words.' Talgameth leaned over Hal and grabbed him by the throat. 'What did you say?' In an instant, Hal stopped laughing and opened his eyes to stare at Talgameth.

'Click.' Hal made the sound, although he had no idea what it meant. At the same time, he flashed his blade across Talgameth's stomach. The slash caused the Dark Mage to release his hold on Hal, and as he did so, twenty or so imps got up and attacked Talgameth, biting and clawing into flesh, robe and bone. Some were flung off, but most made their attack count. Vicious and unrelenting, the imps chewed and sliced at anything that was within range.

Still wheezing and coughing, Hal propped himself back up. 'I said that *my* companions are *not* dead, you dusty old bastard!'

Wincing, he noticed a particularly hungry creature go for Talgameth's genitals. The screams did not last long – Tep made sure that this final assault would be the end of the Great Terror, returning him firmly to the nightmares of children and horror stories – never again to threaten Kalnath.

Hal lay back, watching the feast, in awe of the Weelan street pests. He needed to find De'sal and see if the Queen was okay. Getting up, the pain in his chest was excruciating. His armour, dented from the blow, pressed into his spine. 'Tep!'

'Clack?' The little armoured imp made his way to Hal.

'You're a handy little bunch. The realm owes you much. I'll be sure to let the Queen know.'

'Click.'

'I'll take that as thanks. Could you help me off with this armour?' The little blue imp took a claw and cut through the leather straps and the plate fell from Hal's chest and back, providing instant relief. Hal took a deep in-breath. The ensuing cough made Tep wince in sympathy. 'That's better.'

De'sal kept a keen eye out through the foliage.

'How goes the battle?' the Queen asked quietly.

'I cannot see clearly, your highness, and I worry for Hal. He is a good man and I wish I had met him under better circumstances.' De'sal turned to her. 'You have a lot of living to do. When this is over, we will ask, *what* have we done? We then have to choose what path to take. You know the truth of what happened here. Do not let these souls die for nothing.' There was a rustle behind De'sal. Someone now stood a hair's breadth from him. He saw the Queens eyes widen in surprise. A breath on his slender neck and a sweet scent on the air let him know that Freya had found them.

'Profound words. What a surprise. The filthy Tialan with the Queen of Raniel. Be careful, He has a tendency to take advantage of young women.'

With a flash of steel Freya took her blade across De'sal's ear and ripped it clean off. De'sal recoiled in agony.

Laughing at the event. Freya threw the ear at the Queen. 'There, that's what you wanted.'

'You bitch! My ear!' De'sal cried out and clasped the side of his head. Blood seeped through his fingers. He could feel the warm thick liquid on his neck.

Sinking back against the tree sheltering from the monster that had been her friend.

'Freya, no. Please stop this,' said the Queen.

'Why settle for one when you can have two?' Freya grabbed De'sal by the hair and went to cut his other ear, but at that moment, the Queen broke from her frightened shell and pounced on Freya, driving her elbow into the side of her once adviser's cheek. De'sal fell to the ground still reeling from the attack on his ear.

Both women were throwing lacklustre strikes. Neither had trained for this event. Freya had no energy left to attempt a magical attack. Pools of tears welled in the Queen's eyes born of the emotions that trust and friendship had given her. Now gone, like thin parchment on a raging river.

'Why?' she said as she caught her breath. Her heart pounded and her throat closed up to hold back the grief. Her arms were flailing and not really making contact. Freya saw her opportunity. With effort, the mage pushed the Queen off and managed to gulp in some much-needed air. The Queen didn't attempt a second assault, but lay heaving on her hands and knees. Red, water-filled eyes could only make out shapes in front of her. It was too late to defend herself as Freya's knee made contact with her face. A spray of cherry-coloured blood defiled her gold and silver armour.

Standing, gloating over her prize like a wild hunter, Freya managed a few threatening words. 'My master has brought upon this world the doom of all ages. You were a puppet, a tool to be used. Like the crops in the field, you were to be reaped.' Picking up the blade that had taken the ear from De'sal, Freya pondered the situation. 'We had some fun, but I'm not going to weep for the loss.' Her fingers curled tighter around the hilt. Freya moved to plunge the dagger into the Queen's side. However, a sudden crash reverberated through the branches. Wide-eyed she witnessed Marin charging forward with raised shield and a poised spear, making an intimidating sight. Not having the strength to fight off any soldier, Freya released her weapon, letting it fall from her grasp.

'Raniel is dead,' she spat and ran into the forest. Marin arrived beside the incumbent De'sal and the Queen. Panting heavily, he took in the scene.

'Shit, look at your ear!'

'Thank you soldier, what's your name?' asked the Queen.

'I'm Marin, Hal sent me to find De'sal and help protect you.' De'sal was still groaning in pain. 'We should move before any of Talgameth's cronies catch us. Or worse – one of those imps.'

'You need not worry about the imps,' said De'sal. 'You're safe as long as they like you and they're not hungry.'

Chapter Thirty-Six

After the death of Talgameth, the northern followers no longer felt the crack of the whip that had driven them forward. Suddenly, as if waking up, all they could do was defend themselves. For some, the battle was over, for many more the battle was the end. Hundreds ran, dropping all that they did not need. Those who stayed fought on for their own cause to a futile end, their skills no match for the Kolgothian warriors without the additional strength given by Talgameth.

The remaining demons were let loose on the world with no one to control them. Real nightmares now resided in the shadows.

Scanning the field for those that still stood, Helda raised her shield and crashed her axe against it. She waited for a response. Slowly, one by one, the answer came back. She beat it again. This time there was a louder response, along with cheers and shouting. Even the Ranielians joined in, smashing sword and spear against shields. Though thousands lay dead and the wounded needed attending to, those that survived blessed the gods for their luck. Both races greeted each other tentatively.

'Help the wounded!' Helda's voice carried over the cheering. She needed to find someone.

Marin left the cover of the trees with the Queen and De'sal, relieved to no longer see the towering form of Talgameth lording over his army of lost souls and demons.

'I had friends in these battles and they fought for you.' Marin looked at the Queen. 'They died for you, for what you mean. You are Raniel. I was going to run and I heard their voices in my head, calling me back.'

'All will be honoured for their sacrifice,' she said.

'We don't need your thanks; we need our friends.' At this she shamefully hung her head. Marin bowed and continued to walk onto the outcrop.

'Maleth!' he shouted, as he stumbled over bodies. 'Maleth!' There was no response. 'Mal–' His cry was interrupted as he spotted the robes of his friend. He collapsed at the side of the mage.

'Mal! Mal? Can you hear me?' Marin's eyes began to glass over, his throat closing and lip starting to quiver. He picked up Maleth's body and laid him across his knees. 'Mal?' his voice was soft and full of pain. 'Mal, c'mon. Wake up.' He rocked him and held his head. 'Shit, Mal! Don't leave me.'

'Are you crying?' The faint voice of the mage came sweetly to Marin's ears.

'Ha, you're alive!' Getting up, Marin dropped Maleth back onto the ground.

'What happened? How long was I out?'

'I don't know, but I think it's over.' He couldn't stop his tears now. Marin sobbed into his hands as Maleth tried his best to comfort him.

'We survived. By the gods, we survived.'

A figure approached the place where Guldr lay. Placing her hand on him, she stared at the Guardian's body. 'Well, you fool, you did it. You led your people to victory over the unseen threat and you left me to walk the night plain.'

Helda sank to her knees and looked up to the sky. 'To the honour of our people, you were the best of us.' More Kolgothians gathered and knelt beside Helda, bowing and offering blessings to the Guardian. One old warrior placed his hand on Helda's shoulder.

'His journey is not over; it's only changed direction. Take comfort.'

'Thank you for your words.' She turned to see that no one stood behind her, but there was the presence of someone familiar.

Stepping through the gathering crowd of warriors, Maleth tried to get to the front. There was still resentment from many for the events of this day. With warriors looming over him, he stood in front of Guldr.

'Your Guardian has not passed,' he told Helda. Closing his eyes, he focused a healing spell on the fallen warrior. Helda placed her hand on Guldr's chest and felt him breathe. A single tear shone in the late sun. She looked up at the mage.

'Thank you.'

Guldr woke surrounded by warriors. Most confusing for him was Helda's face hovering over him. He moved a hand to his head, where he had been wounded. Sitting up, almost back to full strength, he noticed Maleth.

'I see that you have saved my life once again, mage.'

Guldr requested to be helped up.

'Gathered warriors, you are all an honour to your tribes and forefathers.' He looked down at Maleth. 'That goes for you too. I was given a task that I could not achieve on my own. I needed the faith and loyalty of my kinsmen.'

'And the women!' Helda interjected.

'Yes, and the women. Talgameth divided this land and divided our kin. We know not what has happened to the Dark Lord. What we do know is that we were victorious today.' A loud cheer erupted from the crowd. 'We have lost many and the hurt will last for a generation. But a new day has dawned. Who among you is willing to lead as Guardian?'

There was a stunned silence – no one wanted to fight for guardianship. 'Then I will choose the next Guardian.' Looks of panic shot between warriors: it would be difficult to follow a Kol of such renown.

'Helda.' There was a shocked look on her face. 'With your strength and courage to rally the warrior maidens, to ride into battle for the protection of our way of life, I pass the guardianship to you.'

'But only a tribal leader can claim guardianship after fighting to the death,' she stuttered.

'Things have to change. He took Heaven's Blade from his belt and placed it in Helda's mud-stained hands. 'You now carry the ancestors with you.'

'I am losing my freedom and my love.'

'The rules are yours to change. Do you accept?'

Helda looked around at the weary faces of her kinsmen. Each one bowed their heads. 'Yes.'

An enormous fire crackled. Embers billowed into the night sky. There was laughing and roaring. Some way off drums could be heard accompanied by the chanting of a Shaman sending warriors on to their journey to the night plain, as they performed the sombre task of stoking the funeral pyres, hundreds of which were dotted along the Wellspring River.

Two friends stood, their faces glowing in the firelight. Saying goodbye was always hard. Harder still was knowing that you would never see them again. Those lost in the battle would be remembered; they would live forever in the memories of their friends.

'He was strong to the end.' Maleth remembered Jack's last moments.

'He was a stupid son of a bitch! Should have stayed down,' Marin said.

'Would you have done?'

'I don't know. Maybe.' There was a deep sadness in Marin, more than the situation deserved.

'What else is troubling you?' Maleth could see this was more than the passing of a friend.

'Until conscription, he was the only friend I had.'

'He'll always be with us.'

'When we get back to Weelan, I'll go and see his father.'

Maleth did not comment on his own return to Weelan. He had felt compelled to pick up the broken pieces of the Emerald Knight. A voice deep within his conscience wanted to learn more of the dark magic. The Citadel would know what to do.

'Each event changes us. We will not leave this field the same as when we walked onto it,' said Maleth.

More gathered at the fire, weary to the point of exhaustion. Some boars were roasting on spits and the Ranielian baggage train had been emptied of food and ale. Any civilian that had made it this far had fled at the start of the battle, along with most of the Ranielian command and Freya's minions. All that was left were survivors, with an unspoken tether that held them together: Kolgoth and Raniel sat beside each other sharing bread and meat, though it would be a long time before true trust could be established.

Conversations stopped and quietness fell. Walking towards the fire came a young woman in golden armour, her head bowed low, yet still with a regal walk. Those standing parted to let the woman through. Someone in the crowd spat at her feet. She paused and moved on. As she approached the centre, her gaze lifted to meet Guldr who stood tall in front of her. Enchanting shadows danced upon his frame in the flickering firelight. His imposing presence made her mouth suddenly dry. Standing before him she knelt with humble reverence.

'I offer you my apologies and my kingdom. It cannot bring back the souls that have been lost and I do not ask for forgiveness.' The Queen was utterly submissive.

'Stand up. You are still a Queen. And it is not me you need to speak to.' Guldr moved aside and presented Helda.

'We have much to discuss, your highness. I am Helda ...' she paused as the words still didn't sit comfortably, '... Guardian of Kolgoth.'

De'sal and Hal had also entered the ring of warriors and soldiers. 'What is a Tialan doing in this hell?' Guldr beckoned them over. 'Come. Sit. What is your story?'

Reliving their accounts somehow took the weight of their shoulders. There was laughter at the antics of the imps and rage at Freya's escape. They, in turn, listened to some exaggerated tales of heroism from various people around the fire. The first battle was not discussed: some of those wounds were too deep and memories raw.

'I've had enough of Raniel, Hal.' De'sal held out his hand. 'I'm heading back to Freehold.'

'With at least one of your ears still attached to your head!' The Tialan gave a thin smile. 'Thank you, friend,' Hal said. 'You stuck to your end of the bargain – you helped me save the Queen.

'I wish you'd stuck to your end, that I'd return without a scratch. I'll have to sell my reading glasses.'

Hal's lips curled in an acknowledging smile. 'I need to support her rebuilding of Raniel. She requests your counsel, to help her chose the right path. There is a seat at the table for you.'

'The wound is deep, Hal – Freya took my ear.' The healers had removed the pain, but everything else was raw emotion.

'I'm sorry that we lost Freya. I want her to pay for her crimes too,' said Hal.

'Then I may be of service.' Guldr stepped into the conversation. 'I have been given a higher purpose. The cult of Talgameth and those foul demons need to be eradicated from these lands: my task now is to see that done.'

'Will you be needing a mage?' Maleth nodded at De'sal and Hal.

Guldr gave a hearty laugh, then added, 'With you around, I'll live forever.'

Maleth gave Marin a questioning look. 'What do you say, brother? For Jack?'

'You're an arsehole, Maleth! All I want is to get back to Simpsons Farm, curl up in the hay and let Treen lick me to sleep.'

'Ah,' Guldr said, 'you have a woman to look after you.' He grinned.

'Well, no ...' Guldr's features expressed confusion.

'She's a cow,' Maleth explained. The whole group roared with laughter.

'Fine, I'll help,' Marin agreed. 'You'll probably get yourself killed without me anyway, Mal.'

That night was for the living: food, ale, song and company. Come the morning, Kalnath would have to sow itself back together. And the hunt for the dark cult and demon alike would begin.

Printed in Great Britain
by Amazon